Tortuga Bay

Pirate of Panther Bay Series
Volume II

SR Staley

Published by:
Southern Yellow Pine (SYP) Publishing, LLC
4351 Natural Bridge Rd.
Tallahassee, FL 32305

www.syppublishing.com

This is a work of fiction. Names, characters, places, and events that occur either are the products of the author's imagination or are used fictitiously. Any resemblance to actual persons, places, or events is purely co-incidental.

The contents and opinions expressed in this book do not necessarily reflect the views and opinions of Southern Yellow Pine Publishing, nor does the mention of brands or trade names constitute endorsement.

ISBN-10: 194086951X
ISBN-13: 978-1-940869-51-3
ISBN-13: EPUB 978-1-940869-52-0
ISBN-13: Adobe PDF eBook 978-1-940869-53-7
Library of Congress Control Number: 2015949079

Cover Design: Jim Hamer
Used in cover iStock Photo 11361998 © jordanhetrick

a

Praise for *Tortuga Bay* and The Pirate of Panther Bay Series

"Isabella, continuing her role as *The Pirate of Panther Bay* from the previous book, is an intriguing character. By casting this young woman as a pirate captain Staley launches a frontal assault on all the female stereotypes so prevalent in literature, media and the entertainment world. He has done a remarkable job of mixing pirates, Royal political intrigue and Haitian voodoo into an entertaining tale."
Col. Michael Whitehead (ret.), author of *The Lion of Babylon* and *Messages from Babylon*

"The action starts on page one and never lets up. Through exhilarating battles at sea and the start of a slave revolution on land, Isabella fights for the success of her ship, safety of her crew, and survival of her lover, who happens to be a captain in the Spanish Army—a sworn enemy. At the same time, she is searching for the meaning of the Prophecy given to her long ago by her now dead mother. Staley's familiarity with ships of war and the history of the region helps readers feel they are part of the action."
M.R. Street, award-winning author of *The Werewolfe's Daughter*, *Hunter's Moon*, and *Blue Rock Rescue*

"SR Staley puts plenty of zip into the action sequences. There's fine description plus conspiracies and colorful characters galore, but what I liked best was the irony of the story. Robert Louis Stevenson would have loved this book."
John Lehman, founder and former publisher of the literary magazine *Rosebud*, writing at BookReview.com.

"I love the heroine in this novel. There's plenty of action, as well as sizzling forbidden romance."
Donna Meredith, award-winning author of *The Color of Lies*, *The Glass Madonna*, and *Wet Work*.

Also by SR Staley

The Pirate of Panther Bay
St. Nic., Inc.
Renegade
A Warrior's Soul

Dedication

To my father:

William J. Staley

Acknowledgements

Much of the action in *Tortuga Bay* takes place in and around what is now Haiti. While many may be aware of this country primarily as a victim of a devastating earthquake in 2010, Haiti has an extraordinary history that provided a rich canvas on which to paint this phase of Isabella's story (which was outlined in 2004). Among the resources I found most useful in giving me the background necessary to chart this path were Laurent Dubois, *Avengers of the New World: The Story of the Haitian Revolution* (Harvard University Press, 2004); Philippe Girard, *Haiti: The Tumultuous History—from Pearl of the Caribbean to Broken Nation* (Palgrave-Macmillan, 2010); Lawrence E. Harrison, *Underdevelopment is a State of Mind* (University Press of America, 1985); C.L.R. James, *Black Jacobins: Toussaint L'Ouverture and the San Domingo Revolution* (Vintage Books, 1989); Kenaz Filan, *The Haitian Vodou Handbook* (Destiny Books, 2007); and Leah Gordon, *The Book of Voo Doo* (Quantum Books, 2006).

Tortuga Bay is the sequel to *The Pirate of Panther Bay*, but, in reality, much more: It's my fifth published novel. While I don't have the space or the memory to acknowledge and thank everyone who has helped me get to this point, several people have provided invaluable input and assistance in getting *Tortuga Bay* into print. Among these amazing friends, supporters, and constructive critics are Michael Whitehead, Terry Lewis, Diane Carlisle, Liz Jameson, Jane Ruberg, and Claire Staley. Claire, in particular, was instrumental in creating the character of Gabrielle. The steadfast support I receive from Chip Staley, Joa Douglas, Ruth Krug, M.R. Street, Donna Meredith, Ken Johnson, Saundra Kelly, and my friends and personal heroes in the Tallahassee Writers Association helps keep my writing on track and provides a continuous source of inspiration.

The staff at Southern Yellow Pine Publishing is extraordinary, and I count my blessings every day to be in their stable. Terri Gerrell's faith in my stories and characters cannot be overestimated as a foundation stone for my career in fiction, nor can the commitment of Victoria Dula, Lindsay Marder, Tom Birol, and Gina Edwards.

I also thank Claire for her love of Isabella and support for my writing, Evan for always keeping it real for me, and Susan for enduring five published books and three other completed or partially completed manuscripts developed over twenty years of writing. This novel is dedicated to my father, Bill Staley, who provided inspiration for many of the ideas embedded in the plot and the ambitions of the characters. It's been a long road, and we aren't even close to the end!

SR Staley
Tallahassee, Florida
July 4, 2015

Map of Hispaniola

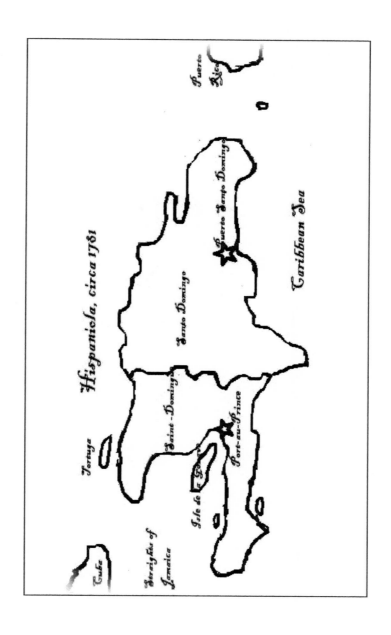

Map of Port-au-Prince

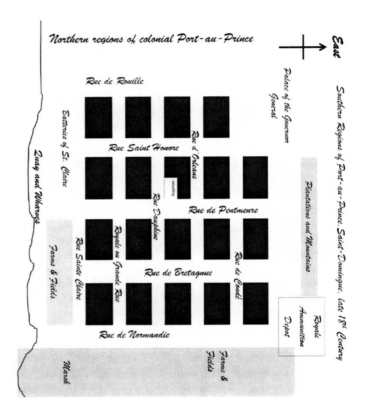

Tortuga Bay

1

Isabella bolted upright from her bed. Something was terribly wrong. She could feel it even though her thoughts weren't yet crisp or her brain alert. Why hadn't Jean-Michel woken her? Had she been rattled awake by rumbling from her ship's cannons or the sharp reports of muskets?

She rolled from her bed, seizing her saber nestled under the thin cotton mattress, in an effortless sweep as her feet hit the hard pine floor of the cramped stateroom. A glowing red sun crested over the horizon as her pirate brig beat westward, but a glare from the *Marée Rouge*'s stern windows kept its bright rays from invading the gray of her cabin.

What trap could they have possibly fallen into? The Spanish Viceroy of the West Indies wasn't that clever. Neither were his underlings save one—Juan Carlos—and she trusted Juan Carlos with her very life.

Muffled cracks and pops from the deck above freed more of her thoughts. Muskets. At least they weren't in the pitch of a ship-to-ship battle.

Isabella patted her body through a brain-weary fog to make sure she was still wearing her shirt and breeches as her mind cleared. She leaned toward the door leading out of the captain's quarters, lost her balance and fell to the deck with a hard thump to her left knee.

"Idiot!" she mumbled, scampering upright, bending her knees this time to rock with the heave of the boat.

Isabella stumbled forward again, looking desperately at the deck. What had happened to her legs? Alarm caught her breath and held it tight in her chest. It wasn't her sea legs that she was missing—the deck was pitched. Sharply. The *Marée Rouge* was under full sail with a stiff wind crossing her beam.

She fumbled for one of her pistols and cursed, glancing over at the wooden captain's table just a few feet away as if her stare alone were enough to pull it into her hands. Feet apart to steady herself, she stepped back toward the table and thrust her hand toward the tabletop. She bent over the table, reaching and clutching until her fingers felt the steel of a muzzle. Isabella grabbed the snout and pulled the pistol up into the cloistered gray light, inspected the flint, and shoved it into the rear of her breeches.

Isabella's mind began a furious, lightning-speed assessment. Musket shots but no cannon. Ambush? Possibly. Mutiny? Not likely, although that scene was uncomfortably familiar; she cringed as her mind flashed back to the feel of a steel blade running through her arm almost a year ago. She had survived only because the windows at her back broke away as she and Jean-Michel tumbled into Panther Bay, her battered body clinging to life. Jean-Michel had saved her, but just in time to be betrayed again as they were captured by the Spaniards and tortured deep in the bowels of El Morro fortress in San Juan. Juan Carlos had saved her there, defying the orders of the Viceroy, thus allowing her to seek revenge on the mutinous Stiles and his dogs.

This time, Jean-Michel was on watch as she slept; he wouldn't let a mutiny happen again. No, the *Marée Rouge* was in pursuit, but of whom?

Wooden planks shuddered beneath Isabella's feet as she heard a report from the ship's nine-pounder. A distance shot from the forecastle. Señor Herrera was busy. Isabella pictured the battle-hardened conquistador-turned-pirate leaning over his most prized weapon's sight, readying the fuse to send another ball through its rifled bore.

Musket shots popped above her from the *Marée Rouge*'s deck again. Softer, less distinctive cracks told her the other ship was now returning fire. Jean-Michel was giving chase.

Anger ignited a slow churn in her stomach. How could Jean-Michel give chase without consulting her?

Isabella leapt toward her cabin door and pulled it open, just as another shot burst from Herrera's gun. No longer muffled by the wood veneer of her cabin, the cannon's report thundered through the vessel, forcing Isabella to stop as if the sound alone could push her back onto her bed.

"Why didn't Jean-Michel wake me?" Isabella muttered as she clambered up the plank steps to the main deck, struggling to repress thoughts that his oversight was calculated. She gripped a beam to keep from tumbling off the steps. She thrust her head into fresh sea air, the last shades of night disappearing into a brightening morning.

"Duck!"

Isabella heard the warning just as she emerged onto the weather deck, and she pulled her head down when the telltale whistle from a cannon ball screamed overhead.

A hearty laugh broke out above her. Isabella fumed. Her fury blotted out any sense of danger. She thrust herself across the exposed gun deck, ignoring the cracks and pops of musket balls streaking overhead. She stood upright, cataloguing her crew while searching for Jean-Michel.

The *Marée Rouge* moaned its complaint as it plowed through the gentle rolls of the morning swells, falling forward over each crest at what must have been close to twelve knots—almost top speed. About twenty of her men stood on the quarterdeck, fully armed and looking toward the bow. The helmsman, rock steady, did not acknowledge his captain. His eyes jumped from sail to sail and mast to mast, all his energy focused on keeping the *Marée Rouge* lean and fast as it cut through the waves.

"Where's Jean-Michel?" Isabella bellowed.

A barefooted pirate seaman, a tar, stepped toward her; medium build with a full beard and hair pulled back in a ponytail, his eyes sparkled with excitement. He clutched a cutlass in one hand and pawed at a pistol in the other. "The quartermaster's forward, Cap'n, in the fo'c's'le, with Herrera."

Isabella turned toward the bow. All hands were ready, fully armed as if boarding their hapless target was seconds away. A sudden doubt rounded the edges of her anger. She looked beyond the bow. A schooner, under full sail and flying Spain's colors, was less than a quarter mile ahead of them, beating a similar course. The *Marée Rouge* was gaining, taking advantage of her position upwind of her target.

"She's trying to outrun us, Cap'n," the pirate said, the image of gold sparkling in his eyes, "but she can't. We've been chasin' her since we glimpsed her masts at light. Been gainin' on her the whole time.

3

She's jus' come in range. Herrera's workin' on her riggin'. They been tryin' to scare us off, but the balls ain't more than flies on a dead hog."

Isabella looked at the schooner. Something didn't fit. Maybe it was luck they happened to cross paths in the wake of their escape from St. Thomas. They had barely escaped a raiding party of Spanish marines, the glints of their bayonets sparkling through the streets as she and Jean-Michel dodged patrol after patrol over the rooftops. Isabella looked out over the water, straining to see the ship's details, telltale clues of her prey's real purpose.

The boom of a cannon threw a puff of smoke and the acrid smell of burnt gun powder into her face as the *Marée Rouge* plowed forward, ever closer to its two-masted target.

"Bring her a little more square to her stern," Isabella ordered the helmsman.

"Aye, Cap'n," the helmsman responded, his voice less certain than his dutiful reply. "Just so you know, though, Cap'n, Jean-Michel wants me to stay just a bit to starboard so Smoothy can train our guns on her better."

Isabella swiveled to the helmsman, casting a disciplined look onto the quarterdeck.

"Just so you know," the helmsman repeated.

Isabella looked up at the crow's nest on the forward mast and spotted a sniper priming his rifle with powder and shot. A second sharpshooter was taking aim at the schooner. The crack of his musket sent a whoop up from a huddle of pirates at the bow.

"Way to take'm out, Jonesy!" someone yelled.

Isabella trotted across the main deck. "Break it up," she ordered. "Spread out!" The pirates, seeing her for the first time, scampered about the deck. "One lucky shot from that schooner and I lose half my crew and any chance at her booty. Get to your stations!"

"You heard the captain!" Jean-Michel yelled, fully visible now that the men were taking up positions near the other cannons. "We should be up alongside her within the hour. Get the cannon primed. Make sure you've got all you need to board her. Where are the grappling hooks? Prepare the grapeshot to spray her deck."

The pirates scattered again, this time with purpose, as the thought of capturing the schooner now loomed real.

Isabella approached Jean-Michel, slowing her trot to a stroll as Smoothy trained the cannon for another shot at the ropes fastening the sails to the schooner.

"Jean-Michel—"

"I know," Jean-Michel said without turning his eyes from the schooner. "*Je connais.* I should have gotten you as soon as we gained sight of her."

Isabella glared at him.

Jean-Michel slid his eyes toward her with a crooked smile. "I wanted to make sure you got your rest before the excitement began."

She blushed.

"After all, you had quite a time in town...before the Spaniards arrived with their bayonets!"

Isabella's embarrassment flashed to white anger; Jean-Michel let out a deep, roaring laugh. "The new tars didn't think a woman could hold grog. They left town broke, betting against you. I warned them!"

Isabella smiled. Jean-Michel was swimming dangerous waters and enjoying every minute of it. She wanted to smack him, but she couldn't. She wouldn't. Not after so much had happened. Their friendship came with privileges although she was hard-pressed to remember all of them now. Jacob's death had united them under the command of the *Marée Rouge*. The mutiny. El Morro. The retaking of the *Marée Rouge*. The battle off Privateer Pointe just six months earlier. She and Jean-Michel had forged a hardy crew, all to honor Jacob. Now, sailing the *Marée Rouge* without the two of them was unthinkable, which was why the Viceroy had put a price on their heads and wanted notices were nailed to every wall and door across the Caribbean.

Isabella turned her eyes back to the Spanish packet; she must be loaded: spices or textiles. A good haul if they could keep her afloat. Her pirates would need patience and a true eye on their guns. Herrera, gunner's mate to Smoothy, was one of the best, even if his thirst for revenge sometimes clouded his judgment. Left for dead in chains in Pensacola, Herrera had plenty of opportunities on the *Marée Rouge* to use his gunnery skills to right the injustices of his Spanish brethren. But Smoothy remained the master of the gun deck.

She searched the weather deck for an older tar, a pirate with a thick mass of red hair and a teacher's patience and sensibility. Smoothy knew each of the guns as if they were his children. The master gunner was making his way down the deck, ensuring the battle readiness of each cannon, leaving the bow chasers in the capable hands of Herrera.

Even with less than an hour since sun up, and despite the spray from the sea, the day's heat seemed to embed itself in the wood deck beneath their feet. This was going to be a miserable day, made bearable only by the strong breeze sweeping them toward a possible prize.

The schooner's lines were sleek, and she was fast. There weren't that many vessels around the Caribbean Islands that could match the *Marée Rouge* empty, let alone weighed down with cargo. Spices and textiles were light enough, but she still seemed fast for an island packet.

Sweat streamed down Jean-Michel, making his beard glisten in the sun. Isabella felt a wet band beginning to form around her waist, under the scarlet sash that kept her saber and pistol firmly in place.

"What do you make of her?" she asked after a few more minutes.

Jean-Michel hesitated, betraying doubt. "A Spanish schooner," he said, knowing he was saying the obvious. "Two masts under full sail? Hard to tell what she's carrying." Jean-Michel brimmed with confidence, something she needed to soothe her own worries.

"When did she set her sails?"

"As soon as she saw us."

"Were we under full sail when she saw us?"

"Aye."

Isabella hesitated. "Jean-Michel, we've been here before."

"Aye, *mon Capitaine*. I know; *je connais*. If she's not what she seems, we'll be ready."

"Are you sure she's alone?" Jean-Michel hesitated again. His silence confirmed her doubts.

"Jean-Michel—"

"*Mon Capitaine*, we have full crews in the crow's nests on the lookout. They haven't spotted anything that looks like a trap or ambush."

"Yet."

"Are you saying we shouldn't go after prizes? We wouldn't have much of a crew if we did that. They're hungry for a payout."

"We're down to just one hundred fifty men on board. We barely escaped Charlotte Amalie with our own hides. We didn't sign up anyone from town before we set sail; did we?"

6

Jean-Michel answered with silence.

A knot appeared in Isabella's stomach. Something wasn't right. Something about that schooner was wrong. She looked at the Spaniard's masts and rigging. She could see its lines more clearly as they closed in on her. She seemed to see gun ports for about six guns on the side. That would give her complement about fifteen or sixteen guns including chasers in the bow or stern.

"Mr. Smoothy," Isabella called toward the bow, trying to mask the concern rising from the pit of her stomach. "What guns are they using?"

The crusty pirate turned so his voice would carry over the deck. "Seems to be a jury-rigged gun on wheels they hauled up to their quarter deck. The men in the crow's nest said the gun's lashed to her rails to keep her steady when she fires." Smoothy stood up from his cannon, turning back to the schooner. Smoothy knew something was wrong, too.

"She's got two chasers in the stern she hasn't fired," Isabella said. "What else haven't they shown us?"

She scanned the vessel's rigging. The packet was running from them under full sail. Or was she? She had two masts. Clean lines. Square rigged. Schooners usually run with triangular lateen sails rigged between the masts. They should have a spinnaker ballooning from the bow, too.

Isabella turned to look at the *Marée Rouge's* rigging even though she didn't have to: Every inch of canvas, its role and its effect on the vessel, was carved into her memory. She knew before she stumbled onto the deck all her sails were set—including those between the masts to provide an extra boost in the stiff wind. The pitch of the deck, the heave of the hull, were all Isabella needed to comprehend its purpose.

"It's a trap!" she murmured. "A bloody trap."

"A stupid trap," Jean-Michel agreed. "We've got her outgunned. She can't match our twenty-four guns. We have four times her crew. The freight runners always run lean on men."

Isabella shook her head. "What we see is not what it seems. Jean-Michel, have the men stand down, as if we're giving up the chase."

"Isabella, we can win this fight."

Isabella stood deep in thought for a moment. "Perhaps. Jean-Michel, let's test this schooner captain. We were outrunning them, right?"

"Aye, we had about two knots on them with these winds."

"Well, let's see what they do if they think we're giving up the chase. Tell the men to stand down. But don't have them secure the guns. Make the order loud, but pass the word quietly that we may still be in for a fight. Take in some of the sail and tell the quartermaster to bring the boat two points into the wind. That should take a few knots off our speed. Let's see what our pretty little packet captain does."

"What if she keeps running?"

"We continue the chase," Isabella said. "We've probably lost an hour, but with these winds we have time to catch her by the afternoon and take her by evening."

"And if she turns to face us?"

"At least we won't be surprised. If it's a trap, she's hiding something. If she's trying to lure us to keep up the chase, she should slow enough for us to set our sails again to keep us after her."

Isabella noticed Smoothy, just a few feet away, with two other crewman.

"If they turn toward us?" Smoothy asked.

"Then we've got a fight," Isabella responded.

Isabella's nerves seemed to bind her insides. She looked at Jean-Michel, hoping to catch a comforting word or expression. His expression didn't satisfy her at all.

Isabella gazed at the schooner, deep in thought, as she reviewed her unusual orders. It would take time to explain the plan, but they had no room for error. Isabella sighed. This was the only time the King's navy might have an advantage over her pirates. The navy could force its crews to follow orders. Pirate crews required diplomacy. They hadn't been pressed. They joined by their own free will, and they were used to picking their captain. She had "inherited" the ship and most of her crew from Jacob after his murder, much as a merchant's son would inherit his father's business. Isabella's captaincy dangled by a thread. The mutiny last year proved that. She wished she had all her vessels now—a fleet of three—a squadron by military reckoning, but she knew it would have been impossible to gather them after they were mustered from the bay yesterday.

8

The *Marée Rouge*'s crew began to mill around the deck, trying their hardest to appear as if they were giving up the chase. Four men started taking in sail, climbing to the topgallant sail, more than one hundred feet over the main deck. Isabella could feel the *Marée Rouge* pitch forward as the helmsmen brought her into the wind and the deck tilted from the shift in direction. Isabella felt all of this; relying on her ears, her feet, the smell of the ship, and the taste of the wind. The schooner was less than a quarter mile ahead of them.

"She's still under full sail, heading away from us," Jean-Michel reported.

"Aye," Isabella responded, her voice cold and expectant. She thought she could see bodies start to move about on the schooner's deck. Then, its deck exploded with activity.

Isabella's heart raced. She twirled and headed toward the quarterdeck. "Beat to quarters! She's coming after us!"

2

Isabella stomped toward the stern. The *Marée Rouge* was in for a fight, and that was the last thing she wanted or needed now. She was short of men, and they were barely rested. The Spaniards would have an upper hand in a hand-to-hand fight even if her pirates had more firepower. Jean-Michel should have known better. Was he so greedy for loot and a prize that he would risk so much? She could understand the crew acting on impulse, but Jean-Michel?

The schooner turned warship, cannon now nudged from the gun portals, remained under full sail as she came about and started to bear down on the *Marée Rouge*. The hunter had become prey. The Spanish captain had turned his ship so it would pass upwind of the *Marée Rouge*, stealing the wind she needed to maneuver. Exactly what Jean-Michel, and Isabella if she had decided to pursue, was planning to do to the schooner.

"Helmsman!" Isabella barked.

"Aye, Captain!"

"The dago's going to pass upwind of us. She's got the speed and the momentum; we're not going to match her. Turn us back to our original course. When I give the order, bring the *Marée Rouge* about to let our starboard guns train on her.

"When we've closed to one hundred yards, I'll signal to bring the *Marée Rouge* around, and we can bring the forward guns to bear. We'll give her a broadside she won't forget."

"That's a risky move," Jean-Michel said. He had followed her back to the quarterdeck.

"Aye, but I don't see any choice."

Isabella looked back at the schooner which had now closed on them. The urgent orders of its captain and officers carried easily over the rolls of the sea.

Isabella's expression was steady and calm. *The Spanish captain knows we've got twenty-four guns*, she told herself. "They must be packing more than we can see. Our best chance is to knock some of their guns out before they have a chance to attack. They think they have the privilege of surprise. I'm going to count on that and a little misplaced Spanish bravado."

Isabella looked at the schooner again, sizing up her rigging and course. Her deck was now thick with Spanish sailors and marines.

"Where did they all come from?" a pirate stammered.

"Hiding below decks," Jean-Michel spat. "Pirate tricks!"

Isabella nodded. "They've been studying us. His Most Catholic Majesty's Emissary, Viceroy Rodriguez, is getting serious about sending us to the hangman's noose! Jean-Michel, coordinate the guns with Smoothy and Herrera. Both their talents will be needed to win our day. Fire as each gun comes to bear. Focus on disabling their guns rather than destroying them to conserve shot. Then have the crews shift to the portside. Let's hope we can get a broadside off to keep them from boarding!"

Jean-Michel ran down the main deck, dispatching orders like the professional French seaman he was before taking up the pirating life. The crow's nest on the Spanish schooner teemed with marines. Isabella heard Jean-Michel order their pirates to start sniping at them, but it was too late. A barrage of musket fire rained down on the *Marée Rouge*. Balls whizzed by Isabella's head.

Isabella checked her limbs and body for the cold feel of blood. She survived the volley unscathed, but two of her tars now lay writhing on deck, deep red splotches growing on their shirts and pools of blood spreading around them. Isabella had long abandoned any attempt to understand the whims of fate during these battles. Another tar scattered sawdust over the darkening wet spots on the deck as the wounded men were hauled below to the surgeon's table. Doc could certainly use an assistant today, she thought.

Isabella turned her attention back to the schooner. She spotted the ship's name etched into the bow and smiled at the name of one of Spain's most storied heroes: *El Cid*. "Let's hope you don't fulfill the legends of your namesake today," she quipped, turning to the helmsman. "Now! Turn her into the wind slow and steady."

The *Marée Rouge* seemed to disengage from the battle. Isabella cracked another smile as she saw the momentary confusion on the Spanish vessel's deck as marines and sailors scampered. *El Cid*'s captain stood by her tiller, steadfast and resolute, unfazed, despite the growing chaos on his gun deck.

The sound of the *Marée Rouge*'s first cannon shattered the air as a twelve-pound shot burst toward the Spanish pirate-hunter. A second cannon fired as *El Cid* fell into its sights, followed by the steady thunder of each carronade as it came to bear.

Disorder consumed the deck of *El Cid* as the deft sighting and orders from Smoothy and Herrera threw round after round into her rigging, blasting through gunwales, and dislodging the moorings of at least one cannon.

"Now, helmsman, bring her hard about so our portside guns fully bear!" shouted Isabella.

The *Marée Rouge* heaved forward and then strained as the wind caught her sails and completed the turn. The *Marée Rouge* shuddered and rocked on her keel as the power of the unified firing of cannons lifted her hull, exposing wood below her waterline. The deck seemed to suspend its pitch, then settled back into the sea in a violent fall. The broadside was a complete surprise; the crew of *El Cid* didn't seem to grasp the vulnerability of the *Marée Rouge* as her waterline drifted back into the water, rendering any Spanish repost ineffective.

El Cid unleashed her first round of shot too late to cripple the *Marée Rouge* but strong enough to rattle the rigging and deck as Spanish balls found their marks. Wails and screams rushed down the weather deck as legs, arms, and hands disappeared from hapless pirates, replaced by bloodied stumps.

"Grapeshot!" ordered Isabella, keeping her voice firm and measured. A volley of swivel guns from the *Marée Rouge* raked the deck of *El Cid*. A score of Spanish marines and sailors seemed to drop out of sight. Isabella turned her attention to *El Cid's* rigging. The sails were beginning to fray, but the yards and spars were still in good shape, and the masts were holding up. The schooner seemed to be drifting, treading water as its crew scampered for cover and its nimble design fell into rudderless uselessness less than one hundred feet from the *Marée Rouge*.

Another broadside roared from the *Marée Rouge*. Smoke encased Isabella as she stood on the quarterdeck, her view of her target obliterated. Musket balls whizzed across the deck again, forcing her to duck. Swivel guns popped as their canisters of lead balls pelted the Spanish sailors and marines at close range.

Isabella held her breath, waiting for the smoke to clear, an eerie quiet settling over the two foes. As the smoke cleared, Isabella's heart raced and chest tightened. *El Cid* had drifted within a few feet of the *Marée Rouge*. She instantly sensed the battle had changed and searched the obscuring fog created by burnt gunpowder for some sign of the sailors and marines. Isabella pulled her saber from its scabbard.

Iron ripped into wood as grappling hooks scarred the railings of the *Marée Rouge*. Isabella's heart seemed to leap from her chest. The Spaniards were boarding her ship!

Isabella bottled the scream tearing at her lungs, tamping down the terror that could paralyze her and destroy her crew. The Spanish commander was seasoned. The sailors and marines were on deck because his plan all along was to board them. Why hadn't she seen that?

The clunk of boots filled the air as Spanish marines dropped onto the *Marée Rouge*. Pistols flared, and the sound of metal against metal enveloped her.

A Spanish marine, sword in hand, appeared as if transported through thin air, planting himself in front of Isabella. He charged through the acrid mist. Isabella pulled her blade up, deflecting a powerful arc from the marine that would have severed her right arm. The Spanish blade came again—a sweeping side cut. She parried and stepped backward. The cutting motion exposed the marine's shoulder. Isabella lunged, forcing her tip deep into his flesh and muscle. She turned to pull the saber from the man's torso, and brought it around in a powerful cut into the soldier's back. He screamed as the blade cut deep into his spine, then fell to the deck, silent.

Isabella twirled again, sensing another body lurking just feet away. She rolled to the deck as a gun ignited and sent a ball past her ear. A figure charged her, but the body carried too much momentum and passed her. Isabella deflected the cutlass into the deck. She brought her blade's tip up, spearing a second Spaniard.

Isabella seemed to feel the hot breath of the soldier as his body slid up her blade, pushing her back with its force. She stumbled backward, falling onto the deck, the mortally wounded body of the Spaniard pinning her legs to the deck. The body gasped, but lacked any real life. Isabella pressed at the deadweight, pushing to free herself.

The sounds of desperate struggles closed in on her—swords clanging, pistols flaring, the pock-pock of muskets. The cannon stood as silent witness to the screams and yells of men locked in hand-to-hand combat. The thud of another body dropping to the deck sent a soft wind across her cheeks.

"Arrgghhh," Isabella screamed, straining against the lifeless soldier's body.

Another figure emerged through the smoke. The squared outline of a uniform told her he wasn't a pirate. Isabella pushed at the shoulders of the body that pinned her to the wood, pulling to loosen her feet, struggling to keep panic at bay.

She looked up at the marine, blade and pistol ready. He hesitated, as if unsure at first of what to make of his dead comrade and the struggling girl beneath his body. Anger furrowed his eyebrows as he brought his pistol, flintlock cocked, up and into line with Isabella's head.

Isabella paused, then twisted her body just as the pistol's hammer flashed against the flint. The ball grazed Isabella's cheek, cutting through tight ringlets of black hair. She thrust her hips up, turning her back just enough to free her pistol. She pulled it from her sash, sweeping it up toward the Spaniard as her experienced fingers cocked the hammer and her brain prayed the flint wasn't too wet. She didn't hear the pistol fire, but the soldier's face turned scarlet as a musket ball tore into it, and his lifeless body fell to the deck.

She dropped the spent pistol and pushed again at the lifeless human that was now an anvil trapping her to the deck. She inched her legs free and stumbled back on her feet. She careened forward, almost tripping over a dead pirate, his pistol resting unspent in his hand. She reached for the gun, letting her eyes skip over his face in case she recognized him, then scoured the quarterdeck for any signs of her crew still alive. The helmsman was just a few feet away, locked in a hand-to-hand fight with another Spanish marine. She lifted the pistol, aimed, and pulled the trigger. The spark created by the hammer scraping against flint seemed to drop the Spaniard in an instant. Another marine appeared from nowhere, forcing the helmsman into yet another duel.

The smoke of battle began to thin, absent the methodic thumping of the cannon. Isabella stepped back to survey the fight. The two vessels, tethered together, their fates bound in an intimate death match, were little more than a massive stage for two relentless foes, one fighting for their honor, the other fighting for their lives.

The *Marée Rouge*'s midship was bearing the brunt of the fight, with sailors, soldiers, and pirates knotted in clusters of hand-to-hand combat. The clanging of swords and knives told the gruesome tales of individual battles, drowning out any thought of using rifles. Isabella glanced up into the crow's nests of *El Cid* where a lone marksman sniped at her crew below.

But the *Marée Rouge*'s quarterdeck was now clear. Her helmsman had survived his duel, and his foe was now cast aside in a blood-streaked tumble of flesh. The Spaniards' backs were up against the gunwales of the *Marée Rouge*, a welcome sign her pirate crew might prevail. They were winning...barely. She needed to end it. Now.

3

Isabella sprinted across the aft deck, her saber secured under her arm, an unspent pistol lodged at her back. She clutched a second firearm in a free hand and jumped onto the railing of the *Marée Rouge*. She sprang from the rail over the water separating the two warships, praying she had timed the pitch of the ship's roll just right. A mist cast up by churning water seemed to carry her through the air. She reached for the deck of her mortal enemy, knowing any deviation from her targeted landing spot would spell death. As her foot touched the railing of *El Cid*, she pushed forward toward the schooner's forecastle, letting her body angle into a roll and allowing the momentum to pull her into a defensive fighting position. She scoped the deck for stray Spanish marines and sailors.

The musket balls whistled toward her, miraculously straying as she fell into an evasive backward roll. She finished in a tuck, her sword's edge outward, and a leg extended behind her with her boot braced against the carriage of an unused cannon. She lifted her pistol, ready to pull the trigger the instant a Spanish uniform made an appearance.

Isabella was struck by how clear the air was and by how many Spanish marines and seaman had stayed on *El Cid*. They seemed to be waiting to reinforce their brethren, just yards away, in a desperate struggle with her pirate crew. Her decision to cross onto the deck of her enemy's vessel was both brash and foolish as more than a dozen Spaniards began to rush her with swords, knives, and pistols. She pointed her pistol at the lead attacker, an officer, and pulled the trigger. He dropped forward, and the two seamen following close tripped over his body. Isabella shifted toward the helm of *El Cid*, dropping her spent flintlock. She pulled the other from her sash and pointed it at the next attacker. The Spaniard recognized the threat and dodged to the side just as the lock ignited the flint, sending the ball into the chest of the marine just behind him.

She shuffled again, positioning herself on the flank of the attacking group. The tiller protected Isabella's flank, forcing her assailants into a line as she lifted her saber over her head in preparation for a downward cut. When its tip passed over her chest, a weight seemed to lock her throat from behind. Isabella pulled the edged weapon down, using the momentum to twist her torso. An attacking blade pricked through her shirt and into her back. She could feel the point flick back outside her shirt with the twist of her body, sending her attacker tumbling past her. She continued her turn, letting the blade of her sword slice into the lower leg of what she now recognized as a Spanish naval officer.

Isabella cursed, using all her power to focus on the fight in front of her and not on how she had missed the enemy behind her.

The slash in the officer's leg did not erase the determination in his look, and he pulled his own pistol up to square it with her eyes. She blinked, bringing her head back as her body bent backward. The crack of the officer's flint sent a ball hurtling past her jaw. Isabella stumbled, unable to catch herself as she fell on her butt, and her head cracked against the stern railing.

The officer jumped to his feet, unfazed by the blood soaking through his blue pantaloons, saved from a crippling injury by the thick, black leather boots protecting his lower leg. The gold buttons on his matching, blue, single-breasted coat were untinged by the smoke and dirt of battle. Isabella caught the movements of his arms as his hands pulled his sword free to launch into an attack, and she knew this was the fight that would end this battle. The coat did not carry the epaulettes typical of a commander of a Spanish schooner. The cuffs on his sleeves had two gold laces—the rank of a frigate captain. This ambush carried more importance than she or Jean-Michel could have imagined.

"Surrender," the Spanish captain ordered, bringing the point of his sword up to Isabella's chest. "The Viceroy will give you a fair hearing in San Juan."

Fury roared through Isabella's insides. "Do you think I will fall for those lies? Rodriguez would just as soon have my head on a pike than bring me to trial. The only thing waiting for me in San Juan is the gallows."

17

"My orders are to bring you in alive...if I can. I swear on my officer's oath that I will deliver you safely if you surrender now."

Isabella remembered the tip of the blade piercing her back as the captain pulled her into a headlock from behind. You treacherous dog!

She hesitated, letting the blade of her sword dip. The feint worked, the captain lunged, thrusting the point of his sword toward her belly. Isabella deflected the blade, letting the Spanish steel slide beyond her. As the blade passed by her waist, she rotated the wrist, turning the cutting edge up under the arm of the Spaniard and slicing through his shoulder and across his chest. She grabbed the hilt with both hands and brought the pommel down in a crushing blow into the captain's face. The captain fell to his knees, staggered sideways, and then pulled himself upright. He glared at Isabella, his arm laying limply by his side.

"Now, Captain, I think you should surrender your ship before my crew decides to give no quarter."

Sweat streamed down the captain's face. He stumbled again as his wounded leg gave out, but he caught himself by leaning on the tiller. The captain slipped his good arm behind his back. Isabella rushed forward, pushing the tip of her blade deep into his chest, sucking the last moments of life from his body. As the corpse fell to the deck, a knife fell from his hand.

Isabella stepped back, looking around her, unsure of whether the captain's crew would rally at his defeat.

4

An unnatural stillness overcame the deck of *El Cid* as Isabella straightened herself over the dead Spanish captain. She prepared for another attack, but the Spanish marines and sailors stood silent, subdued by the death of their captain. Their duel had ended the battle.

Isabella was gratified to be alive, but she was furious.

"A fine prize we have here," Jean-Michel called over from the *Marée Rouge*'s midships. His bulky physique was easy to spot among the pirates securing cannons and the dense mass of captured Spanish sailors and marines. A dozen or so remained on *El Cid*, disciplined by the watchful stare of Isabella's crew.

Isabella struggled to contain herself. She clenched the hilt of her saber, forcing the blood from her knuckles. This was the last thing she needed right now. A prize? They were beating a course north to escape the Spanish. Their crew was half what she needed to man her ship, and now she would have to put another score on *El Cid* to ensure safe delivery to a friendly port.

But now wasn't the time to lament what exists; she had to secure the ship and come up with a plan. They couldn't afford to get caught up in another desperate fight or let her pursuers catch up to her. They had cheated the hangman's noose twice in twenty-four hours—two more times than any pirate could hope for.

Jean-Michel knew she was angry before she even set foot back on board the *Marée Rouge*. "She's a fine prize," he repeated, this time with more force.

"Aye," Isabella acknowledged after a deliberate pause.

Jean-Michel looked at her. "Fast, too."

"We don't need to expand our fleet. Three vessels are enough. Even Blackbeard couldn't handle the four he sailed to America. Where would we go to get the tars to man her?"

Jean-Michel frowned.

Pirating had become risky in recent months. The Viceroy, despite the efforts of Juan Carlos, was pressing the pirates with a zeal stronger than any other time since the British squashed the likes of Bartholomew Roberts and Blackbeard seventy years earlier. The Brits had unleashed a torrent of shot, ships, and men into the Caribbean, the Atlantic Coast of America, and the coasts of Africa. Rodriguez knew history, and it was making her life difficult.

Isabella's victory would be all that much more sweet once the West Indies were rid of the Spanish colonists. And the French. And the British. Rodriguez was forcing her hand a little early. Or so she reasoned.

"We don't need to keep her," Jean-Michel pointed out. "We can auction her off."

Isabella nodded. *El Cid* was a fine vessel that could bring a half-year's fortune to her crew if they sold her in the right city.

"We could run her up to Santo Domingo," Jean-Michel continued. "Perhaps the Spanish navy is in need of a new vessel for their fleet of pirate hunters!"

The quip drew a long, loud laugh from the crew. Isabella scowled.

"Of course, the French may be interested too," Jean-Michel added, hoping the idea of selling the schooner in French-controlled Hispaniola, might bring a lighter mood back to his captain.

"She won't fetch as much at auction in Saint-Domingue," Isabella pointed out.

"Aye," Jean-Michel acknowledged, "but the French don't have much love for the Spanish right now even though they are allied against the British with the Americans. They might be creative with our new-found crew!"

Isabella turned toward the prisoners. "We don't have much time," she said, her back to Jean-Michel. "Let's get underway as quickly as possible. Jean-Michel, assign a prize crew. Lock up the marines and officers in the bilge. Use what sailors you think you can manage to get the ship underway. Offer them a commission in our little navy if you think they can be trusted. I want you to take command of *El Cid*."

Jean-Michel hesitated, but knew it was fruitless to argue with Isabella's back. If he took command of *El Cid*, he wouldn't be able to discuss Saint-Domingue. The tars and soldiers at the Wooden Anchor in Charlotte Amalie were buzzing with talk about slave rebellions and discontent among the island's free blacks: *les gens de couleur.* Jean-Michel didn't normally put much stock in drunken bar talk, but Carl seemed to think it was more than just talk. As the owner of the Wooden Anchor, he heard it all and was a good judge of gossip.

All of Hispaniola was abuzz about a slave girl turned pirate captain who would lead them to freedom. It wasn't just the Christians talking about it, either. Voodoo priestesses were spreading wild prophecies of an African phoenix that would swoop over the plantations and villages, spewing fire and magic to beat back the colonial soldiers, sailors, and governors. He needed to know which rumors were true and which ones were mere bragging. But what could he do now? Another Spanish schooner or brig, maybe even a frigate, could be rounding the north side of St. Thomas. Isabella was right. They had to get underway as quickly as possible. "*Oui, mon capitaine.*"

The sun was breaking through the final black wisps of smoke as Jean-Michel boarded *El Cid* and began organizing his crew. *El Cid* was in good shape. The broadsides had torn loose several cannons, and a fire smoldered near the bow, but her masts and rigging were intact. The sails had survived, although the *Marée Rouge*'s carronades had riddled the main sail and foresail. That would shave a knot or two off her speed, but the bowsprit was as strong as ever. She would have the maneuverability she needed to take full advantage of the winds filling the square sails.

The prisoners were solemn. Isabella fancied she could read their minds. Just a few hours ago, they could not keep their excitement in check as they realized their trap had worked. The anticipation of capturing a pirate prize—the Pirate of Panther Bay no less—with the reward it would bring, and the prospects of seeing a few heads hanging off the yards gave them more than they needed to throw their backs and hopes into the pursuit. Joyous expectation must have melted to dread when they realized they had been captured. Trepidation and fear now etched deep scowls in their faces; any hopeful twinkle in their eyes had been dowsed. She wondered if any of them thought they would see the sunset. They would…unless someone did something stupid.

Isabella's boots fell on the deck as she let the soles grind sand across the wood planks. She dipped her head so her eyebrows masked her eyes, knowing the Spaniards would cower even further before the unseen. Such undisciplined rabble. How could Rodriguez think they could subdue her? Isabella's blade was back in its scabbard, and she let it clank as she watched them.

El Cid was well armed, much better armed than typical for even a Caribbean warship. Rodriguez had commissioned her for the hunt. Isabella's tally of the dead and wounded showed the marines outnumbered the sailors; they had planned to be boarded or to board.

Doubts began to overtake her. Why did Juan Carlos leave their room in the dead of night two days earlier? Did he know the marines were going to raid Charlotte Amalie and the Wooden Anchor? He must have known. How could anything like that, on that scale, go on without his knowledge? Did he direct *El Cid* to intercept her? He couldn't have, she reasoned. They had agreed months ago that he would never divulge the whereabouts of her ship or crew, and that they would never discuss Rodriguez's plans or his orders for Juan Carlos. They both knew trading information would doom them. They wouldn't survive each other, let alone their crews.

Isabella shook her head. Why did she let herself descend into these periods of useless brooding? She couldn't afford to be distracted now. Too much had to be done. She couldn't think of Juan Carlos, at least not as a lover. Right now, on this sea, he was the enemy. His captains, marines, and sailors would kill her on his orders. That was the way the world worked. Her world worked that way almost every day, every hour, save the precious few they shared every month or so in Charlotte Amalie under the cover of the Wooden Anchor and Carl's watchful eyes.

Isabella smiled. Rodriguez. When would he learn? How many vessels would she have to take? How much treasure, real or imagined, would she have to seize?

Isabella lay in her cot, letting the moon's rays cleanse her. She was tired. Near-death experiences wore her down, no matter how many times she faced them. She cherished the hours and minutes that let her relax.

The salt air flowed through the windows of the captain's cabin, soothing her arms, legs, and back; but the light of the moon reached deeper, spreading into the very fiber of her body. She felt suspended, in time and space, as the Caribbean Sea washed underneath the hull of the *Marée Rouge*. Soon, she and her pirate crew would be safe. How many of her crew made it back on board? They would do a full head count at first light. She started down the ship's roster: Jean-Michel, the former slave Sarhaan, Smoothy, Herrera, another former slave, L'Enfant, Stillman....

5

His Most Catholic Majesty's Emissary, Viceroy of the West Indies, José María Ferdinand Rodriguez, stomped up and down in front of the window overlooking San Juan Harbor, his rotund body jiggling with each step. Juan Carlos turned his eyes away, hoping he could keep his mind focused on the Viceroy's mood and commands. The stakes were too high to lose focus. Rodriguez couldn't even guess at the plan at this point. It was too early. He hoped.

Rodriguez turned. "How could this have happened?"

Juan Carlos kept his head bowed, as if ashamed and in deference to Rodriguez's authority.

"Answer!" Rodriguez roared. "Tell me what happened!"

Juan Carlos looked up at his superior. Rodriguez had gained at least fifty pounds since he started the relentless pursuit of Isabella throughout the Caribbean. His wig barely covered his round, chubby head, giving him a childlike quality difficult to square with the authority King Charles III had bestowed upon him in the New World. The tailors hadn't assembled a bigger coat for the ever-expanding Viceroy, so the vest pulled tight around his belly while the lace stretched almost to the breaking point.

"Your Excellency, all I can do is apologize."

He looked at Juan Carlos. "That's not good enough, Capitán Santa Ana. I expect much more from you than a whining apology."

"The marines were within minutes, perhaps seconds, of catching the pirate and her horde of criminals."

"Their orders were to capture her! We had good intelligence. She was there, in Charlotte Amalie, wasn't she?"

"Yes, Your Excellency, but we didn't know which boarding house she was staying in. We had five pubs and inns identified, but rogues in town kept her hidden. If she had been in the first one or two, we would have captured her. Unfortunately, this time, she just happened to be in the fourth one on our list."

Rodriguez peered into Juan Carlos's eyes as if he sensed Juan Carlos's betrayal.

Juan Carlos shifted his weight, keeping his eyes locked on Rodriguez. He couldn't waiver, no matter how dark, deep, and black Rodriguez's eyes seemed. "Señor Rodriguez, we were very close. She has many friends in Charlotte Amalie and among the islands."

Rodriguez turned his back to Juan Carlos. "How can that water wench slip from our hands each time?" Drool dripped from the corners of his mouth as he slammed a goblet to the tabletop, the splatter of wine creating glinting dots on the finished wood, and walked around the large mahogany table imported on the last slaver from Africa. "That whore must be sleeping with every barkeep in the town. How else could she keep that den of criminals so tightlipped?"

Juan Carlos cringed as blood swept up his spine and into his face. He clenched his teeth as he resisted every urge in his body to send the tip of his sword into the base of Rodriguez's neck. He hoped his deep tan hid the flush of rage.

Rodriguez's desk was cleared of paperwork. The only visible sign of any work at all was a blotter, quill, and inkwell. The table and writing tools were overwhelmed by the expanse inside the stone office carved out of Spain's most impressive fortress in the Americas—El Morro.

"We will get her the next time," Juan Carlos tried to say with a reassuring tone.

"You're assuming there will be a next time, Capitán Santa Ana."

"*Su Excelencia?*"

"You've had three opportunities to catch that wench within the last six months, and you've blown each one."

"But, Señor Rodriguez, my reports…they explained everything."

"When you were dispatched by His Majesty, I naively thought they had sent the best. Your credentials and your bravery on Spain's battlefields, particularly Portugal, seemed to speak for themselves, but you have been nothing but a disappointment ever since you stepped off that lousy fishing boat after the *Ana Maria* was sunk. And then, that embarrassing engagement off Privateer Pointe! You lost two schooners and your flagship was pulverized by a scraggly bunch of pirate misfits!

I would have thought your pride and ambition would have driven you to capture or sink them by now."

"Your Excellency, your frustration is my shame. I am putting all my efforts and energy into capturing Isabella and her crew. I have to admit, the transition to the Leeward Islands of the West Indies has been more challenging than I expected, but I assure you, Your Excellency, I am up to the task. I will not let these pirates continue to flout your authority in these seas and disrespect me, our King, and God! When the two frigates arrive next week—"

Rodriguez huffed. He looked at Juan Carlos. "As I said, Capitán Santa Ana, I don't think there will be a next time. I suspected you would fail, once again, so I dispatched *El Cid* to intercept the *Marée Rouge* in the event she evaded your capture again."

Juan Carlos's heart quickened. A trickle of sweat emerged under his forehead and began to move toward his sideburn. His pressed military uniform seemed tight, hot and excessive, its brass buttons lining the double-breasted jacket a glittering annoyance and the red sash marking a hollow army appointment in a doomed career.

Juan Carlos clutched his bicorn hat as he remained at attention before the Viceroy.

"I...I...don't know what so say, Your Excellency."

Rodriguez let a satisfied smirk lighten his face. He seemed recharged by the sight of his lieutenant, the King's envoy, drowning in the sweat of his own incompetence. "*El Cid* has been outfitted to look like a merchant ship, but her booty includes one hundred Spanish marines and a full complement of cannons. Her orders are to act like an innocent merchantman to draw the pirates into a trap. She will use the pirates' own tricks to do them in!"

Rodriguez's confidence forced Juan Carlos to catch his breath. Rodriguez's boldness meant only one thing: He must have already received word of *El Cid's* success. Juan Carlos let his lungs fill with humid salt air. Isabella. Had Rodriguez's plan worked? Had she been captured? Or, better for her, killed? "You've received word from *El Cid*?"

The Viceroy's smirk bled into a full-blown smile. "A packet entered the bay this morning. *El Cid* engaged the *Marée Rouge* yesterday on the north side of St. Thomas, and they executed their plan perfectly. I thought you might want to hear the report yourself. Perhaps you can learn a little something about engaging pirates, Capitán Santa Ana."

Juan Carlos felt his face flush from embarrassment as the blood in his cheeks transformed from rage to hot humility. "Yes, sir." Isabella. He prayed Rodriguez couldn't see the fear and anguish that had overtaken his thoughts. The smile on Rodriguez's face showed him that he did.

"I see you're worried," Rodriguez said with a frown. "You should be. Your assignment in the West Indies has been nothing short of a failure. If I were a more prudent administrator, I would have you arrested and tried for incompetence. Perhaps your sentence should be exile to that God-forsaken pirate hellhole on St. Thomas."

Right now, Juan Carlos thought, that would be a blessing. He had more friends there than in the capital of Spain's vice royalty in San Juan. But living in Charlotte Amalie without Isabella? He could not stand the thought, and his heart sank deeper. He was not even conscious of the fact his shoulders had slumped from their disciplined military stance.

A heavy knock on the door announced the arrival of the message from the packet.

Rodriguez nodded. "Instead, Santa Ana, I will likely ship you back to Spain with a recommendation you stay in the field. You should thank me for my generosity. *Entrar!*"

Juan Carlos stayed facing Rodriguez as a marine entered the room from behind him. The heavy soles of the soldier's boots seemed to count down a death sentence as he approached. The messenger handed Rodriguez a sealed packet, and with a swift flick of the wrist, Rodriguez sent him out of the room.

Juan Carlos stood as Rodriguez opened the letter and began reading the report. He wanted to sit down but knew it would be unacceptable. He would have to stand and hear the news even as his legs felt like they would melt through the stone floor of the fortress.

Rodriguez's mood began to shift as his eyes finished each line of the letter. Juan Carlos thought he could see his eyes skip back and forth, line to line, as if he were re-reading each word to make sure he understood it. Is Isabella alive? Or dead? Is the *Marée Rouge* afloat? Or had it been sent to the bottom with her crew? Which crew was getting the fifty doubloons per tar reward? Juan Carlos's head became light. He swayed. He summoned all his will to steady himself. He dared not say a word.

Rodriguez sat down in a plush chair, forcing its legs to creak as he settled himself. He drew in a deep breath, laid the letter down on his desk, and brought his hands to his plump face. "Capitán Juan Carlos Lopez de Santa Ana," he said, his face still buried in his hands, "you are either the luckiest man in the Caribbean, or I am the unluckiest administrator who has ever governed this watery hell."

Juan Carlos's spirits picked up. "Your Excellency?"

Rodriguez let his hands drop to the letter again, his eyes awash with anger. He lifted his fist and brought it down on the tabletop with a loud clap. The quill jumped from its holder, leaving a line of black ink on the blotter while the inkwell wobbled but by some supernatural force didn't spill. "Damn that filthy wench. She's like a cat with nine lives!"

Juan Carlos kept his face calm and struggled to contain an overwhelming sense of relief...and joy. Isabella was alive! And, based on the Viceroy's outburst, she had escaped.

"She escaped *El Cid*?"

Now Rodriguez became uneasy. His round face was often red from the effort of moving his corpulent body around in the old fortress and in the streets, but the crimson color now in his cheeks and forehead was much more pronounced. Whatever was in that letter was embarrassing, and not just to Rodriguez. It was a slap at Spain and at his King.

Rodriguez leaned back in his chair. "Apparently, Capitán Santa Ana, God has seen to it to ensure your work is not yet done in the West Indies. That filthy slave pirate captain has captured *El Cid*."

Juan Carlos's jaw dropped as his lips parted in stunned silence. He tried to muster a response. How could that be? *El Cid* was better armed. It had trained marines. It was one of the most disciplined ships and crews in the Caribbean squadron! "I don't understand, Your Excellency," Juan Carlos stumbled with his words, unable to hide his own sincere curiosity.

Rodriguez snapped. "What is there not to understand? She captured the vessel!"

"I'm sorry, Your Excellency," Juan Carlos said, bowing his head, trying to burrow his glee from the news and to project humbleness.

Several minutes passed in what seemed like hours. Juan Carlos then realized Rodriguez was expecting him to say something. He was supposed to have a plan, but he didn't have one.

"Your Excellency," Juan Carlos said, "these unfortunate events clearly call for rethinking our strategy. The last several months seem to have emboldened the pirates."

Rodriguez looked at Juan Carlos with steady eyes. "You think her success is about her attitude?"

"Blackbeard captured many prizes simply by instilling fear in the ships he approached."

"Unseasoned, untrained merchantmen are not the same as a Spanish warship manned by well-trained sailors and one hundred marines."

Juan Carlos now blushed with embarrassment. He had hoped Rodriguez would appreciate his knowledge of pirate strategy. Instead, he did little more than confirm Rodriguez's suspicions of his inexperience and poor thinking. And Rodriguez was right. Isabella was no ordinary pirate. "No, Your Excellency."

"This pirate is like nothing I've run up against in these waters. It's almost as if she has a spy in our midst."

Juan Carlos's heart skipped. What did Rodriguez suspect? Had Rosa said anything to him? She didn't know that it was he who helped Isabella escape from El Morro almost a year ago, but Rosa was there when he dressed Isabella's wounds after she was tortured and whipped. And Rosa thought he had been much too easy on Isabella, a slave on the run of all things, during his interrogation. Besides, Rosa was angry with him for not courting her. What was Rosa telling Rodriguez?

Rodriguez lifted himself from his chair and began to pace without looking at Juan Carlos. "You are obviously too inexperienced to capture her."

Juan Carlos stood, stiff at attention, unsure of his next play.

"Unfortunately, I don't have much of a choice. You're all I've got. I'm sure His Majesty believes I have more than enough resources to capture this pest and her motley crew. Asking the King for more ships and men would merely point to my incompetence as the administrator of these colonies. I will not return to Spain in disgrace!"

"No, Your Excellency," Juan Carlos responded. "That would be unacceptable."

Rodriguez sighed.

Juan Carlos lifted his head. "Your Excellency, perhaps we need a shift in strategy. We have tried to engage her at sea, and each time we have been stopped from capturing her. Perhaps we need to focus on capturing her on land."

Rodriguez tilted his head suspiciously over to Juan Carlos. "Wasn't that what we tried to do in Charlotte Amalie?"

"Only partly. We tried to attack by land, but we ignored the sea. Off Privateer Pointe, we attacked by sea but ignored the land, and with both the *Ana Maria* and *El Cid*, we attacked at sea. In each case, except Charlotte Amalie, we fought on her battlefield, playing to her strength."

Rodriguez's expression softened as he pondered and studied his advisor's words.

"We came closest to getting her in Charlotte Amalie," Juan Carlos continued. "A land operation, not a sea-based one."

"But she still escaped."

"*Sí Señor*, but that's because we ignored the sea."

Rodriguez nodded. "Go on."

"Next week, we will have two frigates arriving from Spain. That gives our fleet two frigates, a brig, five schooners, and a dozen ketches. The next time the *Marée Rouge* makes anchor, we block her escape to sea by blockading the bay. We send the soldiers ashore to block exits from the town, and we send the marines into town to capture Isabella."

Rodriguez thought for several minutes, then grumbled agreement. "Interesting. It just might work."

Juan Carlos felt a wave of relief and self-satisfaction flood his body. It wouldn't be until hours later, sitting in his room overlooking San Juan harbor, that the full implications of what he had proposed would hit him. With its success, he would have to be ready for his whole world to fall apart.

6

Isabella's mind reeled. The first cannon flared just as the sun dipped below the horizon. Now she lay helpless, unable to rally her crew for a final, if desperate, defense of the *Marée Rouge*, her glorious guns silenced by the steady sweep of Spanish cannons.

Isabella peered through the slits of her eyelids as haze swirled through her eyelashes and stung her cheeks. She lifted an arm to shield her forehead, matting black waves of curls against the sweat pouring down her face. She had to get up. She had to rally her men. The Spaniards couldn't take her alive. Not now. Not ever!

Crackling musket fire pinned Isabella to the deck. Praying the balls would miss her, she rolled over onto her knees, feet tucked under her, back and head low to the deck. She frowned. Here, on the quarterdeck, she was exposed to all her enemies. She had to move—fast. Isabella pushed her toes into the wood, thrusting her body forward in a mad scramble across the splintered deck, hoping the wood wouldn't cave in under her feet as cannon balls blasted through the gunwales of the *Marée Rouge*.

Where was Jean-Michel? She depended on him to be by her side during these fights. Was he still alive?

Isabella screamed as a lead ball broke through the sleeve of her thin woolen shirt. She reached up to touch her right arm. The edges of the seared fabric warmed her fingertips, but she didn't feel anything wet or sticky. She ducked again as the crack and snap of the mizzenmast gave her yet another clue to the fate of her floating home. How could this be happening? Four years roaming the Caribbean Sea, stalking slave and merchant ships, doing the bidding of the colonial demons, and this was her payback?

She looked down at her hand as blood dripped from her fingers into her palm. The trickles of red found a ridge that extended from her index finger to a few inches above her wrist—her lifeline. The blood fell into a deep ridge and then spilled onto the base of her hand after it disappeared above her wrist. The lessons her mother had taught her, dismissed by a headstrong child, now rushed into her consciousness: She was going to die. Today.

Anger charged through her veins. She opened her eyes wide to catch the final showdown. Juan Carlos had betrayed her! Who else could have done this?

The scene around her seemed to melt into a fuzzy mesh of colors and sound. The spectacle of a nighttime firefight was different from any other experience. How many times had this sight energized her as her crew boarded some hapless merchantman? Now, with her vessel in shambles, a different kind of excitement gripped her. Flames oozed from one end of the boat to the other, pushing reds and yellows into the sky and across the deck. The haze shifted with each second, carrying the acrid odor of burnt gunpowder and the nauseating smell of burnt flesh into every crack of wood and caulk.

Isabella clutched her sword. The dagos would board at any moment. She could see their shadows moving behind a pulsating curtain of colors, pushed to and fro by the flames and smoke, a kaleidoscope of death. If this was her destiny, she had to embrace it. She would fulfill her mother's prophecy. Betrayed by her lover, forsaken by her confidant, this was the end. Isabella would face her death as she had faced it the night of the slave rebellion. That night, four years earlier, had set her on her course of piracy—and freedom. She would embrace that fate. She had to embrace her fate—in defiance of her former masters!

Isabella lifted her body, straight and upright, defiant and confident. She raised the tip of her sword at the outlines of Spanish marines as they clustered for a final assault. "Come on!" she cried. "I'll not go alive!"

She tried to step forward, but pain shot up through her legs. She stumbled backward and onto the deck as her legs gave out. *No!* She screamed to herself. *I can't pass out. Not now. They can't capture me alive.*

Isabella struggled to lift her sword. She couldn't let them take her. *Focus!* Push the tip up. Run them through. *They're coming. They're coming!*

32

Isabella's head fell backward, striking the gunwale like a deadweight. Her eyes closed, but she forced them open again. *No, no, no*, she pleaded to herself. *Don't let them take me! Don't let them take me.*

Isabella's eyes peered deep into the sky, her body useless. A dark mist clouded the outlines of the flailing rigging of the *Marée Rouge*. Flashes lit up the smoke in pulsating balls of yellow, red, and now a strange, pale blue-green: so many colors. *How beautiful*, she thought as she gazed from the deck, arms lying helplessly by her side. She was tired, too tired. Fatigue oozed through her body, pulling her head down to her chest. No. She had to resist. *No! I'm not ready to go yet!*

Isabella forced her eyes up again. Could He hear her? "Please," she whispered. "Don't take me yet. I have not fulfilled the prophecy. This can't be the prophecy...your prophecy."

A blinding flash of gold burst through the smoke over her head, then disappeared. The fires now cast a pale yellow against the ever-changing mist. Isabella's eyes remained fixed on the smoky abyss, captivated by the wisps and puffs of the air as the flames pulled the smoke one way, then another. The wisps turned and twisted, creating lines and circles, but they didn't disappear. They began to take on shapes, resistant to the gusts created by explosions and deck fires. What was happening?

Energy began to surge back into Isabella's hands. She glared down at them. Her lifeline seemed to be elongating, connecting her palm to her wrist. Almost unconsciously, by instinct perhaps, Isabella gripped the hilt of her sword. Then, she felt her arms regain the power they had just hours ago when the battle had begun. Next, her legs strengthened. The newly discovered energy set her mind racing.

She snapped her head back up to the sky. Could it be? Could her prayers really have been answered?

"Did You hear me?" she screamed. "Do You understand the prophecy? Is that my destiny?"

The pale smoke twisted and churned, but she could see a shape emerging. It wasn't a man. It was a woman. No, it was a man. Was it both? Or neither? The smoke turned blue, then green, and the shape transformed into a woman again. It lifted an arm, and it was holding something. A gun? A sword? No, a trumpet! The figure in the blue-

33

green mist was calling to her. She pointed the trumpet toward Isabella and lifted it to her lips. Then, the ghost-woman disappeared.

The man emerged again in the smoke, and his arms churned the air with fury. His eyes burned bright red, piercing through the burnt powder haze as if nothing could stop them. His arms grew bigger, pulled apart by the breeze and fire, his fingers stretching toward her.

Isabella scrambled to her feet and thrust her sword at the ghostly figure. "No! You will not take me. You will not take me now, or ever!"

The ghost's head bucked as it laughed at Isabella's feeble defense.

Isabella's eyes shot open as sweat poured down from her forehead and cheeks into the coarse cotton pillow. The window peeking into her closet of a captain's cabin remained open, letting the soothing sounds of the *Marée Rouge* lifting over a Caribbean wave rock her bunk. Her cabin was dark, save for a moonbeam's pale square cast against the base of the closed door at the foot of her bed. No fires. No smoke. No cannons belching flame and death. No ghosts.

Isabella closed her eyes and drifted back into a slumber even as her brain registered the soft hiss of a voice in the darkness. "The prophecy is real!"

7

Isabella watched the sea as the *Marée Rouge* glided closer to shore, unwilling to believe her eyes. It couldn't possibly be true. How could the sea become darker and colder as they approached the southern shores of Hispaniola? The water should be shallower, clearer, more blue and warm. Isabella sighed, tapped the quarterdeck railing of the brig, and turned her eyes back to the deck. The ghost was a dream. She couldn't be spooked by a dream. She didn't have the time.

The capture of *El Cid* had drawn their stores to dangerous levels, and they needed provisions. And information. That meant she would probably have to go on shore. Setting foot onto Hispaniola, even the French-controlled western side, sent a chill down her spine.

"Calm down, *mon cher*," comforted Jean-Michel.

"I can't. It's too close."

"The Spanish plantations are hundreds of miles from here."

"Slaves still work the colonies of the French. As do the free blacks."

Jean-Michel sighed. "Oui. But no one is sure how much longer it will last. The rebellion in the American colonies has started a lot of talk on that island. I've heard many stories of discontent in France as well."

Isabella shook her head. "The French will never free their peasants or their slaves in the New World."

"*Peut-être*; perhaps. But they may have no choice. Saint-Domingue has more black freedmen than anywhere else surrounded by these waters. They want rights, too."

"Rights to own slaves?"

"Rights to riches and opportunity. I think the only rights they care about are their own. In Saint-Domingue, the French have given the free blacks the full rights of citizenship on paper. But, remember, many of those black slaveholders were slaves themselves. That bond will never disappear."

Isabella shook her head. "I wish I had your optimism."

Jean-Michel's hand lifted to her shoulder. "Patience, *mon cher*. You are right, of course. No one should experience the evils you faced on Spanish Hispaniola, Santo Domingo, but freedom like what you want—what we want—is still a dream for most."

"Oh, Jean-Michel!" Isabella laughed. She pulled him closer. "A philosopher pirate? You haven't been reading those Englishmen, have you?"

"Non! Of course not. I would never read an Englishman. They are Scotsmen, and the Scottish hate the English as I do." Jean-Michel let loose a barreling laugh.

Isabella shook her head, letting her smile stay just a little longer to shake the sense of foreboding that pitted her stomach. Free blacks—former slaves no less—running plantations. The thought disgusted her. She reached up to her shoulder to touch the tough, uneven bands of raised skin under her blouse. She could remember each lash of the foreman's whip as she worked the sugarcane fields with her mother. She was terrified the night of the slave revolt, but it gave her a first taste of freedom, a taste she would never forget. And Jacob...dear Jacob...gave her the courage to accept herself.

Isabella closed her eyes as she let the rugged features of Jacob's face, red locks dancing in front of his eyes, project themselves onto the backs of her eyelids. She saw the smile that first pulled her into his arms, the sparkle in his eyes that told her she was all he needed. She let her hand fall to the hilt of her saber. And Jacob had taught her to fight.

Isabella opened her eyes to see lush mountains rising above the deck of the increasingly tiny boat: the eastern rises of La Chaîne de la Selle. Jean-Michel said Saint-Domingue was different from when she had worked the fields on the eastern side of Hispaniola, and she prayed he was right. Still, she couldn't cast off the vulnerability she felt each time they hauled in close to shore and dropped anchor. Rodriguez's gunboats would make quick work of them if they were discovered.

But the *Marée Rouge* needed provisions. The early morning surprise in Charlotte Amalie hadn't given her crew time to stock up on chickens, pigs, and other livestock. She also needed to score a cache of lemons to keep the scurvy from picking off the crew. Their best hope, she knew, was with the farmers on Hispaniola's southern shores. They were used to pirates and would trade freely as long as they thought they were getting a fair deal. The French colonials kept their army on the north shore, to protect the sugar and coffee plantations, and Port-au-Prince. Besides, their hands were full, helping the Americans against the British in the Northern colonies. Still, no point in provoking them. Isabella sighed. She wished she could stay on board.

The *Marée Rouge* crawled against the current, closer and closer to the Caribbean's highest mountain range. The peaks rose from the sea, much higher than Saint John and Panther Bay, like a giant, green wave ready to swallow her up. She tried to convince herself her fears were illogical and irrational, the silly feelings of a superstitious child. But she had also heard the stories—of rebellion and freedom, prosperity and death. She had lived through that before, and most of her friends and family had died as a result. She was lucky.

Isabella gripped the rails on the starboard side of the boat as it cruised along the shore. They had decided to skirt around the western side of the island once they were provisioned and make their way north to Tortuga Bay, just a few sea miles off the northwest coast of Hispaniola. She was glad she had listened to Jean-Michel when he argued to let L'Enfant captain the *El Cid* to Santo Domingo and negotiate her auction.

The long boat nudged to a stop, its bow captured by the sandy shore. A gentle wave lifted the boat slightly, giving the four oarsmen one more opportunity to push its keel further onto the beach. As the boat settled, it leaned to the port side, giving Isabella her opportunity to hop over the gunwales and into the ankle-deep water. Jean-Michel followed her, followed by three more of her crew. Each was armed with a saber or cutlass and a pistol. Two also carried rifles, their flints dry and their hammers ready to fire in an instant at the sign of trouble.

Jean-Michel signaled a fourth tar to stay with the boat and moved toward the front of the group. "A little anxious, aren't we?" he asked. Isabella ignored him. "I think it's best you follow me."

37

Of course, he was right. Isabella had not intended to blaze the trail into the jungle. She hated the jungle, the gnarled trunks of mangrove trees near the shore, and the endless vines that seemed to snake around her feet. She could hardly believe she called this land home at one point, playing in the forest and hunting down wild pigs with Gamba. Now, she couldn't believe that she had not run into the escaped slaves, the maroons, who lived among the jungles. Perhaps she didn't know the ground that well after all.

Jean-Michel knew the territory. As a Frenchman and European, a free man, he had knowledge of Saint-Domingue that she could never have.

"I don't understand you," she said as they pushed leaves and bushes aside to clear a narrow path into the hills. "How does a good Christian man like you become such good friends with a voodoo priestess?"

"Hah," Jean-Michel laughed, oblivious to the loud noises he was creating. "I've spent more than twenty years at sea, almost ten as a pirate. Serving on a French man o' war and merchantman took me to these ports more than once. I was an adventurous tar!"

Isabella still didn't like the idea they were going so deep into the jungle. The leaves and foliage darkened their path, and the setting sun would mean they would be traipsing in pitch black darkness within minutes. Isabella patted the handle of her saber as if to make sure she hadn't left it on the *Marée Rouge*.

"Don't worry, *mon cher!*" Jean-Michel must have heard the rattle of her metal weapon. "If they wanted to kill us, we would be dead already. Our long boat would be feeding a nice bonfire by now, and they would probably be making sure our flesh was well done before they ate us!"

"Merci, mon ami," Isabella said, the sarcasm thick in her response. "I feel much better knowing that!" She heard the light rattle of men checking blades and pistols behind her.

Their climb was steeper now, and Isabella began to breathe more heavily. She hoped they wouldn't get attacked. She didn't know how she could fend off an assault, fighting for her breath like this. She worked through a strategy in her mind—first, she would fire her pistol, hopefully wounding any assailant. Then she would retreat down the path, keeping her blade in front of her, cutting large swaths to keep other attackers at bay. She sighed. Somehow, she seemed to know each of these strategies was feeble at best. If they were attacked, she and the others would be dead in seconds. They couldn't fight well against anyone who understood these jungles. She remembered that much from her days hunting wild boar on the plantation.

Jean-Michel's pace slowed. Blackness completely enveloped the small band of buccaneers. Isabella seemed to feel the nerves of the three pirates behind her. She prayed they wouldn't do anything rash or stupid. The last thing they needed now was to waste balls and powder on a ghost.

"We're here," Jean-Michel said, his voice low. His tone was not as confident as Isabella would have liked.

Isabella couldn't see anything in the blackness. No amount of time would let her eyes adjust to this light. "I don't see anything. Where are they?"

"They're here," Jean-Michel said out of the darkness. "They're watching us."

"They must be bats."

Jean-Michel chuckled. "That's one way to describe them. They can see in the dark. They say Madame Rêve-Cœur can see through the darkest of the dark. Like a bat. Some say it is a gift; she says it's a spell she conjured up as a voodoo priestess."

Isabella shook her head. "Magic? I don't believe in magic."

"You don't believe in magic, but you believe in prophecies and dreams?"

Isabella felt a rush of heat overtake her body and overwhelm her cheeks. "The prophecy was from my mother, not me."

"Aye," Jean-Michel acknowledged, "but it exerts a powerful force on you, too."

"I don't believe in prophecies," Isabella said, her eyes deflected into the dark, wet soil.

"Dreams?"

"Everyone has dreams."

"An odd comment from a woman with your background."

Woman? That was the first time Isabella heard him call her a woman. "My background? What do you mean by that? I was a slave."

"Voodoo is part of you. Just like the prophecy."

"I don't believe in voodoo."

"No," Jean-Michel said. "Just like you don't believe in God. Or the prophecy."

Isabella struggled to control her anger. "How do you, a Christian, know so much about voodoo? Isn't it considered blasphemy? Would the Church burn you at the stake, throw you on a rack, or do something else if one of your priests or monks heard you talk like this?"

Jean-Michel laughed. "Oui. But I don't believe in voodoo. My faith doesn't waver. I don't have to believe in voodoo to understand it."

"Somehow," Isabella retorted, "I don't think your Church would agree with that. To understand is to know the truth. To know the truth is to believe."

Silence surrounded them. "You are getting much better at these debates," Jean-Michel said, a hint of approval evident in his tone.

The five pirates stood in the path for several minutes, listening to the noises of the jungle. Isabella began to fidget. She gripped her flintlock as the leaves rustled to her right. She peered in the direction of the noise, struggling to see into the darkness. She couldn't spot anything, and her nerves sent her fingertips into a steady drumbeat on her hips. An owl hooted deeper in the woods. The low buzz of mosquitos began to swarm around them.

Isabella grabbed her pistol, pointing it into the darkness.

Something was indeed watching them.

8

"Please, continue arguing! It's much easier to kill you when I know exactly where you are!"

Isabella waved her pistol in the thick carpet of darkness, unable to pinpoint the source of the surly voice.

A laugh bellowed from another point in the jungle. "Captain!" the voice soared playfully. "You can't possibly hit us with that pistol, let alone kill us!"

How did he know she had her pistol ready? She couldn't see anything even after slogging a half hour through the dark jungle.

Jean-Michel laughed. "*Bon soir*, Peter! I wondered when you would finally reveal yourself."

A small flame flickered in the woods, immediately drawing the barrel of her gun, but Isabella couldn't tell if it was one foot away or one hundred feet. The darkness had obliterated her senses. The flame seemed to dance, moving and stopping, and finally growing into a yellow glow. The glow transformed into an orb and began to move toward them, illuminating a bigger and bigger spot around her band of pirates as it approached.

"Please, Captain, put your weapons away. We were expecting you."

The boxy shape of a lantern emerged, followed by a hand, and then a man's body. The orb unveiled the clearing where Isabella's pirates had clustered. The man holding the lamp was slightly shorter than Jean-Michel, about five feet, eight inches tall. While the light wasn't bright, it revealed brown, shoulder-length hair, a solid frame, and what appeared to be a clean, loose-fitting cotton blouse. The man's pants fit close to his skin, but high-top leather boots cut them off just below the knee. He was dressed for the jungle. Clean, honest lines defined his face. Isabella found herself attracted to him.

She lowered her pistol, let the hammer click safely onto the flint, and exhaled.

Suddenly, the dim light caught the flicker of a knife blade as it passed into the beam toward Isabella. She stepped back, dropped the useless pistol, and brought her left hand up to slap at the thrusting arm, deflecting the blade just inches from her chest. She wrapped her right hand around his arm, letting her weight pull it and the knife toward the ground.

A man's body sprawled onto the jungle floor, his face pounding into the dirt and leaves, as Isabella brought her leg over his back. She pushed her knee into his spine, forcing a garbled yell. She grabbed a handful of his hair and yanked. The man yelped again. She leaned forward, peeled the knife from his fingers, and let the handle slip into her palm with the tip pointed down. She raised her arm, ready to plunge the knife deep into the back of her attacker, now lying helpless under her. Just as she began to pull the blade down, an unseen force grabbed her arm and hand, stopping her in mid-air. Isabella pulled, trying to wrench her arm free. Time seemed to crawl forward as Isabella kneeled next to the man, waiting for the gunshot, or worse, a cut from a cutlass that would lop off her head and send her body, lifeless, to the ground.

A loud, throaty laugh rumbled through the jungle from the man underneath her.

"Peter!" Jean-Michel bellowed from behind Isabella. "You stupid fool!"

Isabella relaxed and her arm was released. "Jean-Michel! What are you doing?" She wanted to punch him or perhaps skewer him with her sword. Or at least draw some blood. She slapped the back of Peter's head, letting out an exasperated gasp.

Isabella pushed herself upright, letting her knee sink into Peter's back before picking herself up.

Peter turned over and looked at Isabella in the faint light, a grin spread across his round face. He seemed to be enjoying the entire spectacle!

"Peter," Jean-Michel said, "I told you Isabella is as good a fighter as any rogue. What were you doing?"

"Just a test," Peter cackled. "I was never one to trust the French on matters of battle."

Rage rushed through Isabella as she jerked her arm up, knife still in her hand.

Peter's look turned to panic when he saw the blade.

"No," Peter pleaded, bringing his hand up. "No, Isabella, don't!"

Isabella fumed. "I won't put up with treachery!" The scars on her back received in the dungeons of El Morro and the memories of the mutiny that sent her there burned into her brain. Isabella snatched her firearm from the ground, cocked the hammer, and swung it into line with Peter's forehead.

"Isabella, no!" yelled Jean-Michel.

"It was a simple test," Peter pleaded again. "A stupid test."

Isabella's brows furrowed as she glared into the stricken face of her erstwhile mutineer.

Peter diverted his eyes to the ground. "Jean-Michel had talked about your skills...the Pirate of Panther Bay...I...I...."

Jean-Michel's boots stepped up to her side. "Isabella," he said, "Peter was being stupid, but he wasn't trying to kill you."

Isabella looked at the top of Peter's head, his eyes still directed to the ground, shoulders slumped forward. She let the pistol's muzzle drop, uncocked the hammer, and tucked it into her breeches.

"Jean-Michel was right," Peter said as he lifted himself off the ground.

Jean-Michel moved out from behind Isabella and approached Peter, anger in each fidget of his fingers and feet. "You idiot!" Jean-Michel sent a solid punch into Peter's stomach. Peter doubled over from the pain and dropped to his knees. "You should feel lucky. I should have let the Pirate of Panther Bay show everyone here what she is capable of."

Peter, looked up at Jean-Michel, and then over to Isabella. "I'm sorry."

Isabella kicked a lump of dirt with her deck boots. She turned to Jean-Michel. "What are we doing here, Jean-Michel? We don't have time for this."

Peter lifted himself from the ground. "I'll take you to Madame Rêve-Cœur immediately."

The remainder of the trek passed with unexpected quickness. Isabella wasn't sure if it was the adrenaline left over from her duel with Peter or the small cluster of makeshift huts that showed how close they were to their rendezvous point. Either way, she was struck by how fast they found themselves in the middle of the buccaneer village. One moment, she saw the dull glow of the lantern bobbing in the darkness in front of her. The next moment, they were in the middle of five or six thatched roof *bohíos* illuminated by a fire. She couldn't figure out how the fire could burn so brightly but still be invisible from their path. Perhaps there was something to the voodoo magic she had heard about from her mother before her escape from the plantation.

Peter waved, signaling them to stop near a large fire. "Let me make sure Madame is ready for you," he said turning to Isabella first, then Jean-Michel. Isabella looked around the small camp while Jean-Michel gave Peter the nod to go ahead.

The fire burned hot, but they didn't mind as long as the mosquitos, gnats, and other flying pests were kept off their skin. That blessing was worth the extra drops of sweat bleeding into her shirt and breeches.

Wooden walls framed the *bohíos* that surrounded them. Dense layers of palm leaves knitted thick roofs, insulating the residents from torrential downpours. Windows were carved out of the walls, with leaves and thick panes of wood serving as shutters. Isabella didn't see any sign of people, but the camp could accommodate a score of residents or more.

Isabella stood, mesmerized by the flames. The forest was quiet. Only her instincts kept her aware of the maroon men, women, and children scouting the encampment, observing their small band from their leafy camouflage. The smell of burning wood betrayed its presence as they approached through the thick brush. They couldn't see any of the huts until they stumbled into the clearing.

Every few seconds, a pop sent another ember flare into the sky. Isabella watched one as the heat from the flames pushed it upward. She thought for a moment she would see it ascend into the heavens, a lone spark against a dark gray hole.

The rising ember reminded her of "her" star, the one that kept her focused on the prophecy as she lay wounded in the jungles after the mutiny. She hadn't thought of it in months, and only a few times since the battle off Privateer Pointe. Every couple of days, perhaps weeks, she would watch the sunrise from her perch on the aft mast of the *Marée Rouge* and look for it. Most often she found it, but she was surprised how often she could not. At first, she felt her heart tumble into a panic—how could a star disappear? It was so bright that night she escaped from Stiles and his mutineers. It had helped keep her focused as the wretched dagos tortured her in El Morro. She wanted to see it. She wanted to find it. She felt alone, even abandoned, without it. She never seemed to think of it when she was with Juan Carlos. Like four nights ago.

The muffled thud of a closing door drew Isabella's thoughts out of the heavens and back to the flames. Peter re-emerged at the edge of the morphing light and waved Isabella and Jean-Michel into the one of the huts. Madame Rêve-Cœur was ready.

The air inside the hut seemed thin and cold compared to the embracing heat of the bonfire's flames. A small shiver shimmied up Isabella's body as she ducked into the grayness of an inside room. Shadows teased her from the walls and ceiling, tossed away from the light of the oil lamps. She stood in front of a small, rough-cut desk, home to two lamps and three bowls of herbs, and wondered if her shiver was just the cold. She glanced over to Jean-Michel. He caught her glance, and his eyebrow ticked up in curiosity. Isabella smiled and nodded, acknowledging the irony: Jean-Michel, the Catholic, sitting calmly, even contented, in a voodoo den!

The two pirates waited for a few minutes before rustling beads announced a small woman, not much older than Jean-Michel, wearing a brightly colored smock draped over her like a dress. The beads drooped around her neck, and a red, yellow, and black bandana was tied to her forehead, keeping a mess of flowing black locks bound behind her shoulders.

"*Bonjour*," she said in a sugary voice, opening her arms with a dramatic flair and smiling like a panther stalking its prey. "*Bienvenue.*" She motioned to Jean-Michel and Isabella to sit down next to her at the table. "Jean-Michel," she said with a bow toward the quartermaster, "is always good to see you."

The French accent took Isabella off guard, although it shouldn't have. Growing up on the eastern side of Hispaniola, Santo Domingo, she rarely ran into Frenchmen. Most of the tars she entertained at the pubs on those nights she slipped off the plantation were Spanish and English, with an occasional American thrown in to spice up the fights and grog. She'd picked up enough Spanish, but the French came harder, until she met Jean-Michel. Now, the French, thick on Madame Rêve-Cœur's tongue, jolted her off center, forcing her to remember that the west side of the island was a different place altogether. Different rules. Different customs. Different world.

"Madame," Jean-Michel said, bowing, "*Tout le plaisir est pour moi*; the pleasure is all mine, as always."

Rêve-Cœur clucked through a smile. Isabella fought to keep from rolling her eyes, but managed to smile anyway. The priestess's eyes darted toward Isabella. "You doubt me?" she asked, playfulness lacing her response.

Isabella hesitated.

Rêve-Cœur watched Isabella intently, letting her eyes roam from head to foot.

Isabella suddenly felt naked. Her heart skipped. "We need supplies," she blurted.

Isabella caught her breath; she didn't have to see Jean-Michel roll his eyes. She felt them push her back toward the door.

"Ayayayie," Rêve-Cœur muttered in a curious and studious tone. "I know. Boats, especially pirate boats, don't come up to my shorz close-hauled to wave at parades!"

Isabella's face reddened. She hoped the dim light and her dark skin would hide her embarrassment, but one look at the priestess's satisfied face and she knew it had not and would not.

Rêve-Cœur stepped over to Isabella. Her moves were quick, so fast Isabella did not have time to flinch, despite all her years of fencing, jousting, and swordplay.

"Don't worry, mademoiselle," she said. "I won't be letting you bleed today." She looked up at Isabella's face. "*Je suis curieux*. You are curious, too." She smiled. "You chose wisely, Jean-Michel. *Mon ami. Mon fils.*"

The words—*mon fils*—seemed to sting Isabella's ears. Did she just call Jean-Michel her son? Isabella shot a look at Jean-Michel, but his face was calm. No, Isabella thought. It couldn't be. This woman could not be more than ten years older than Jean-Michel. Isabella looked at Rêve-Cœur again, trying to study her face and expression. It was useless.

Rêve-Cœur picked up Isabella's hand, turned it over, and looked at her wrists and arms. She moved her hands up and down the wrists and forearms, her fingers hovering over the skin, feeling joints and muscles. "Strong arms and hands. Very strong."

She looked up at Isabella. "You have a large family."

Isabella couldn't help but roll her eyes again.

"Do not dismiss the Loua so easily, Captain," the priestess continued unfazed.

"Loua?"

Rêve-Cœur cast a disappointed glance toward Jean-Michel, as if saying "How could you have not taught her about the voodoo spirits?"

Jean-Michel looked down at the floor's loose planks and shifted his weight. "*Excusez-moi, Madame,*" he said. "She is stubborn. She only listens to what she wants to hear."

The priestess laughed. "Of course. I should know. I can see it. I can see des spirits in her eyez."

Isabella knew she could no longer hide her doubt, but she had to try. They needed supplies, and she needed to get the *Marée Rouge* to Tortuga.

"Tortuga will wait," Rêve-Cœur whispered as if reading her mind. "You have bigger problemz right now."

Isabella's heart seemed to jump out of her chest when Rêve-Cœur said "Tortuga." The priestess still held her arm, a thin smile softening her face. "Don't worry, mademoiselle. You will be fine. You have survived much in your short life."

"How do you know about my past?" Isabella glared at Jean-Michel.

"Non. Jean-Michel does not tell me about his girlz! He makes me guess each time." Rêve-Cœur shook her head with a motion that seemed more playful than scornful. "But mademoiselle, you know about our wayz." Isabella pulled her shoulders up. The priestess gave her a reverent nod. "Your mother taught you many things. You try to

47

hide them, but honor what has been taught in the mountains of Hispaniola."

"Jean-Michel doesn't have much to tell about me," Isabella protested, knowing her words sounded as hollow as the truth behind her objection.

"*Mais non*," Rêve-Cœur corrected. "He haz much to tell, if he chooses to tell. He chooses not to tell, but I read." She wagged a knowing finger at Isabella. "And the spirits talk to manbo. Your spirits, your ancestors are loud. You cannot ignore them!"

Isabella felt her lungs deflate and her chest lighten.

Rêve-Cœur continued to work Isabella's arms and hands. She stepped back to her table after a few moments and began moving shells on the tabletop, arranging them in patterns. "You are beginning to believe."

No, Isabella thought. *I don't believe.* But she couldn't resist Rêve-Cœur's draw.

Her anxiety gave way to a presence in the room she couldn't fathom. The air was thick. Maybe this woman knew something? The prophecy. Isabella needed to know. What did the prophecy mean? Her mother had told her, long ago, at night around the fire near the slave huts, as she showed her how to read a person's life by reading their hands. She taught her daughter the ways of their ancestors. The prophecy stalked her. It followed her when she escaped during the slave uprising outside of Santo Domingo. It bore down on her with every prize she took as captain of the *Marée Rouge*, but what did it mean? Isabella closed her eyes, thinking back to the battle just six months earlier that united her with Juan Carlos. The idea of the prophecy—her greater destiny—allowed her to rally and retake the *Marée Rouge* from Stiles and his treacherous crew. But she killed Stiles. She had to. It was The Code. But was the prophecy also the reason she preserved the life of the vile mutineer Perez during the battle off Privateer Pointe? Isabella's head began to spin.

Rêve-Cœur felt the shells with the tips of her fingers, appearing to use a light touch that did not press down with too much force. She pulled a darkened lamp close, lifted the glass, and lit the wick on a candle. She lit five other candles in front of her—one red, two yellow, and two black—forming a horseshoe around the shells. She put a bowl containing the dried leaves of herbs that Isabella did not recognize in the center. She had heard about these rituals as a child. The priestess ground the leaves into a powder. Then she took one of the candles and dipped the flame into the powder, coaxing a tendril of smoke into the air near her. Isabella drew in a deep breath as the hut filled with a bitter smell from the smoldering herbs.

Rêve-Cœur leaned back in her chair, palms down on the table, eyes closed, lifting her face toward the ceiling. "Your family is strong, Captain. West Africa talks to you willingly. They have strong voices. They come from across the ocean. Over the waves and the death ships that carried your mother. They are warriors, and they are proud."

Isabella braced from the clarity of the priestess's voice. Her voice was strong, unwavering, absent of any accent known to her. She couldn't peg it; it wasn't Spanish, or French, or English. She had heard a Scotsman before, but that was different, too. The tone seemed to most resemble the voices of Americans who had sailed from the north.

Rêve-Cœur's eyes remained closed, her face placid. She seemed content and accessible, at peace. "They know your blood is not pure African." Isabella's heart skipped again. "They know that in your veins flows the blood of African, Spanish, and English. They are proud. That makes you stronger. You can embrace much more than yourself."

Isabella looked over to Jean-Michel. He was looking at Rêve-Cœur, studying her, processing her statements.

Rêve-Cœur smiled. Isabella began to wonder if she could read her mind. The priestess's eyes remained closed, her face serene. "They see you rising, rising, rising. Your strength is much bigger than you know yourself. The fire that set you free is but a small campfire, bringing water to a boil, necessary for a feast unknown in the islands or the world."

The fire? Was she talking about the slave rebellion? The one that set her free and unleashed a murderous frenzy across hundreds of miles of Hispaniola?

"Feast?" Isabella said. "What feast?"

The entranced woman laughed. "Good, good my child. Talk to us. Talk to your ancestors. We have wisdom. Wisdom you will need. Wisdom that will fulfill your destiny. A destiny for yourself, your family, and your people."

Isabella couldn't help but feel the strength of Rêve-Cœur's draw. "People?" she whispered.

"A great sea warrior will bring together energy and spirits that cross oceans, and deserts, and jungles. You have spirits inside you that are strong. Too strong for anyone to control. You can suppress us, but you cannot control us. Let us inside you; embrace us and your destiny will be fulfilled."

Isabella's heart zipped at lightning speed. Sweat beaded on her forehead and cheeks. She leaned over the table as if trying to get closer to the spirits.

The priestess leaned away from Isabella as if the spirits were keeping their distance. Rêve-Cœur's fingers were trembling. Her palms began to agitate, flipping from palm up to palm down. Then, as if moved by some invisible force, each hand grabbed a seashell, a small conch in one hand and a smooth, circular sand dollar in the other. She closed her fists around them. The voodoo priestess gasped. "Aiyiayiahi," she chanted. "Aiyiayiahi. Aiyiayiahi."

Isabella stepped back, almost pushing Jean-Michel into the wall. Jean-Michel grabbed Isabella's arm, steadying her while keeping her turned toward the priestess. "Watch," he ordered in her ear. "Listen."

Isabella wanted to run. She wanted to run from the chants. Run from the spirits. Run from the crazy woman telling her she had a prophecy to fulfill. She had wondered for years what the prophecy was, what her destiny was. Now, as these otherworldly noises flowed from this woman in colorful garb, hidden on a mountaintop, she wanted to get back on her pirate ship and look for more loot. She had Spanish ships to sink, ports to raid.

This woman, this hut, these chants, these rituals were bringing back a rush of memories and images she did not want to remember. Not now. Isabella wanted all those mysteries to stay buried, unknown. Why did she have to have a destiny? Why did there have to be a prophecy?

Jean-Michel stood behind Isabella, his body unmoving. She wished his steady, trusty hands were not so solid or dependable right now. Why couldn't she just go back to the boat and set sail for Tortuga? They could find their supplies somewhere else.

Isabella stood in front of the table, watching Rêve-Cœur's body twist, wind, and sway. Her chest heaved as each moan became a stronger chant. "Isabella, Isabella. Aiyiayiahi. Isabella, Binta, Isabella, Binta, Aiyiayiahi."

Isabella stared at Rêve-Cœur, stunned, disbelieving. How could this woman have known about Binta? Only Isabella's mother and the other elders called her that. Isabella gasped. Did Madame Rêve-Cœur know her mother? Impossible! Their plantation was on the other side of Hispaniola, hundreds of miles from this forsaken mountain, Le Morne Bois-Pin. Rêve-Cœur spoke French, not Spanish, and her accent was thick with no hint of Africa. Yet Rêve-Cœur was about the same age as her mother...when she died in the fires set during the slave revolt.

"Binta...Binta...you have the destiny of your ancestors. We are calling you. You must not forsake the generations before you or the generations ahead of you. Press on. Trust your heart. Draw strength from us. Press on. Press on! Liberate yourself and the spirits of those that have come before you and those that will follow you. Aiyiayiahi. Binta."

Isabella stood, transfixed by the words and chants, failing to notice that the priestess was now floating into the air, her back arched so that her chest rose and her head drooped over the back of the chair. "Aiyiayiahi!"

Without warning, Rêve-Cœur's body fell into the chair. The force of the drop snapped her head forward, bringing her forehead down on to the tabletop with a hard thump.

Isabella reached for the priestess's head to steady it, but Jean-Michel grabbed her arm before she could touch the priestess's body. "Leave her, Isabella," Jean-Michel coached. "She'll be okay. This is normal."

Isabella sent a piercing look at Jean-Michel. She wrenched her arm from his grip and turned toward the door.

"Isabella!"

But it was too late. Isabella stormed out of the hut, leaving Rêve-Cœur's unconscious head on the table and Jean-Michel standing alone.

9

"Isabella!" Jean-Michel's call was desperate as Isabella stormed out of the thatched hut. "Come back!" he pleaded as she faded into the jungle.

Each step ratcheted up Isabella's fury as she bolted down the path, beating her way back to the *Marée Rouge*.

She was well into the jungle when Jean-Michel's strong hands pulled her to a stop. She struggled, twisting her arms, trying to loosen his grip, but he was too strong. He pulled her close, bringing his arms around her chest. She twisted, bending her body so that she could face him.

"How dare you!" she yelled. "How dare you do that to me!" Her anger fueled another surge of strength. She pushed against his body, managing to free one arm. She clenched her fist, brought her arm back and punched it as hard as she could into his chest. "How dare you!"

The punch seemed to tap her last bit of strength, and she collapsed into his arms. Jean-Michel held her, secure and protected. Isabella felt the power of her anger ebb. "How dare you," she repeated in a low voice, a muffled sob rising from his chest.

"*Mon cher*," Jean-Michel whispered. "I didn't know."

Why did she feel so wasted and spent? How could Jean-Michel not know what Rêve-Cœur was doing? He knew Rêve-Cœur. He knew Peter. "I don't believe you."

"I have not lied to you before, and I am not lying now. I did not know."

"You've never seen her possessed by spirits before?" Isabella asked, her skepticism obvious in her voice's pitch.

Jean-Michel chuckled. "I have seen that before. The spirits are very strong in Madame Rêve-Cœur. That is why she is so respected in the mountains and villages, even in Port-au-Prince. The spirits are so strong that she could command the entire south if she wanted. The whites would fear her too, but they dismiss voodoo as a pagan religion."

Isabella felt her blood flow through her veins again, fed by fear. Betrayal. "Then what didn't you know?"

Jean-Michel sighed, stroking Isabella's hair as she kept her head buried in his chest. She clutched his shirt, succumbing to fear of what he was going to say.

"The spirit possessions take different forms each time," he explained. "This is the first time I have seen her rise completely from her chair or off the ground. So many spirits this time!"

Isabella pulled at Jean-Michel's shirt. She shook her head, feeling her emotions recede and strength build, using his shirt to blot out the few remaining tears. He relaxed his arms, sensing her anger had left.

"You're Catholic," she chided. "You don't believe in spirits."

Jean-Michel grinned. "Have you ever heard of the Father, the Son, and the Holy Ghost?"

Isabella pulled her head back. "That's different. That's one ghost. These voodoo people believe in a whole slew of ghosts!"

"Ever heard of angels? Every human spirit can become an angel. Every soul can go to heaven. What's the difference?"

"Christians believe you're dead when you die. Your soul goes somewhere else, not your body. It doesn't come back to encourage your children to lead a revolution!"

Jean-Michel laughed. "Oui, *mon cher*. There's much truth in what you say; *c'est vrai*. Sometimes I think you are more Catholic than I am!"

Isabella giggled. She felt blood rush into her cheeks and pushed herself away from him. "Oh no!" she teased. "Don't even think that. I will never be as Catholic as you."

She stepped back, a sudden seriousness overcoming her. "How can I adopt the religion of the men that enslaved me and beat me? People who murdered my family? All in the name of a Christian God?"

"Men are born into sin," Jean-Michel said. "Many don't understand God and his will, or the teachings of his Son. Do not hold Jesus and God accountable for the foolishness and ignorance of the fallen."

Isabella tapped Jean-Michel's chest, letting him know she was not going to argue. It would serve no point, and there was no humor in it. Not after El Morro and the beatings, the torture they'd both endured. "Okay."

Jean-Michel regrouped. "Besides, those who practice voodoo don't really think they are different from Christians in a real way. Each Loua has a Saint."

"Hah!" Isabella joked. "I think my patron saint is the one for lost causes!"

Jean-Michel smiled. "That would be Saint Jude."

"Aye," Isabella said, pleased with herself. "It certainly isn't Saint Francis. I can't handle peace and love."

"Saint Jude is not a match for you," came a voice from behind them, forcing them to spin and face the village.

Madame Rêve-Cœur stood behind them, a shawl pulled around her shoulders. Her face was round and smooth in the dull light sifting into the jungle from the bonfire. She seemed shorter, only five feet tall, and her frame much more slight. Her presence, not as powerful outside the hut, seemed frail and unimposing, displaying none of the power that seemed to overwhelm the insides of the *bohio*.

She walked up to Isabella and touched her elbow. "Isabella, I'm sorry. We sometimes forget that these experiences can overwhelm those who have not been educated or prepared."

Isabella looked at Jean-Michel. "I would have thought someone would have done a better job with that."

"Isabella," Jean-Michel said, "I didn't know Madame Rêve-Cœur was going to summon your spirits. We were here to get supplies and to introduce you. Nothing more."

Rêve-Cœur chuckled. "Jean-Michel is right. Don't judge 'im too harshly, mademoiselle."

The three stood in an awkward moment, the priestess refusing to leave, as if recognizing unfinished business.

"Madame," Isabella began after a few more moments.

"Yez, child," Rêve-Cœur said.

Her motherly tone caused Isabella to hesitate. "How did you know to refer to me as Binta?"

Rêve-Cœur seemed genuinely surprised. "Binta?"

Isabella paused. "Of course. You called me Binta."

"Madame," Jean-Michel interjected. "During your communion with the spirits, you referred to Isabella as Binta."

The priestess closed her eyes. Her face tightened, as if she were straining to conjure up distant memories, even though just minutes had passed since Isabella had abandoned the hut. "Oui, oui. I remember; *Je me rapelle*." She stood for a few minutes, eyes closed. "What do you know about the name, Binta?"

Isabella's heart dropped. She cursed to herself. How could she have thought this woman really had any special powers? Isabella smiled and shook her head. "It's nothing. I thought you might know something about it."

"You do not trust me?"

"If you knew anything, you would tell me. I would not have to tell you. After all, didn't the 'spirits' talk to you?"

The priestess laughed. "No, no, child." She emphasized the "d," as if giving it more importance than normal. "The spirits do not talk to me. They talk to you. I do not always know what they say. I do not always hear."

Rêve-Cœur stepped close to Isabella. She raised her hands to clasp her arms with a gentle firmness. "Captain Isabella, the spirits are strong in you. At first, I thought Lasiren was speaking to you."

"Lasiren?"

Rêve-Cœur laughed again. "You have so much to learn. Lasiren is the Queen of the Ocean. I know her well, because she speaks directly to me. She calls me every day to Ginen, the home of my ancestors deep below the waves. Tis a choice many of us would have made had we known our life on this island."

Isabella's brain snapped. Her mouth became hard and her eyes cold. "You're a fraud, a fake. How could I be possessed by a queen of the ocean? You say that because you know I captain a pirate ship, but my blood was turned on the land, not three hundred miles from here."

"Aye," Rêve-Cœur nodded. "That confused me as well. Lasiren is a mermaid, and she calls to all of us on land to Ginen, to the home of our ancestral spirits." The priestess then became quiet, deep in thought. She looked at the headstrong woman brought to her by Jean-Michel. "Her song is strong in you. But she is not the strongest siren calling you and that confused me."

55

Isabella lifted her hands to her hips, looking hard at the small woman in front of her. Why couldn't she help but feel drawn to her? She was a fraud, but something about her voice made Isabella want to know more.

The voodoo priestess seemed human in the jungle. In the hut, she seemed to control the world. Doubt could not exist. But now, under the pine trees high on the mountain ridge, in the dead of night, Isabella felt a presence more vulnerable and deep.

The priestess's claims were preposterous! A ghost? Calling her? A mermaid no less! Isabella had sweated for fifteen years of her life under the hot sun of the sugarcane fields, first on her mother's back and then cutting the cane herself. The closest she got to water was the stream running through the plantation. She played in the water, building small rafts to float a few hundred feet, but the creek wasn't wide enough to carry anything bigger than a small canoe and being caught off the plantation carried a death sentence. She didn't see the ocean until that fateful morning, the dawn after the revolt, when ashes and smoke cast an ominous shadow over the normally festive colors of the rising Caribbean sun. A siren of the sea? Speaking to her?

Isabella closed her eyes, suppressing a shudder from the memories of the bizarre morning, as she recalled standing transfixed on the bluff overlooking the most beautiful sight she had ever seen—the white bubbles of the waves fading into ribbons of lighter and deeper aqua blues—while realizing her life had changed irrevocably.

But what if the priestess was right? What if there was some truth in what she said. After all, wouldn't it explain her mother's prophecy?

Madame Rêve-Cœur stood calmly, clutching Isabella's arms like a mother to a child, as if preparing to impart some great words of wisdom. "Lasiren is not the only voice calling for you. The loudest voice is the strongest of all—Papa Legba!"

Isabella sensed Jean-Michel step backward in the darkness. She kept her focus on the priestess. "Papa Legba?"

The priestess's laugh was so loud and deep it seemed sinister. "Oui, Papa Legba. He governs all the spirit world. His voice was loud, but I was confused because his voice was mixed with Lasiren."

Isabella's eyes drifted to the darkness of the jungle. She tried to make sense of the priestess's words. She brought her hands up and crossed her arms over her chest, furrowing her eyebrows.

Rêve-Cœur shook her head. "Jean-Michel, what have you been teaching this girl? She knows nothing?"

"Madame," Jean-Michel said. "You know I am not a believer."

The priestess shot a daggered stare toward Jean-Michel. "You are a believer, Jean-Michel. You cannot escape it." She turned back to Isabella. "Girl, it is rare to find Papa Legba and Lasiren speak to the same person. You have a gift that will carry the world."

Isabella felt her belly lurch. Her mother's prophecy. It was true! She felt the pit in her stomach begin to grow. "How do you know? You know nothing of me."

Rêve-Cœur nodded, now studying Isabella's face, its lines, her lips, her eyes. "I know all I need to know. The spirits speak through me, and they tell me you will be great in these waters. Perhaps you will be great all over the world."

"Ridiculous," Isabella said, looking over to Jean-Michel.

The priestess turned to Jean-Michel, nodded, and returned her gaze to Isabella. "My girl," she said. "Did not your mother tell you?"

"Of course not," Isabella snipped. "She died when I was young, the night of the uprising in Santo Domingo."

"Oui, I know that," Rêve-Cœur said, calm steadying her voice. "Binta. Your mother did not tell you anything about your name?"

Jean-Michel tossed a curious glance toward Isabella. The pieces began to fit together better, slowly, and bit by bit.

Isabella shook her head.

Rêve-Cœur nodded, as if acknowledging she finally understood. "She wanted you to find the meaning for yourself. She was a smart woman."

The priestess reached for Isabella's arms and pulled them away from her chest. She turned the palms up and inspected each crease, line, and curve in the night air and sky as if they were illuminated by a bright, mid-day sun. Rêve-Cœur cupped Isabella's forearms in her palms, letting her thumb rest on the center of her upturned wrists. She then ran the thumb from the wrist to the crook of the elbow and then back again. She tapped Isabella's arms.

Rêve-Cœur stepped back, stopped, and seemed to meditate. After what seemed like an hour, she reached into a pocket hidden in her dress and pulled out a white key and a wooden cross, painted red. The priestess put one object in each of Isabella's palms and gently used her thumbs to close Isabella's fingers, securing the objects in the privacy of her hands. Isabella felt her body deaden, as if the cross and key had taken on the weights of her heaviest cannonballs, but she could not let go. She did not want to let go. These were part of her.

"I have been carrying these for many days," Rêve-Cœur said with reverence, her thumbs still closed over Isabella's wrists. "I knew not what they were, but trusted the spirits to tell me at the right time. Now, it is the right time. You are The One."

Isabella stared at her wrists. Her body no longer felt like lead. In fact, she felt light. Her breath became shallow, and she thought her hands would begin to tremble as her legs weakened. "I don't understand."

"Of course you don't. You are still but a little girl. You have a presence that is rare in these waters. I believe you may be the only one with these powers."

"What powers?"

Isabella became aware of Jean-Michel again.

"Saint Peter," Jean-Michel said matter-of-factly.

"Saint Peter?" Isabella mumbled.

Rêve-Cœur nodded.

"Saint Peter," Jean-Michel repeated. "One of the twelve apostles of the Jewish prophet Jesus." Jean-Michel seemed lost as the words came out. "Peter was, with Paul, the first leader of the Christian church."

"Aiyiayiahi," chanted the priestess, her voice low, soft, and reverent. Her eyes closed, but she held Isabella's wrists fast. "Aiyiayiahi."

Pangs of doubt and revulsion began to well inside of Isabella. She pulled her hands from Rêve-Cœur.

Rêve-Cœur opened her eyes and looked at Isabella. "My girl. You cannot escape it. Papa Legba, Lasiren. You have a destiny beyond your experience. Do not push the spirits away. Embrace them, my child."

The priestess looked into Isabella's eyes. "My child of Africa. Binta 'with God.' Girl, you are with God."

10

His Excellency Viceroy José María Ferdinand Rodriguez pounded the map, his fat, stubby finger falling with a force that should have splintered the mahogany tabletop. "There!"

The finger was a curious one, clean and dressed with the best jewels and the most exquisitely worked gold. Even the grotesque could be covered by a thin veneer of importance. The well-manicured fingernail rested on Western Hispaniola, just southwest of the colonial capital of Port-au-Prince.

Capitán Juan Carlos Lopez de Santa Ana tried to control the shiver working its way down his spine from his shoulders. He thumbed the brass hilt on the sword hanging from his waist, as if it had been lulled to sleep by the casualness of his unbuttoned jacket. His hat rested under his arm in formal deference to the Viceroy's position. Juan Carlos mustered all his military discipline to keep from spitting in disgust. How could His Majesty not recognize this incompetence? "Your Excellency, do you have evidence that the French are aiding the pirates?"

"Evidence?" Rodriguez bellowed. He looked up from the map. "Evidence is your job...my Most Eminent Counselor on Military Strategy."

Juan Carlos paused, keeping his tone respectful. "Sí, but I am still a student of His Majesty's empire. I am experienced on land. I can advise on tactics. I can lead our troops into battle, but I do not know the politics of the New World as you do, Your Excellency."

Rodriguez sniffed. "I had hoped you would have learned more by now. You've been in these seas and on these islands for almost a year, and we've made no progress. The pirates still run our channels and capture our ships, my treasure. Your job is simple. Destroy those pirates with the Caribbean fleet. Crush that wench calling herself the Pirate of Panther Bay."

Juan Carlos winced at the harsh orders he was now, duty-bound to carry out. "Of course, Your Excellency." He paused. "I will need five hundred marines for our landing party."

Rodriguez shot an impatient glance toward his military advisor. "Five hundred? Are you sure that's enough?"

"One hundred and fifty marines for each of the frigates, fifty for the brig, twenty each for the schooners, the rest spread among the ketches."

"You're taking the entire fleet? I can't let you have all those ships! I still have to protect Havana. His Majesty has made me responsible for St. Augustine and Pensacola in the Florida territory as well."

Juan Carlos stiffened to avoid stepping back. "Your Excellency, I thought we had agreed that a joint, land-sea operation was the most effective way to catch the pirates and secure the port."

"Humph," the Viceroy huffed. "I can't leave San Juan unprotected."

"El Morro protects the bay. A half dozen ketches will be more than enough to protect San Juan and Havana until we return. The entire operation should take less than two weeks."

"If you can find the wench."

"We'll find her."

Rodriguez shifted his rotund body. "I should ship you back to Spain. What the devil have you been doing this past year?" He shook his head. "I'll give you a frigate, two schooners, and a ketch. That should be more than enough for one pirate."

Juan Carlos stood, knowing there wasn't any point in responding. Pirates were an annoyance, pests to be exterminated, one noose at a time. He agreed, but Isabella was different. She wasn't like the others. She was smart. Her bronze-colored skin gave her an exotic beauty he could not have imagined until he saw her with his own eyes. How could she have ever been a slave? How could anyone with her passion and will to live have worked the sugarcane fields under someone else's whip?

Juan Carlos's eyes tracked Rodriguez as his mind drifted back to the room at the Wooden Anchor in Charlotte Amalie, just weeks earlier. He could still feel the rough cotton of the bed sheets he had left in the dark hours of the morning as Isabella slept at peace. He felt again, even as Rodriguez was directing him to kill her, the hollowness in his heart as he abandoned her. He had sensed turmoil, a churning, in his world, and he had to return to San Juan, his regiment, his ship, and this slothful Viceroy as soon as possible.

He had warned Charles and Jean-Michel as he darted into the alley behind the inn, but he couldn't be sure they believed him. He was, after all, in service to his King. Could they really believe he loved Isabella? Could they understand his first loyalty, to God? Did they fully understand the risks he took every day, every minute, to keep them safe and Rodriguez guessing about their whereabouts?

"Capitán!"

"Yes, Your Excellency!"

Rodriguez eyed Juan Carlos, his lower lip quivering as he fingered the wire-coiled handle of a dagger on the desk. His other hand supported what seemed like a three hundred-pound weight as he leaned over the map of the Caribbean Sea, Spain's possessions marked in flowering black ink.

Juan Carlos caught his breath and stretched his index finger one hundred miles due south of San Juan on the map. "Here is where *El Cid* was taken. She was sailing west with the trade winds away from St. Croix. I think she is continuing to sail west, skirting the southern shores of Hispaniola. I think she is headed toward Santiago de Cuba."

"Preposterous, Cuba is Spain's territory. Why would she go into the jaws of her enemies?"

Rodriguez's military advisor resisted the temptation to look up at his superior in disgust. "Cuba is an immense island. Most economic activity goes through the northern port of Havana, over five hundred and fifty miles away and impassible by land. Santiago is a large city, a major port for the plantations with a garrison, but the southwestern shores are difficult to navigate."

Juan Carlos traced the shoreline southwest of Santiago de Cuba to a finger of land that carved out a wide bay below the central part of the island. The map showed an archipelago of barrier islands that shielded these shores. Juan Carlos started on the eastern edge of the bay. "This part of the bay is a treacherous lowland of swamps and sand. The area is useless, but these barrier islands and reefs protect the bay from the worst of the storms."

"But why there? They are vulnerable to the garrison and our ships in Cuba."

"Our warships, when they are available, are in Havana. Santiago has just a few vessels, ketches with eight or ten guns, not enough to deploy to catch the Pirate of Panther Bay. Her brig has twice the armament and three times their crew."

"Santiago? You're grasping at air."

"Confer with your commanders," Juan Carlos said, frustration rippling through his voice. He moved his finger back to the point of land, forcing his tone to remain even, and he made a circle that encompassed the peninsula. "Escaped slaves have established *palenques*—their own villages—without permission from the Crown, throughout these hills and mountains. The terrain makes them fortresses, impenetrable from the land. The plantation owners have given up on recapturing the slaves who inhabit them. They believe it's better to import more slaves than to spend the time and money to attack these makeshift forts. Even if they recapture their slaves, the cost would be too high."

Rodriguez nodded. "I'll send a request to His Most Catholic Majesty for another regiment of soldiers to garrison Santiago and three more brigs to patrol the waters of Cuba and Florida."

"Sí, Your Excellency. But the task will be very difficult, and we have very little time. The entire island's population is about six hundred thousand. Half are European, mostly Spanish. Over one hundred thousand are free blacks. They will be more than happy to harbor a fugitive slave-turned-pirate from Hispaniola."

Rodriguez turned and stepped to the side, his portly body catching the corner of the table and sending a waft of wind to turn up the corner of the map. "Then destroy them before they reach Cuba."

Juan Carlos smiled. "Sí, Your Excellency." He tapped his finger on the island that separated Cuba and Puerto Rico. "Hispaniola is the key. Isabella—the Pirate of Panther Bay—escaped from the Spanish sugar plantations on the eastern side of the island near Santo Domingo. She won't go there."

Rodriguez nodded again. "The French."

"Exactly. I think she is going to stop in Port-au-Prince. She knows the French have no taste for hanging a pirate raiding Spanish ships. Port-au-Prince has a large, free black population, and I have heard they are restless for more freedoms. The American revolutionaries have inspired them. It's a stew an escaped slave would be hard-pressed to avoid."

"Your plan? Western Hispaniola, Saint-Domingue, is controlled by the French."

Juan Carlos tried not to smile. "A land and sea operation can still work. We chase her into Port-au-Prince and blockade the port. Then, we send marines in to capture her, either on land or on sea."

"The French will never agree to that."

"We send them in without their Spanish uniforms."

"Spies?"

"A small, targeted extraction."

Rodriguez paused. Juan Carlos couldn't tell if he was confused or was really weighing the risks and benefits.

"It's a bold plan," Rodriguez said after a few minutes. "I will write up an official letter to the Governor General of Saint-Domingue, Guillaume Léonard de Bellecombe. He's new to his post and licking his wounds after surrendering to the British in India. He will be looking for a quick diplomatic victory to restore Louis XVI's faith in his appointment. Capturing this pirate wench and her crew should be an easy win and an early feather in his colonial governor's hat. She is a criminal, and he should know the consequences of harboring a criminal. Once you have chased her into port, deliver the letter with a detachment of marines."

Juan Carlos bowed, facing the table.

"But remember, Capitán. If you fail, the consequences will be swift, direct, and clear. My patience is running out."

Juan Carlos stared at the stone block floor of the hallway as the door to the Viceroy's office slammed shut, sending dust off the walls and onto his boots. His knuckles glowed white as he gripped the hilt of his sword, keeping its rattle from adding to the echoes. He was risking everything. For a bunch of pirates! He had already risked his life and commission to save Isabella, but how loyal was she to him? Would she make the same choice now that she had off Privateer Pointe six months ago?

"Santa Ana," Rodriguez had warned him as he was dismissed, "I need results! If I don't get them with this next expedition, I won't ask for His Majesty to recall you to Spain. I will *reassign* you my way. The Caribbean Way."

Juan Carlos felt his chest freeze. The Caribbean Way. The Viceroy would kill him. There would be no trial, no hearing. There would be no public execution. He would simply "disappear."

Juan Carlos's mind hummed with the discipline and precision of his army training. He had risen through the ranks for a reason. How could he ignore his orders? Didn't he have an oath to uphold to his King? Of course, Rodriguez was a bumbling fool. He prayed for the Fever to take Rodriguez out. But Juan Carlos was an officer of the Spanish Army, and his loyalty and commitment to his job needed to come first. He sighed, but what about his loyalty to Isabella?

Juan Carlos opened the door to his quarters. The sun was high above San Juan, sucking up the sunbeam that had illuminated his floor in the morning hours, but the room was full of light, and he walked over to his desk. He picked up a scrolled map and smoothed it out over the tabletop, scanning the islands and reefs of the Caribbean Sea from Cuba to the Leeward Islands. He bent over the map, surveying distances, tracing lines, letting his palms brace the weight of his body over the desk. He put his index finger on Charlotte Amalie, then traced the path of *El Cid* to the battle with the *Marée Rouge*, and then up to the southern and west coast of Hispaniola. He hesitated and then dropped his finger on the tiny island just a few miles off the northwest corner of Hispaniola.

"Tortuga," he whispered. "Isabella, you are as smart as you are beautiful."

The pirate haven had been cleared out sixty years ago, but that gave it advantages. A clever and respected pirate can repair ships, restock with illegal guns and ammunition, and even hire more crew just miles off the coast of Hispaniola.

But my clever girl, can you get there before my fleet arrives at Port-au-Prince?

11

Juan Carlos clutched the envelope sealed with the governor's signet ring as he straightened his sword and patted the wrinkles from his tunic, making sure the gold lace on his double-breasted coat was sharp and clear. He would make sure that boarding the frigate waiting in San Juan harbor would include all the ceremony his rank deserved as the chief military advisor to His Most Catholic Majesty's Emissary, the Viceroy of the Caribbean colonies.

The midshipman sent to pick up his trunk had told him the *Santa Mónica* was set to sail with the outgoing tide. Juan Carlos nodded as he looked out the window of his room into the pristine blue of the Caribbean Sea. The warship was new, commissioned in 1777, but with just twenty-six guns. He wondered if she could match the *Marée Rouge* in a one-on-one duel even with heavier armament. Isabella would be outgunned, but the spirit of her crew could break a prize with the smoke of one broadside.

He lifted his free hand to silence an unfastened button on his tunic, and Juan Carlos suddenly found himself leaning against the stone wall. He smiled. Saint Monica. The mother of Saint Augustine was revered for her patience and forgiveness. Somehow, that seemed like an odd name for a vessel that was going to lead a fleet of warships into a foreign port on a quest to destroy hundreds of human beings.

"Are you sure you want to button that?" said a playful, sweet voice. A woman's soft, pale arms slipped around his waist. She turned her palms in toward his stomach, her bright red nails and exquisite fingers drawing his hands into hers. He could feel her cheeks rest on his back as she turned her face and sighed.

"Rosa," Juan Carlos whispered. "Not here."

He turned to look into round, playful eyes. Rosa's well-coiffed black curls framed a supple, round face. He couldn't see what she was wearing, but the simple cloth and embroidery meant she had left her formal dress in her quarters. The dress she wore now was loose and comfortable. He had dreamed of women as beautiful as Rosa in the halls of the royal court.

Rosa pulled her hands up to his chest. "Then where?"

Juan Carlos reminded himself to be gentle. The Viceroy's daughter could be vengeful when she felt she had been wronged. "We've discussed this," he said, forcing a smile.

"And I don't believe you. How could anyone put God and King over me?" Rosa smiled. She lifted her hands to his shoulders and pressed her body up against his, lifting her eyes up to his face, moving her lips closer to his.

"Rosa!"

"Ssssh," she said, lifting her finger as if to clamp his mouth shut. "No one can see us. We're alone."

"I have orders to deliver—"

"All the more reason to sneak our kisses now."

"We can't do this."

"Yes, we can. I'm the daughter of the Viceroy. I can do whatever I want. No one will say a word. They don't want to go to the gallows." She moved her lips to within a breath of his.

Juan Carlos lifted his hands to grab her shoulders and pushed her away, careful to keep the envelope from slipping from his hands.

An angry spark flared through Rosa's eyes then gave way to disgust and contempt. "It's that pirate trash, isn't it?"

"Don't be ridiculous. How could I care about her? She's an enemy of my King."

"Is she an enemy of your God?"

The question surprised Juan Carlos, leading him to hesitate.

Rosa lifted her hand in a fist. "Arggh! I can't believe you!"

"Rosa," Juan Carlos pleaded. "How could you think that I have any feelings for a pirate?"

"Capitán Juan Carlos Lopez de Santa Ana, don't lie to me. I know what you did in El Morro."

"What?"

"Don't play games with me. I know how that pirate girl escaped, and I know what you did. I was there in the dungeon of this fortress, tending to her wounds. Her lashes were deep. She could not have escaped without help. Your help!"

Juan Carlos forced a laugh. "Now I know you are bluffing! I was nowhere near the dungeon when she escaped. I was writing her execution orders. The guards were ambushed in the streets as they were taking her to the gallows."

"You coward!"

"Rosa, please. How could I care about Isabella? How could I do my job, stay loyal to my King, if I cared about her?"

Rosa's head turned toward Juan Carlos, her piercing dark eyes reminding him of stakes ready to be driven into his heart. "Isabella? You dare talk about her using her given name?" Her cheeks flushed with rage. "How could you fall for that cheap little whore of a slave?"

Juan Carlos clenched his fists. Sweat flooded into his breast coat, dampening along the gold braid and soaking into the finely woven wool. He had to stay in control; he mustn't let her win.

"Rosa, there is nothing between me and Isabella." Juan Carlos raised the envelope to her face and waved it. "Your father gave me these orders—which I accepted—to find her and crush her. There's no confusion about my duty as long as I remain in the service of my King, and I have chosen to remain in the service of His Royal Majesty King Charles III!"

The scarlet cheeks faded to a soft blush as Rosa stepped closer, lifting her hand to his chest. "Then why do you push me away? Why don't you want me?"

"Rosa," Juan Carlos said, invoking his most tender voice. "You are beautiful and smart. You deserve much more than a lowly army captain who serves as an adjunct to your father."

Rosa smiled again, slipping her hands around Juan Carlos's hips, and pulling him to her. "I think you are a fine example of the gentleman warrior His Royal Highness hopes every one of his officers can become." Juan Carlos could feel the wall around his heart soften as the beat quickened. "I'm sure my father would approve."

Juan Carlos found his hand lifting itself to Rosa's face, cupping her cheek with a tender touch. She turned her lips into his palm and kissed it. Juan Carlos closed his eyes. Not now. And especially not with Rosa.

67

When he opened his eyes, he could see a glint in Rosa's eyes. "Well, maybe I was wrong. Maybe I can steal your heart away from that feisty, little pirate girl."

Guilt overwhelmed Juan Carlos. Rosa thought his sentimentality was for her! How could he forsake Isabella like that? But did he have a choice? Death was surely waiting for Rosa's hand to usher it in the door if she guessed the truth. No doubt, it would be swift and vengeful.

Rosa patted Juan Carlos's chest lightly with her fingertips. "I can wait a little longer." She glanced at the envelope. "I can wait for you to complete Father's task. The pirate whore is a nuisance. The sooner you get rid of her, the sooner we can move on. For King, God, and Country."

Juan Carlos's head was in a whirl, and he was barely aware of Rosa lifting her head and kissing his lips. Then she disappeared through the door to his quarters, leaving Juan Carlos feeling exposed and naked, holding the envelope with a letter respectfully asking the French colonial governor for permission to destroy the Pirate of Panther Bay.

12

Isabella opened her eyes, a flurry of questions ready to bubble from her mouth, but Rêve-Cœur had disappeared, vanishing into the jungle without a trace. The only signs of her presence were the key and the cross.

"*Mon cher.*"

She had all but forgotten about Jean-Michel.

He put his hand on her shoulder. "I don't know what to say. *Je confuse.*"

Isabella nodded.

Jean-Michel reached and grabbed Isabella's fists, using his thumbs as if to pry open her fingers, but she released the objects with ease. Jean-Michel inspected them, feeling their fronts and backs, examining their silhouettes against a spot of clear night sky between trees arching over their path.

"Madame Rêve-Cœur didn't give these to you lightly, *mon cher.*"

"*Oui, je connais;* I know. But what do they mean?"

"They are the voodoo worship objects of Papa Legba. As Madame Rêve-Cœur said, he governs all the spirit world. They believe he is the ancient spirit that traveled with the slaves as they were hauled to the African port where they were sold and sent to these God-forsaken islands. Papa Legba is the keeper of the gates. A guardian of the crossroads."

Isabella chuckled. "You don't believe that do you?"

"Of course not," Jean-Michel said without much conviction. "Voodoo is a pagan religion. I believe in one God. The Father, the Son, and the Holy Ghost."

"So you do believe in spirits," laughed Isabella.

Jean-Michel scowled. "I don't believe in voodoo!"

Isabella laughed again, taking the objects back. "A key and a cross. What do they mean?"

"Voodoo superstition. I wouldn't put any meaning in those objects."

Isabella shook her head. "Jean-Michel! How can you say that? I've seen you pray to your God. I've seen your cross in your cabin and around your own neck." She hesitated before adding, "Although I still don't know how a Christian can be a pirate."

She couldn't see his expression in the dark, but she knew the disapproving scowl was there.

"It's not the same," Jean-Michel insisted. "The Christian cross forces me to admit my sins. To let myself be judged before God. To remind me of the sacrifices Jesus made for our sins."

Isabella looked at the key and cross again. "I have a cross. Why can't it serve the same purpose? I must be held accountable to a higher law, too, right? A universal law? Why can't this cross serve the same purpose for me?"

She could tell Jean-Michel was getting angry even though the blackness of the jungle still hid his face. Her mouth turned a small smile at the thought of his anger creating a glow bright enough that it might illuminate their path.

"This cross meant a lot to Madame Rêve-Cœur," she said, turning the object in her hands. Its image was crisp and clear in her fingers as she traced its outlines and the ornate angles of its whittled sides. As she turned it over, feeling its dimensions, the cross seemed to calm her. "Perhaps I can learn to use it like your cross." She sighed. "But the key."

"Every object has a meaning in voodoo," Jean-Michel said. He paused.

"But what?"

"I don't know. The meaning is connected to one of their gods."

"Who else would there be other than Papa Legba? Lasiren?"

Jean-Michel remained silent.

"Jean-Michel, who else would this key represent?"

Finally, after several more moments, Jean-Michel shook his head. "Lasiren is the voodoo queen of the ocean, but her symbols are not the key. They are female objects. A mirror. A comb. She calls to her followers from the ocean, so believers also think she will use the music of a trumpet to convince them to follow her to the bottom of the sea."

"That sounds risky," Isabella said, remembering a vague dream of a ghost, a man, blowing a trumpet. "She tricks them into drowning? She doesn't seem like a merciful goddess."

"That depends on where you sit. Or where you are chained."

The anguish of Isabella's plantation life rushed over her. There were days, even weeks, when she would have given her heart and soul to leave the terror she lived on Earth with her mother. She clutched her chest as she thought of her mother pleading to keep her daughter away from the foreman's whip. "How can she take care of me?" she would cry at the overseer, trying to get him to the see the consequences of lower crop production when his slaves were incapable of working.

Isabella's legs weakened. She fell to her knees and bowed her head as the tears welled in her eyes. She lifted the cross to her lips and cupped the key against her cheek. She tried to hide her sobs as she remembered her mother scolding her for leaving the camps at night. Her mother tried to protect her. Every day. But Isabella rebelled, as if she wanted to feel the lashes of the overseer's leather on her back. Those lashes burned into her flesh, but she did not care. That hotheaded fifteen-year-old was sure she could control the world...someday. The overseer and his henchman would get what they deserved.

She rolled the cross and key over in her hands as she knelt in the jungle darkness. Her mother would have followed Lasiren into the ocean if she weren't trying to keep her daughter safe. And alive. Tears began to fall across her cheeks as her nose seemed to close up. How could she have made her mother's life so miserable? Now, she was dead, a victim of Isabella's stupid dream to become a legend in the Caribbean.

Isabella sighed deeply, wiping the tears with the backs of her hands.

Two large arms swept her up and pulled her close into Jean-Michel's chest. "*Mon cher, mon cher.* I'm sorry she is gone."

Isabella couldn't hold it back any longer. In Jean-Michel's strong, comforting arms, she sobbed. For her mother. For all those who had died on that terrible night when flames rose from the sugarcane fields to lick the skies of Hispaniola. A point in time that would forever stain Isabella with the blood of friends, family, and enemies.

But even as she sobbed, she knew the tears would have to dry soon. She felt the weight of her destiny more than ever—the prophecy was real—and she understood that she would soon face the test that would determine her fate, the fate of her crew, and perhaps the fate of all those living under the European laws of His Most Catholic Majesty King Charles III of Spain.

13

Juan Carlos let his hands glide down the polished rails of the *Santa Mónica* as he watched the turrets of El Morro recede into the horizon. Their light frigate tacked northwest with the trade winds, ready to turn south in one day's time once they had left the rocky shores of Tortuga and sighted the western tip of Cap Saint-Nicolas. He stopped to tap the railing as he felt the winds at his back sweep them toward an inevitable confrontation that would, in all likelihood, destroy him. Juan Carlos looked past the lone sailor guiding the ship, firm hands on a massive tiller and eyes darting from sails to spars to masts to the horizon of their destiny.

He closed his eyes, letting his mind drift to smells and sights of Isabella sleeping beside him. He fastened his tunic and let his hand fall to the saber fastened to his belt. His chest thumped, and a knot settled in his stomach as he felt the western shores of Puerto Rico drift further away, nudging his flotilla of pirate hunters toward eastern Hispaniola. Perhaps the trade winds would be too strong as they turned south toward Port-au-Prince. Perhaps their spies were wrong, and Isabella had sailed east instead of west. Perhaps—

"I would not worry," interrupted a confident voice from behind him.

Juan Carlos turned to meet the chiseled face of Capitán de Navio José Maria Cordoba Muñoz. The captain had abandoned his formal uniform for the sturdier wool and comfort of battle dress. Sword strapped sharply to his side, his regulation epaulettes provided all the authority he needed to rule his three-masted, one-hundred-fifty-ton warship armed with its twenty-six cannons. They were cutting through the rolling swells at a steady clip of fifteen knots, just enough to coax the occasional groan from the reluctant oak anchoring the main sails.

"We'll have the scurrilous sea wench hanging from our yardarm before the end of the week."

Juan Carlos bridled at the thought of Isabella's limp body, head unnaturally pitched over a noose like a torn rag doll, twenty feet above him, swaying with the light rolls of the sea. He filled his lungs with air to stop the ball in his stomach from rising into his chest. He sent a sharp look toward Muñoz. "Our orders are to bring her back to El Morro."

Muñoz huffed. "Alive...or dead?" He smiled, dismissing Juan Carlos with a quick nod. "My words were figurative."

"I think the Viceroy would like to see her hang from the noose in person."

A slight cock to Muñoz's head betrayed a skeptical curiosity in the young army officer who served as strategic counselor to the Viceroy. "She's already escaped from that so-called fortress once, Capitán Santa Ana."

"Her crew is loyal, a trait I'm sure you can appreciate, Capitán."

The naval officer smiled. "Sí, Capitán. Much better to keep her in the chains of His Majesty's navy; I'm not sure your soldiers will do a better job holding her a second time."

Juan Carlos's back stiffened. "Capitán Muñoz, I am sure you will have a much better chance of keeping her in chains when hundreds of miles of shark-infested seas are her prison walls and a squadron of His Royal Majesty's warships serves as her prison guards. A city of tens of thousands creates many more challenges."

Muñoz's jaw tightened. "I think Viceroy Rodriguez will be just as happy if we brought her head displayed on a pike to his front steps."

"Should we send the ketch back to the Viceroy to ask him for his preference?"

"Humph." Muñoz waved his hand toward the thin line that was Puerto Rico at the end of the widening wake plowed by their ship. "Remember, Capitán, I have fifteen years and three ranks on you. I am in charge of this mission and responsible for this fleet. The Viceroy knows full well that I can make whatever decision I feel is necessary to complete our mission."

Juan Carlos bowed his head. "Of course. I didn't mean to suggest any disrespect, Capitán de Navio Muñoz." He tried to push aside the urge to slap himself for not recognizing the slight the Viceroy had thrown when he refused to appoint Muñoz to admiral once he was given command of their squadron. No other naval officer in the Caribbean had as much authority or responsibility—or experience at command—as Muñoz, and his failure to be promoted to *Almirante* was weighing on him. Captain of the Navy was a promotion over Frigate Captain, but not by much. "I am, of course, at your service."

Muñoz let Juan Carlos stand at attention for several seconds. "I did not take your words as disrespectful, Capitán Santa Ana. I'm sure they were meant as misguided banter."

Juan Carlos bowed again.

Muñoz shook his head. "For the life of me and His Majesty, I can't understand why the Viceroy has put so much faith in you. You are too inexperienced for this hell."

"With respect, Capitán Muñoz, he put you in charge of the mission."

"Your failures are becoming the laughingstock of this post. They started before you even set foot on Puerto Rico! The transport ship bringing you to the vice admiralty was captured by this rogue pirate locals call the Panther. You escaped—much to your credit, Capitán— but you were unable to use the knowledge of this pirate wench, gained as a prisoner, to bring her to justice. And then her escape from El Morro! As an army officer experienced in interrogation, your orders should have ensured her public execution. Instead, she escaped. And then that travesty off Privateer Pointe! His Majesty's ships brought to a draw by a pirate!"

Juan Carlos bowed his head again. "An embarrassing turn of events."

"You should have boarded her rogue boats and personally cut off her head."

"The loss of life and—"

"You embarrassed His Majesty and Viceroy Rodriguez!"

Juan Carlos glared into Muñoz's eyes.

Muñoz smiled, cold contempt sending its dagger tip into Juan Carlos. "An embarrassment to our King!" He shook his head. "Is this what they taught you in our army?"

Juan Carlos's chest expanded with a sharp breath as his shoulders drew back and his stare hardened. "Capitán Muñoz, my record stands on its own."

"I haven't seen any of that record in this mosquito-infested hell." Muñoz turned to face the bow, noticing for the first time the deck hands had managed to inch their work closer to the back of the vessel while the helmsman kept his gaze narrow and forward. He turned on his heels to face Juan Carlos. "I'll expect much more from you on this mission, Capitán. You will be responsible for capturing this so-called pirate, and I will personally put you in charge of flogging her until she can resist no more." A smile crossed his lips. "But make sure you don't kill her. We'll want to make sure she is healthy enough to cry as we flog her for the Viceroy and hear her whimper for mercy as the noose is put around her neck at the gallows in the public square. We'll make it a spectacle. We'll make it clear to all in the Caribbean admiralty that pirates have no place pillaging the trade of His Most Catholic Royal Majesty's merchant ships on these waters!"

14

Isabella woke from a dreamless night, her wool blanket damp from the sweat pouring from her body into her shirt and onto her face. She reached up to clear her eyes and reset her senses to the reality of the tiny captain's quarters carved out of the stern of the *Marée Rouge.*

Dreams, even the nightmares, were comforting. At least she felt alive as she slept. Now her sleep seemed empty. Was this blank sleep something Rêve-Cœur conjured up? God, she prayed for those dreams again.

Isabella lay on her cot, feeling the waves roll under the keel of her two-masted brig. The motion was soothing, a much-needed comfort now that her sleep had been robbed of its calming benefits. Her eyes dipped as she found herself teetering toward the dreamless abyss, only to have the fall of the stern over an uneven wave jolt her back into the cabin.

The moon would fall below the horizon soon, chased by a sun that would scream at any thought of getting more sleep. She took a deep breath and brought her fists to her eyes, rubbing as sunlight nosed its way over the horizon, sending reds and oranges streaking from one end of the sea to the other. She was so tired. She looked at the windows, a stream of pale, yellow light piercing her gray space. Perhaps Jean-Michel could have one of the crew put blankets over the windows. But the blankets would dam up the stench of unwashed pirates and soiled clothing, leaching in from the main deck only to be boiled by the sun as it rose. "Arghhh!"

All she wanted was a little sleep! And perhaps a little dream. A nice dream. Something that would keep her mind off the blackness of the night and still her thoughts.

Isabella lifted herself upright on her bed, one hand shifting to rub her temple as the other became a tent pole to keep her vertical. It was all part of the puzzle. The prophecy. Shouldn't Rêve-Cœur's hocus pocus have given her clarity? Or at least new clues? A gift! A gift of nothing. No, a gift of worse than nothing because it now tortured her memories and confused her future.

She closed her eyes and leaned back to stretch her legs across the cot. She had removed her breeches at some point during the night, hoping a breeze would cool her as she slept. Her cotton shirt, smudged and stretched during their jungle escapade, draped her body, letting her pretend modesty that was impossible in the stifling quarters of a boat barely one hundred feet long, housing one hundred fifty pirates.

At least she had her own cabin. The rest of the crew lived with hammocks slung from the beams, swaying over a two-week inventory of supplies, and among the cannons and shot. Last night, they probably slept on the main deck, catching the sea breeze as hammocks stood watch for dreams that never came. The *Marée Rouge* let the wind push her over the rolls of the sea until she tacked north toward Tortuga. Then sleep would be impossible as they worked against the northeasterly trade winds sweeping in from the Atlantic.

Isabella shook her head, clearing the fog from her brain. Weeks at sea with rotting food, pirate hunters over every breaker or horizon, or marines rushing through narrow streets to arrest her as she slept—is this what she bargained for when she fled the flames of the plantation burning to the ground on Hispaniola so many years ago? She shook her head, focusing on the bunched-up breeches on the floor. Turning to the deck boots, she caught the glint of her saber dangling from the chair next to the washbasin.

She felt the blood rush into her hands, drawing her fingers into a clenched fist. She would rather hang from the gallows for taking down Spain's filthy dago tyrants than submit to them. Again.

Isabella pushed herself onto her feet and stepped over to the washbasin, catching the glint of her face in a craggy mirror suspended from the wall by a leather string. She had been through too much. She had seen too much. Her mother had sacrificed too much. Jacob, her pirate lover, had sacrificed his life so she could live, and now, was Juan Carlos doing the same? Giving up God, King, and country for her? She could not, she would not, let those sacrifices go. Ever.

Isabella felt the blood stream through her arteries as the light brightened her quarters, building strength and livening her heart. She grabbed at the clumped breeches and pulled them over her legs then clutched at the loose tails of her shirt, anger catalyzing a new power in her arms. How could these people do this to her? How could the Africans let themselves be tortured and worked to death—to death!—without resistance? Isabella's teeth ground as she pulled her shirt tight against her body, every stitch leaving an impression against her hips, stomach, and flattened breasts.

Spaniards! Dago filth! This will not be allowed! Not while I live! Not as long as she commanded the *Marée Rouge*. Not as long as she had one gun crew, one person, willing to take the fight to them.

Blood surged into her cheeks and through her head. She turned, looking for something to grab—anything that could allow her to channel the anger gripping every vein and muscle in her body. The walls, the desk—anything that would release this fury.

Juan Carlos's face popped into her mind so quickly, so concretely, Isabella's heart seemed to flip to a stop. "Arrrgh!" How could she be in love with a Spaniard? A dago army captain at that! How many times did she have to tell herself it wouldn't, it couldn't, work? He believed in the plantations. He worked for the plantations. His loyalty was to his King—His Highest and Most Royal Power—His Most Catholic Majesty King Charles III of Spain. How could she imagine that his so-called love for her could trump twenty years of purebred loyalty to a monarch?

She drew in a deep breath. She let her lungs fill, and, as she exhaled, a door seemed to open showing her the empty bed weeks earlier above the Wooden Anchor on St. Thomas. His sword was gone. His tunic, breeches, and boots had been swept from the room. All that remained was a wisp of his scent and a lingering memory of the warmth of his lips as she descended into a contented sleep, but he was gone. By the position of the sun, he was already on the sloop whisking him back to the offices of that oaf commanding the Vice Royalty of New Spain.

Isabella's anger began to ebb, flowing into a darkening emotional lull.

"Faith," she murmured, as her fingers began to knead her arms. He believes in you. He could have ordered his squadron to sink the *Marée*

Rouge off Privateer Pointe. He could have ordered his men to board her ship and butcher the crew, but he did not. *Instead, he brokered a truce so we could stay together; so we could be together. One or two days, perhaps even a night, we could be in each other's arms.* She would feel the passion of his kiss, the softness of his hands, the firmness of his embrace. Wasn't that what she was living for now?

Isabella stood up and looked at her bed. A year ago, its feathers swallowed her, encasing her in a soft cocoon that removed her from this diseased life of cat-and-mouse, post and repost, fire and brimstone. Her crew, especially the Africans, had little choice. They could starve on land, suffer the lashes of the overseer, or hold out living a life hovering at death's door and fueled by the bounty of their high-seas prey. Isabella saw the sparkle in the pupils of her crew's eyes as they boarded her ship, cleaned the barrels of the cannons, stacked the guns, and secured the shot and powder. They dreamed of the gold and silver the *El Cid* would fetch in Santo Domingo. They were already retiring to the lush hills of some Caribbean island or plot of land near Charlotte Amalie, St. Croix, Kingston, or Port Royal.

Isabella looked down into the makeshift washbasin carved from a driftwood log. Half the water had lapped out onto the floor overnight. She lifted her face to gaze into the grainy mirror that swayed with the pitch of the swells. Gold and silver were not enough for her. She'd realized that as she had lain on a slab deep in the bowels of El Morro, her back stripped of its flesh, as Juan Carlos coaxed her back from oblivion.

She lifted her hand to move a clump of tightly matted dark hair from her eyes. Her bronze skin had deepened in color since their run through the dusty clouds in the jungle and back to the long boats. She dipped her hands in what murky liquid remained and lifted it to her face. She felt the dust dissolve from her cheeks, and her eyelids opened as water dripped from her temples and chin, recycling back into the bowl. Another splash and Isabella felt refreshed; her eyes lifted again into the mirror and she inhaled fresh sea air.

Pursing her lips, she inspected the fleshy cheeks, round eyes, oddly curled hair of the girl everyone else seemed to know was different, even when she worked the sugarcane fields at the foothills of Spanish Hispaniola, Santo Domingo. Now, so many years later, she still didn't know why she was different, and the prophecy didn't help. "Binta," her mother had called her. "With God." But what God? Whose God?

Isabella narrowed her eyes as she remembered the flames overrunning the stars and crisp night sky so many years ago. Her cabin was a white ball of fire, and the master's house was alive with rollicking flashes of deadly light and the bark of exploding timber as air escaped from the intense heat. White-hot embers lifted souls far above the earth, disappearing into the heavens. She knew she was the cause of their deaths, but no one had told her the details. Just that her family was gone. And Gamba—innocent, naïve, obsessive, love-struck Gamba—was one of the first to perish.

Isabella gripped the sides of the basin, just a few droplets clinging to her jaw as they resisted nature's final tug into nothingness. She had to fulfill the prophecy. She had to make the Spanish pay for what they did to her mother. And Gamba. They had to account for the stolen childhoods, lost loves, and the pain of backbreaking work in the fields and the sugar processing plants.

"We're in the Straits of Jamaica." Jean-Michel's words drifted in a way that made it clear his eyes were focused somewhere else. Isabella looked off the bow of the boat's starboard side. The *Marée Rouge* was tacking north, letting the northeastern winds sweep across her canvas sails, as the wind beat around Cap Saint-Nicolas, one hundred twenty miles further up the passage and south into the narrow channel that separated Cuba from the French-speaking western shores and mountains of Hispaniola.

Isabella stepped up to Jean-Michel and scanned the horizon. "What's our speed?"

"About ten knots when we checked an hour ago. She's slow today. Don't know why. Maybe we took on some undersea hitchhikers on our hull. We'll scrape her keel when we get to Tortuga, Île de la Tortue."

"Looks like about three day's sail to Tortuga at this rate," Isabella mumbled, her words trailing off in discouragement.

Jean-Michel nodded. "Coming downwind would be faster, *mon cher*, but we're sailing against the trade winds. Coming from the north, we could fly down these straits, Détroit de la Jamaique, in less than a day!"

Isabella smiled. "That would be quite an enjoyable sail, *mon ami*." She turned to inspect the rigging. "She's holding up well. She's almost in top form again. You've done well, Jean-Michel."

"*Merci*." Jean-Michel looked toward the bow. About two dozen deck hands were straightening up ropes and rigging, bringing the sails in tight enough to buy another hour or two before they would have to tack east. "We'll sail tight to the wind until we see the coast of Cuba. Then we'll head back toward Hispaniola. We should clear the northern shores of Île de la Gonâve, the island at the mouth of Port-au-Prince Bay, by about twenty miles. We'll have to turn toward Cuba again, but once we pass north of her shores, we should be able to sail due east right into Tortuga Bay."

He turned back toward the northern horizon.

"What is it?" asked Isabella.

Jean-Michel shook his head. "I don't know. Something doesn't feel right."

Isabella laughed. "I think our voodoo priestess spooked you!"

Jean-Michel sent a disapproving glance toward Isabella. "Madame Rêve-Cœur knows a lot about these mountains and Saint-Domingue."

"We'll see," Isabella said as she began to walk toward the bow. Now that they were heading into the wind, the bow heaved over swells, and the deck seemed to jolt with each wave. Isabella gauged her steps, adjusting to the rhythm of the sea. The wind nipped at her cheeks, and the gusts seemed to keep the heat at bay for now. "I haven't seen much to convince me voodoo will keep me out of trouble."

"Don't dismiss her warnings, Isabella."

As they approached midships, Isabella lifted her hand to his arm and gave him a light squeeze. *"Merci, mon ami."*

Jean-Michel smiled. "Three days. I'll be happy when we are firmly under the safety of the guns of Tortuga Bay."

"And the protection of your homeland."

"How sure are you that the *Marée Rouge* is in the Straits of Jamaica?"

Capitán Muñoz looked at Juan Carlos and shook his head. "You know, Capitán, as well as I do, we have to trust our intelligence sources. The pirates were on St. Thomas just three weeks ago. *El Cid* was sold in Puerto de Santo Domingo for a sum that would make any sane person retire from the pirating life. She is in these straits."

Juan Carlos turned his head and looked down the weather deck of the *Santa Mónica*. He knew Isabella wouldn't dare run close to Puerto Rico. She was bold but not stupid. Muñoz appeared to have figured that out, too.

"The pirate wench is a lot of things," Muñoz said as if reading his mind, "but she doesn't take unnecessary risks. My bet is she is somewhere in this strait."

Juan Carlos looked up into the frigate's rigging. "I see you've doubled the watch in the crow's nests." He counted two marines on each platform, eyeglasses peering south.

Muñoz nodded. "I want to see her first and run down on her before she knows what's coming."

Juan Carlos nodded, only a slight tightness in his upper lip revealing the unease building inside his chest.

Isabella hoisted herself through the hatch just as pellets of rain began to splatter on the pitched deck of the *Marée Rouge*. A gust of wind snapped at the flap of her overcoat, nearly spinning her onto the hardwood slats that kept the deck below dry. The gathering storm covered the sun, casting a dark gray over the pirate vessel as it heeled under the force of the storm. She scanned the deck, noting as each pirate transformed into an expert seaman, securing the cannons and fastening ropes at each station. Three tars now manhandled the rudder as another gust pushed the *Marée Rouge* even further on its keel. Isabella made her way to a figure clutching at a rail, looking into the fury of the storm-swept sea off the ship's port side. They had come about and were now tacking back toward Hispaniola.

She grabbed Jean-Michel's arm as she lodged her foot against a raised wooden vent. "Cuba?"

Jean-Michel shook his head. "We had to tack earlier. This squall is the leading edge of a bigger storm. This course should let us ride it out." He paused and lifted a spyglass to his eyes. He looked east and then scanned the waves to the west.

"What is it?" Isabella yelled.

"Sails." Jean-Michel's tone was firm and noncommittal, but Isabella knew from experience to be worried.

"Why are we running?"

"I don't like a fight in the middle of a storm."

"That gives us the benefit of surprise!"

Jean-Michel let the telescope fall from his eye and looked at Isabella. "Let's just get to Tortuga."

The *Marée Rouge* shuddered when a wall of water lifted the hull as if scooped up by a giant hand. Isabella felt the deck heave toward her, buckling her knees and bringing her hip crashing against the hard wood. She grasped the wind as if it were an invisible rail. Her foot, lodged against a raised vent, flipped up, releasing her from her makeshift anchor to the deck just as the boat rolled down the backside of the wave. The deck pitch reversed, and Isabella rolled into the left gunwale. She grabbed at the ropes and stayed, holding the aft mast in place and looking up, half expecting the ship's rigging to collapse and bury her on the deck.

Jean-Michel hugged the ropes fastened to the gunwale, holding his body steady as another wall of water crested the railing and swept the deck clean of any loose rope, tools, or sailors. He looked toward the stern and saw sailors draped over the tiller, holding the *Marée Rouge* steady and on course.

Isabella spat out a mouthful of seawater and lifted her arms to clear her eyes. "Those waves must be twenty feet high!"

"Closer to thirty by my reckoning."

"At these winds…they're enough to roll us!"

Jean-Michel shook his head. "We're close, but not that close." He looked up the two masts at the three levels of spars that could hold three layers of sail: the large main sail, the mid-size topsail, and the smallest topgallant one hundred feet over the deck. Jean-Michel turned his eyes to a sail held fast to a boom extending from the rear mast almost to the stern railing. The wind kept the mizzen sail taut and out of harm's way, even though the tip of the boom holding it steady seemed to graze the tops of the largest waves. As long as they stayed on this line, with the wind across the deck, they wouldn't have to worry about being knocked overboard by a sudden shift in the blocks!

Another wave lifted the *Marée Rouge* into the gray light twenty feet higher than a calm sea. Isabella pulled herself up to Jean-Michel. "Shouldn't we shorten sail?" She looked up at the masts and rigging. Jean-Michel had already reefed the topgallants and the main sail, leaving only the main topsails halfway up the masts to keep the ship on speed and on track.

"I don't like that other ship. She had three masts. If she's a man o' war, she's at least the size of a frigate."

"What if she's a merchant ship?"

Jean-Michel shook his head. "Now look who's being reckless? I remember *El Cid*. We were lucky, and I don't want to rely on lady luck again on this trip."

Jean-Michel lifted the spyglass to his eye and scanned the waves again.

"Damn this storm!"

Captain Muñoz clutched the railing as the crest of a wave spun the frigate's bow across the wind again. The stern fell from under his feet as the back of the ship plunged off a receding wave. "Keep her bow downwind."

The helmsman looked as if he would throw a sword through Muñoz's heart if he weren't more afraid of being swept off the deck by the next wave. The wooden beam that kept the ship on course snapped to the side, pulling the helmsman off his feet as two more sailors threw their bodies against the tiller to steady the ship. They had barely turned the rudder back to its rightful place when the back of the ship heaved up under their feet to ride another twenty-foot roller.

Juan Carlos braced against the capstan before the helm, wedging himself between two bars as he prepared for the frigate to roll.

"Ha!" exclaimed Muñoz as he saw Juan Carlos bracing against the pitch of the storm. "I would hold on tight, Capitán! We wouldn't want to lose the Viceroy's senior advisor to the seas, would we?"

A wall of water crested the gunwale, washing across the deck as if a dam had finally broken, only to escape through the scuppers at the base of the railing.

"You'll learn," called Muñoz. "Even the sea can't wash you through those miserly holes. It'll take quite a bit to suck your body over into the water."

Muñoz's tone seemed disappointed, but Juan Carlos was too busy keeping himself tied to the deck to return a look.

"Can you see the *Marée Rouge?*" Juan Carlos's question immediately twisted Muñoz's face into a scowl.

"She's there!" the naval officer grumbled over the wind.

Juan Carlos looked over the starboard side of the ship as they crested another wave. The wind and rain swept across the deck, slammed against his back with a stinging slap, and chased the evil brew of salt and fresh water rain into the blackness over the rails. Juan Carlos lifted his sleeve, realized the futility of clearing his eyes with rain-soaked wool, and swept the water with his hand. He shook his head. "I don't see her!"

"She's there," growled Muñoz again, his grasp of the rails and ropes firm and seasoned. "Once the waves die down, we'll be on her."

"Are we headed east?"

Muñoz sent another scoffing look toward Juan Carlos. "At least you haven't lost your skills for navigation." He looked up into the darkened sky, a nod to the difficulty in knowing which direction the ship would be heading in such a tempest. "Those pirates are smart. They're headed for Port-au-Prince."

Juan Carlos tried to hide the satisfaction that warmed his insides at the thought of Isabella and Jean-Michel resting comfortably in the calm waters of the Baie de Port-au-Prince. "We've got to catch them before they make it to French waters."

Muñoz nodded. "The French have reinforced the colony."

"I've been instructed by both His Royal Majesty's Court and Viceroy Rodriguez that our mission is not to call into question France's lawful control of Saint-Domingue as long as she respects our control of Santo Domingo."

"Agreed," Muñoz said. "But Governor Bellecombe may not see us as so friendly. The *gens de couleur* are advocating for more rights, and the French governor is concerned about how these free blacks might encourage a revolt by the slaves on the plantations."

"They have put down slave revolts before; they will do it again. We have always found the free blacks to be allies in helping us govern our colonies."

"Exactly, and that's why Bellecombe suspects us." Muñoz looked at Juan Carlos and shook his head. "You have a lot to learn about the politics of the West Indies, Capitán."

Juan Carlos looked toward the rain-beaten figure of the naval officer, Spain's most seasoned commander in the Caribbean, and shook his head again. He hoped the newly minted Capitán de Navio was wrong.

"We've got to turn into the wind!"

Isabella knew her desperate plea was useless even before she saw Jean-Michel shake his head. He turned toward the three tars at the helm, and their forms seemed to melt into the wooden tiller as they used all their might to protect their course from the steady crash of waves against the rudder. Each roll seemed to push the *Marée Rouge* to the cusp of heeling over, but she always came back to center.

"Steady!" Jean-Michel yelled toward the helmsmen and his crew. He turned back to Isabella and pulled himself toward the port railing where she stood, wrapped in ropes, braced for another wave. The deck angled again as the waves and wind pushed the *Marée Rouge* onto her beam.

Isabella resisted the urge to look at the rigging; it wouldn't help. Jean-Michel had rigged her for the storm. If he had made a mistake, there was little they could do now.

Isabella looked at Jean-Michel, her eyes wide with questions.

Jean-Michel shook his head, cutting off whatever protest Isabella was trying to muster. "We don't have any choice." He pointed over the railing, which had descended to a far less-threatening angle, but revealed the charge of yet another monster wave. "The closer we get to Île de la Gonâve, the safer we will be."

"How do you know they are out there?"

"I saw three masts just before the rains started. The waves were already at ten feet, maybe even fifteen feet. If I could see her masts, she was very close. A frigate by my reckoning, and she could overtake us easily in strong winds."

Isabella shook her head. "We might not even make it to that island in this storm!"

"We'll get through," Jean-Michel said, lifting his hand to her shoulder. He let his hand slip past her and onto a rope, wrapping his fingers around it and pulling his body between Isabella and the gunwales. The deck seemed to lurch upward, pressuring their knees to buckle. Another liquid mass overwhelmed them as they held fast, just long enough for the deck to flood, and then they watched the water recede through the scuppers into the churn. "I don't want to fight a Spanish frigate…or an English one for that matter…in this weather. We're better off running for Port-au-Prince."

Isabella laced her hand through Jean-Michel's arm, grabbing a rope behind his back and bracing for another blitz of briny water. "I hope you're right," she sputtered through another submersion.

"We don't have much choice, Isabella." Jean-Michel's tone was apologetic. "Another hour and we should be well under Cap Saint-Nicolas. Another hour after that we should be protected. We'll sail south of the island and right into the Baie de Port-au-Prince."

Isabella closed her eyes, letting the rain wash the salt water from her face and off her eyelids. *I hope you are right,* mon ami. *Otherwise, this sail will be our last.*

As if on cue, the winds melted into the waning afternoon sky twenty miles east of the point the *Marée Rouge* would have crossed under Cap Saint-Nicolas. The fury of the storm-whisked sea faded into great rolling waves, pushing then pulling the brig eastward. Jean-Michel mustered scores of tars into the yardarms to unfurl more sail as soon as the foam-capped walls of water were held in check by their vessel's gunwales.

"Ship?" he called to a pirate scouring the horizons from the aft crow's nest. The silence was all Jean-Michel needed to know as he turned his attention to the pirates scrambling to restore order on the deck. He walked toward the bow, inspecting the ropes, blocks, and cannons to ensure they were secure.

Isabella looked into the tempering froth of the sea, wondering if Papa Legba or Lasiren had yet another surprise in store for her band of pirates. The squall had become a mini tempest as her winds hurled their small warship toward the Baie de Port-au-Prince. Perhaps they had been tossed from harm's way.

"Sail!"

Isabella's head snapped upward to the sound of the warning. The figure's telescope was directed to the rear, and Isabella followed the imaginary line to the horizon.

Jean-Michel lifted his hand to his eyes, shielding his face from what was left of the afternoon sun, its winds fighting to clear the last puffs of storm clouds descending on victims to their south. He shook his head. "I don't see them." He turned up to the flying top. "How many?"

"Tough to make out from here. She's got at least two masts. I can see the topgallants, but that's all."

Isabella turned from the pirate in the crow's nest to Jean-Michel. "I thought we were being chased by a frigate. A frigate would have three masts. And she would have more than enough sail to catch us."

Jean-Michel's face tightened as his thoughts twisted. He whirled toward the bow. A small rise of green and brown was growing from the horizon in front of them: Île de la Gonâve. "I reckon we're making fifteen knots, maybe sixteen. If our chaser is a two-master, she's probably a brig if she's a warship. She can match our speed. If she's a frigate, she can probably gain on us at a knot or two more speed." He looked over to Isabella, as if he knew she needed reassurance. "We should make it into *Hôpital* by then."

Isabella's eyebrows turned up at the old name for Port-au-Prince. "You remember the *flibustiers*, rogue pirates from Tortuga who settled Saint-Domingue?"

Jean-Michel laughed. "Only by reputation; the stories of old pirates. They're farmers now, sons and daughters of those wandering pirates who built the hospital on western slopes. That's where they got the name *Hôpital*."

"I thought the pirates were purged when France moved their capital from Cap Français to Port-au-Prince in 1770."

A wry smile lightened Jean-Michel's face. "So says His Majesty Louis XVI."

Isabella nodded. "Our insurance policy."

"Our voodoo priestess doesn't just live in her hut on a ridge."

Isabella leaned back against the portside railing, gripping a rope to steady herself as the pitch of the *Marée Rouge* steepened with steady gusts of wind that boosted her speed by two more knots. She thought of Lasiren and Papa Legba. She closed her eyes and saw the young African girl she had dreamed of in the stories her mother had told late at night after the overseer had gone to bed. "Binta." That's what her mother had called her so long ago, and Madame Rêve-Cœur knew it. Somehow. She reached in her blouse and wrapped her fingers around a cross and a key. Another gust swept over the deck of the *Marée Rouge*. Isabella folded her arms, pulling the wool sleeves close to quell the chill and ward off the shiver that had just swept down her back.

15

Isabella sat perched in the bowsprit as the *Marée Rouge* glided to its assigned mooring. The point of dropping anchor several hundred yards from the nearest pier was a clear enough signal that the harbor captain needed proof of their peaceful intentions. Fair enough, she thought. She didn't want to spend any more time in Port-au-Prince than absolutely necessary.

"A Spanish frigate," Jean-Michel said as if answering a question she had floated toward him.

Isabella kept her gaze on the port, founded four generations earlier by *flibustiers*—pirates searching for their own piece of land—and a stop away from the crowded Tortuga. The squared fronts of two-story wooden warehouses lined the waterfront before her, and merchant ships lay tethered to the docks on the north side of the bay. Loads of sugar, bundles of cotton, and barrels of indigo inched up planks and into the holds of schooners ready to whisk them to ports in the Americas and Europe.

"Not a white back under those loads," Isabella said.

"Aye. I've heard talk among the tars that the *gens de couleur* are growing restless. They hear what is happening in the Americas and read the news from France." Jean-Michel placed his hand on Isabella's shoulder, and she leaned back into his chest.

"Revolution is bloody," she said.

Jean-Michel squeezed her shoulder. "Aye." He leaned over and kissed the maroon bandana covering her head. "But sometimes, *mon cher*, we have no choice."

Isabella closed her eyes. "The Americas in revolt against the British. Peasants rising up against the lords and princes? Maybe 1781 will be the year for freedom."

She lifted her hand to her shoulder and covered Jean-Michel's fingers, her tips just touching the hard calluses over his joints, seasoned by years at sea. "The bay is so calm. The slaves are doing what they are told. Nothing seems amiss in the warehouses."

"At least not that we can see." Jean-Michel sat next to Isabella. He pointed to the hills rising hundreds of feet above the port. "The trees mask the truth under a canopy of palms. The plantations are busy, but the hills hide another plan, another plot."

Isabella let her hand slide down Jean-Michel's arm and rested her head on his shoulder. "Is that what we'll find when we go into town? A hidden plot?"

Jean-Michel reached over to her knee and gave it a firm pat. "I don't know what we'll find, but we'll have to go in at some point. We have only enough food for so long."

Isabella brought her knees up to her chest and wrapped them with her arms as she looked out over the bay into the last few minutes of daylight. "A frigate."

She didn't have to see Jean-Michel's nod to know he was confirming her suspicions. "A Spanish frigate?"

"Aye."

"Just one?"

"Unfortunately not. We spotted two schooners and a ketch, all armed, flying His Most Catholic Majesty's colors. They are just outside the bay."

"Will the governor of Saint-Domingue let that stand? A Spanish squadron constricting their most precious artery? That seems like a diplomatic breach."

"The Treaty of Ryswick has kept the colony secure in French hands for seventy-eight years. The new governor is an army general and former colonial governor in India. Guillaume Léonard de Bellecombe took over from Jean-Baptist de Taste de Lilancour last summer. Lilancour knew the invisible maps of all the players in Western Hispaniola. It led him to three appointments as acting governor of Saint-Domingue."

Isabella laughed. "How do you know all this?"

Jean-Michel smiled. "Jacob was a good teacher. He knew politics as well as anyone, and he was a master at navigating the personalities of these islands."

Isabella lifted a hand to her eyes, anticipating the tears welling inside. "I do miss him."

Jean-Michel stretched an arm around her shoulders and pulled her closer. "I know. I miss him, too. He was a good man."

"For a pirate."

Jean-Michel smiled. "Aye, for a pirate." He turned and kissed the side of her head. "He loved you, Isabella."

Isabella sniffed, wiping away the lone tear that had managed to escape.

The reds and oranges unleashed by the setting sun cast a rich pastel pall over the bay, the wooden hulls of merchant ships with furled sails, and the closed fronts of warehouses. The lush green of the jungles darkened as yellow spots appeared, lanterns lighting the streets and flickering through the windows of inns and bars. The wharves were empty of workers, but the streets were dotted with moving black specks as men and women made their way into the night, disappearing into the layers of wooden storefronts, saloons, shops, and bars. Isabella was sure that they would soon hear the noises of sailors from merchantmen making sure hard-earned pay was used to maximize their pleasure for a few hours off the ships.

"I'll set the watch," Jean-Michel said, lifting himself from the bowsprit. "I don't trust those dirty dagos to leave us alone or respect French sovereignty. We'll keep everyone on board tonight. Perhaps tomorrow we can make a call to the harbor captain and arrange for shore leave for our crew."

Isabella sat watching the lanterns transform from flickering spots to pulsating waves of yellow. The merchant ships idled at their moorings, as if keeping a lazy watch over their tethers as they swayed to the shifting tide.

She let her shoulders drop as exhaustion overwhelmed her. The storm had battered her physically and making port against high tide had added even more stress. Strong winds had allowed them to keep headway, despite the tides—a benefit of having just a one-and-half-foot drop in water levels so close to the equator—but their Spanish stalker had plenty of time to close the gap.

Isabella patted the spar extending from the prow out over the water. *Thank you, Jacob, for giving me such a fine vessel. Her clean lines saved our lives yet again.*

Juan Carlos inventoried the thin lines that made up the masts of a half dozen ships moored in the bay outside Port-au-Prince. The light was fading, but Isabella and Jean-Michel had made it. He closed his eyes and drew a deep breath before letting out the air that would deflate his lungs, loosen his muscles, and lull him into a relaxed sleep in a few hours.

"Damn these tides," Captain Muñoz muttered.

"The *Marée Rouge* is a fast packet, Capitán Muñoz," Juan Carlos said, letting his eyes slide up to meet his commander.

"You talk about her like she's a merchant ship carrying ordinary mail," Muñoz scoffed, holding the scene firm in his view.

"She's a fast vessel. Before she was outfitted with guns, I think she would have made a fine courier."

Muñoz chuckled. "I suppose a soldier would see her as a merchantman first, not a warship."

"What is our next move?" Juan Carlos asked, keeping his eyes on the naval officer.

Muñoz didn't turn toward the army officer. "We wait."

"I'll take the cutter and a landing party into port in the morning."

Muñoz shook his head. "The acting governor probably is not pleased with our presence. Let's wait and see how patient this pirate is. We'll station our warships across the bay. Nothing will get in or out without my knowing about it. If the *Marée Rouge* even hints at an escape, her decks will stoke the fires in our galleys before she can spread full canvas!"

"What if they resist? You know how stubborn the French can be. And Louis XVI hasn't shown much interest in keeping the Caribbean in check, even if he has sided with Spain and the Americans against the British."

"Not to worry, Capitán. My patience can last only so long. The French may have the world's second largest navy, but I command the largest fleet in these waters. I am more than willing to find the appropriate means to fulfill my obligations to my Viceroy and my

King." He turned to Juan Carlos. "Capítan Santa Ana, I may have need for the army's services after all."

Juan Carlos's half-hearted nod would have alerted a more observant commander to his true intentions. But Muñoz had turned to the bay, watching the tides, assessing the *Marée Rouge's* prospects for getting under sail once the tide turned.

Meanwhile, his squadron of pirate hunters rested, moored just to the east of Île de la Gonâve, licking the wounds laid bare by the tempest. Juan Carlos looked at the wharves, their planks and wooden ramps barely populated as the sun dipped below the dark silhouette of the hills rising above the island. He hoped Isabella and Jean-Michel realized they could not afford the time to rest.

16

"How long will they wait?"

As the morning light washed over Île de la Gonâve, the swaying masts revealed predators at the mouth of the bay resolved to block her escape.

Jean-Michel's chortle was nonchalant, as if chiding Isabella for being so naïve. "Until they get bored."

Isabella grimaced. "That's not much help. I could use some insight from the master naval strategist that Jacob relied on to get us out of these messes."

"*Mon cher*, you worry too much. I thought you would be appreciating the beauty of the sunrise."

The sun's rays had crested the mountains east of Port-au-Prince, igniting white sparkles across the bay as they rippled with the changing tides. The show had started with yellow streaks bursting from the crags and uneven peaks in the looming mountains, touching the hills of the island before spreading into a line across the horizon that descended to the sea. Yellows gave way to pulsating whites, purples, pastel greens and blues, as the bay seemed to come to life. The beauty, as natural and welcoming as its pull could be, was unable to shake Isabella's gaze from the three masts of the Spanish frigate *Santa Mónica* and the three armed sloops of war serving as escorts.

"I want to make a run for the sea."

Jean-Michel's laugh carried a hard edge this time. "Patience, Isabella. If we leave now, we'll play right into their hands."

"We can take a Spanish frigate."

Jean-Michel brought his hands down on the wooden rail with a thump. "Those thoughts will get you killed. And me. And the other one hundred pirates on this boat!"

Isabella let her head fall into her hands. "I'm tired of running."

"We're all tired of running, but what choice do we have? The Viceroy has a pretty steep price on your head. We rise and fall with you."

"Let's go into the mountains, live with the maroons in the jungles. The armies won't dare pursue us."

Jean-Michel turned to Isabella so he could see her face. "Rodriguez would track you down. He would burn the jungles until he found you."

Isabella's eyes softened. "What about Juan Carlos?"

Jean-Michel lifted both hands to her cheeks, letting his thumbs sweep imaginary tears from below her eyes. "He loves, or he does not. You can do nothing if he does not. Stay with those who can."

Tears, once imagined, now glistened over dark eyes. Isabella pulled Jean-Michel close and let her head fall into his shoulder as his arms folded around her.

In any other port, at any other time, the call from nearly seventy-five feet in the flying tops overhead would have been cause for eager anticipation, thoughts of lace, fine woven cotton, silk, gold or other coin from hapless victims, coaxing even the laziest tar from his hammock. This time, sitting at anchor in the bay of a vibrant port city, the call of "Sail!" generated curiosity more than concern for pirates...except for Jean-Michel and Isabella.

The warning sent Jean-Michel's hand into his topcoat as Isabella stepped toward the railing to scan the mouth of the bay. He pulled a spyglass from an inside pocket, but hesitated before lifting it to his eye.

"They're sending a sloop," Isabella said, watching the boat's canvas fill as it cleared away from the Spanish frigate and chased the tide into the bay.

"Aye, a cutter from its lines," Jean-Michel responded with a distant tone. "She must have come up alongside the frigate during the night."

"Good news, I think. They must have decided to keep their distance."

Jean-Michel sighed. "Aye." The telescope fell to his side, and he turned to Isabella with a taut jaw. "But it's not a normal meeting with the harbor captain. She's heading our way, and she's ferrying more than a Spanish naval captain. Captain Juan Carlos Lopez de Santa Ana is also on board. Call to quarters!"

Isabella's heart thumped, and each beat seemed to tighten her chest another notch to keep air from escaping her lungs or blood from nourishing her organs. She dared not pace, even as her feet seemed to step on their own before her brain forced them back into form, shoulder width apart, knees with a slight bend to absorb gentle rolls from under the keel. She kept her arms to her sides, letting her hands catch each other behind her, stiffening her back to project her authority without betraying the turmoil that roiled inside her. She closed her eyes and pictured the approaching boat. Its sails were full as it carried a human cargo of two Spanish officers, six marines, and four sailors toward the *Marée Rouge*.

Not long ago, she and Juan Carlos had shared a room above the Wooden Anchor in Charlotte Amalie. Jean-Michel and Charles had kept steady watch as they stole precious hours alone. She imagined his strong jaw, her fingers lacing through his dark locks as he held her in his embrace, their lips touching for what seemed like hours, as she invited his fingers to knead away the tension in her body, built from fortnights spent apart. She slept well that night but felt the emptiness as soon as he slipped away in the early morning hours to return to his royal mission. She knew they would be together again but had prayed it would be under the protective cover of friends. She drew in a deep breath as she steeled herself for a confrontation that could not, under any circumstances, betray her real hopes and desires.

"Prepare to be boarded!"

The order didn't come from the naval officer, dressed in the Spanish regalia of the fleet, or the younger army captain lodged a step behind him.

Jean-Michel peered over at the sloop-rigged vessel, no more than thirty feet in length, a boat clearly intended for little more than ferry service in calm waters, not fighting pirates. "We don't fly under the colors of Spain, and we are anchored peacefully in a neutral port," he called down to the invaders. "You have no authority to board our ship."

The cutter paused in the water, as if waiting for its own orders.

"Hardly a ship," called the naval officer. "Your vessel may be armed as if it sailed with three masts, but I see only two. You don't rate as a ship. Given your armament, I would say you are a pirate, and pirates are rogues in these waters no matter what port they rest in."

"We've not been asked to leave," Jean-Michel responded. "Until I see the letter from Governor General Bellecombe himself, I am happy to stay where we are, and who boards this ship is our choice and that of my captain. I can't vouch for your safety if you try to board without permission."

The cutter had turned away from the tide, its bow facing the open water as its crew adjusted the canvas to capture just enough wind to keep it abreast of the *Marée Rouge*. A few more moments passed before the officer responded. "Then I request permission to come aboard."

Jean-Michel looked over to Isabella. She remained two steps behind him, giving her a view of the sloop without revealing the full form of her own identity. Jean-Michel arched his brow, as if asking for her answer. "We could tell them to go back to their ship."

Isabella nodded. "How will the harbor captain react to a Spanish squadron cruising the mouth of the bay?"

"*Pas de joie*," his skeptical expression making his words unnecessary.

Isabella let her fingers grip her clasped hands, glancing toward Juan Carlos in the makeshift ferry. She nodded again.

Jean-Michel looked over to two tars waiting a few steps down the deck. With one nod, one began to unhinge a rail while the other scurried to a passel of ropes tethered to the side of the boat. He stepped up to the gangway and lifted a hand to his mouth. "Aye, sir, you have permission to board—as my captain's guest!"

"Welcome aboard the *Marée Rouge*, Captain," Isabella said, reading the braids on Captain Muñoz's coat sleeves. She kept her arms to her sides, her forearm cradled between the hilt of her sword and a scarlet sash strapped around her breeches.

Captain Muñoz looked at Isabella, over to Jean-Michel, then back to Isabella. He nodded, keeping his arms to his side, the two gold laces on each cuff making his rank clear, and his hands resting on the hilt of a sword and the handle of a flintlock pistol. His blue, gold-laced bicorn hat remained lodged on his head.

Blood surged through Isabella's veins, and her look at the naval officer hardened as she carved his face out of what was becoming a crowd. "Capitán," she said, emphasizing the Spanish pronunciation and giving a pause for emphasis. "You are on my ship as my guest."

Muñoz looked at the pirates assembling around his boarding party. Spanish marines stepped to both sides of him, hammers pulled back on their flintlocks, ready to ignite sparks in the powder and send balls from their barrels with the twitch of the trigger.

Isabella smiled and shook her head. "I have one hundred and fifty sailors on this ship, Captain. I'm sure your marines are well trained, but each would have three blades pierced through their guts by the time they could lift their bayonets even if each ball found a mark." Isabella extended her hand. "I am Isabella."

Muñoz's hands stayed at his sides. "I know who you are. You are a pirate, and I've been sent to bring you back to Viceroy José María Ferdinand Rodriguez to face the judgment of the court of His Most Royal Catholic Majesty Charles III."

Snickering trickled through the pirates, and the soft shuffle of feet prompted Jean-Michel to lift a hand with an open palm facing away from him. The shuffling stopped, but the lone sound of someone spitting over the side railing drew a critical look from Jean-Michel to one side of the group.

Muñoz thrust quick glances around the crowd, but he held his stand. He looked at Isabella's extended hand and started to lift his hand from the grip of the pistol, just as Isabella retracted hers to her waist. Muñoz straightened his shoulders. "Do you really want to challenge Spain?"

Isabella continued to smile. Juan Carlos stood behind Muñoz, stiff but relaxed. The heat was rising as the morning sun cruised the bay, but none of the soldiers seemed to notice. Her own crew, most barefoot, were dressed in well-worn wool shirts and breeches, standard attire for tending the ropes and sails of a working warship. Isabella tried to keep a knowing smile bottled up as she assessed the contrast between the outnumbered professional warriors and the ragtag scrappers that made up her crew. Juan Carlos had dressed the part for Rodriguez and Muñoz. She had seen him, felt him come closer to her. She looked around at her tars, and her chest filled with pride. None would betray Juan Carlos. None would betray her. She turned back to Muñoz and nodded. Muñoz lifted his chin, not realizing her gesture was for someone else.

"I'm sure you know about my last experience with your Viceroy's hospitality."

"I'm sure we can do a better job accommodating you this time."

Isabella's laugh was light but full. "I'm sure you could, Captain." She looked at the marines, still standing at the ready, and she shook her head. "Can you at least give me the courtesy of knowing the name of the Viceroy's emissary?"

Muñoz looked at Isabella as if trying to resist, but she knew that the Spaniard would have to relent if he had any chance of moving the negotiation forward. "I am Capítan Muñoz. I have the authority to negotiate on behalf of Viceroy Rodriguez, and I am in command of the West Indies fleet."

Jean-Michel cast a doubting glance toward Isabella, but a snapping glare kept him silent. She turned her attention back to Muñoz. "I don't doubt that for a moment."

Isabella stepped to the side of Muñoz and looked around the boarding party, counting the marines and noting the missing sailors. She saw Muñoz tracking her movements, and she caught the rigid professional pose of Juan Carlos out of the corner of her eye. She didn't need a complete gaze to recognize the familiarity of his five-foot, ten-inch frame, his hair pulled back in a ponytail, making his well-defined patrician features even more evident. She had called him "elegant" one time, knowing full well it would challenge his military bearing, eliciting the reaction she intended, much to his embarrassment and her entertainment. His uniform showed the respect he had always given to his calling, despite the humble conditions of a small warship at sea, chasing down pirates.

She forced her fingers around the hilt of her saber, steadying it as she stepped around the encircled marines, knowing her real desire was to touch the cheek of the man she wanted to pull into her arms. She sent a sideways glance toward Muñoz and shook her head. "Capitán Muñoz, I'm surprised."

The captain's jaw remained set as his eyes met Isabella's.

"Your two most senior officers are on my ship," she said, her hand flicking toward Juan Carlos. "Do you have that much confidence in a frigate lieutenant that he could lead your squadron into this bay, defeat me, and take my head to the Viceroy?"

The captain's eyes twitched toward Juan Carlos before steadying his glare back onto Isabella. "My officers are well trained. You are underestimating the King's navy."

Isabella tapped the hilt of her sword. "It seems like a fool's risk. After all, I've escaped from your fortress before, and I've defeated your Viceroy's squadrons."

"A draw is not a win," the captain said, his shoulders straightening.

Isabella smiled. "For me, a draw gives me another day to fight on the sea. I'll count it as a win."

Muñoz's eyes snapped toward Jean-Michel, then back to Isabella. "A draw is not a win."

Jean-Michel stepped toward the captain, edging the toe of his boot just in front of Isabella. "Captain Muñoz, unlike my captain, I have no issues with ordering my crew to cut your marines down with shot and cutlass."

"You would invite certain death."

"This crew has been through tighter scrapes than the one you have presented to us this morning." Jean-Michel squared himself in front of the Spanish captain. "Don't forget, Capitán Muñoz, our men have nothing to lose. Death in battle simply builds our legend."

"And don't you forget," Capitán Muñoz said, keeping his focus on Jean-Michel, "I have everything to lose if I return to San Juan without the Pirate of Panther Bay."

Jean-Michel smiled. "Well, then, perhaps we should alleviate you of that worry." Jean-Michel lifted his arm, and the clicks of a score of muskets echoed across the bay. "You see, Capitán, almost half my crew are brethren to the Pirate of Panther Bay, men who have escaped the chains and whips of the fields your King grants without respect to the God-given rights of those who work his plantations. Whether they die now, or in a day, does not matter to them, as long as they do not die in

102

the shadows of El Morro or by the hands of the court's appointed masters."

Muñoz's eyes darted from face to face behind Jean-Michel. The marines stood, waiting for their commander's order. One of the pirates lifted his musket, aiming it at one of the marines. Muñoz's eyes steadied on Jean-Michel, and the marines tightened their ranks.

"I don't think this is what His Excellency hoped would come of our meeting with these pirates, Capitán Muñoz." The firm tone of Juan Carlos's voice seemed to cut through the tension with the ease of a knife through butter. He stepped forward, nudging past Muñoz as the toes of his boot inched in front of the Captain of the Navy.

Jean-Michel nodded, but kept his glare cold. He sized up Juan Carlos, taking in the white coat, the blue collar, lapels, and cuffs giving his physique clean lines. Two epaulettes marked his rank as captain in the island regiments of the Vice Admiralty of the West Indies. A white gorget covered his throat, the royal arms stitched into the fabric.

Juan Carlos removed his bicorn hat, but kept his eyes trained on Jean-Michel. "Señor, I think we should talk. The death of Capitán Muñoz would only invite disaster, and I'm sure that Governor General Bellecombe would be quite displeased to find his port engulfed in a pitched battle between His Most Catholic Majesty's fleet and a wretched band of pirates."

Jean-Michel stared at Juan Carlos, turned his gaze toward the marines, and then looked at Muñoz. "I think Capitán Muñoz is ready to die for his King right now."

"Of course," Juan Carlos said, keeping his eyes trained on Jean-Michel, as if nothing else on the deck of the brig mattered. "He is loyal to his King and country—as we all are—but setting this bay on fire will accomplish neither of our goals."

An eyebrow turned up as Jean-Michel brought his arm down to his waist. The pirates didn't lower their weapons, but the air seemed to lighten. "An Army captain? Aren't you stepping out of turn?"

Juan Carlos turned to Muñoz, acknowledging him with a slight bend at the waist, and then turned back to Jean-Michel. "We were both sent on behalf of the Viceroy to negotiate your surrender to the court."

"Surrender?" Jean-Michel's guffaw sent a wave of laughter through the pirates. "I really don't think surrender makes much sense."

103

Muñoz shifted his weight, his fingers taking a deliberate track to his sword and pistol grip.

"But you don't know our terms," Juan Carlos said.

Jean-Michel looked at Muñoz. "I think your captain made his terms very clear."

Juan Carlos smiled. "Sí! Always start negotiations from your most extreme position; a classic negotiating tactic! But, of course, pirates don't negotiate…often. Perhaps we can make an exception. After all, the British provided amnesty for pirates more than a century ago, and hundreds found that choice better than going to a watery grave at the hands of the Royal Navy."

Jean-Michel continued to look at Muñoz. The naval captain's eyes glistened with intensity. Jean-Michel lifted his palm to the captain like an offering.

Isabella stepped toward Jean-Michel, providing a fourth edge to what had become a square as they faced each other. She looked at Jean-Michel, lifting her hand to his arm, and then to Muñoz, her eyes avoiding Juan Carlos. "Who is this army officer?"

Muñoz seemed to grit his teeth. "A captain in the Puerto Rican regiment. He also serves His Excellency."

"Oh," Isabella said, letting her eyes fall to the deck, as if acknowledging the odd relationship and awkwardness of the Spanish captain's chain of command. She turned her eyes back to Muñoz, knowing that the insult of a glance toward Juan Carlos could trigger the deaths of dozens of sailors and marines. "Does your mission call for the death of the two most senior members of your squadron?"

"Of course not!" Muñoz grumbled.

She allowed a darting glance toward Juan Carlos before fixing her eyes on the squadron commander. "Then perhaps we need more time."

Juan Carlos nodded. "Capitán Muñoz…with your permission…, I would like to stay on board with these pirates to discuss terms for their surrender."

Jean-Michel shook his head. "And what will that accomplish, pray tell?"

Isabella snapped her gaze back to Jean-Michel. "The loss of eight men and possibly more." She looked back at Muñoz. "But I agree with my first mate. By the time your cutter returns to pick up your army captain, we'll know if we are going to die by the sword or run the risk of dying on your gallows."

Muñoz and his marines had barely pushed away in their launch before Juan Carlos and Isabella had slid down the ladder into the hold below the gun deck. Another fifty tars had been waiting below, cutlasses and pistols ready, in case a fight had started. Now, with the Spanish captain safely on his way back to his frigate, the muffled clinging of blades and stocks of wooden muskets were the welcome signs of a warship returning to normalcy.

Juan Carlos followed Isabella as they made their way past the few pirates who recognized his face, through the stateroom and into her cabin. Jean-Michel lingered, barking orders to the crew to organize the return to their peaceful beds.

As the door to her cabin closed, Isabella slipped her arms under Juan Carlos's shoulders and pulled his chest into her turned head. She lifted her fingers so she could cup his shoulders, careful to avoid the hard wood of the epaulettes, as his arms wrapped around her and his chin fell to the top of her head.

"I am sorry, Isabella."

She lifted her face, his dark eyes glistening with tears he would not release. She lifted her lips to his, and they kissed. His hands found the nape of her neck and ascended into her hair before rounding the lines of her jaw to cup her cheeks as he pulled his kiss away. Isabella kept her eyes closed, letting his touch meld into her face as his thumbs skimmed her lips, opening her mouth to taste the salt of his skin.

She released a long shallow breath, letting her arms fall to his waist, as Juan Carlos gave her forehead a light caress and then brought their lips together again. They held this kiss, their bodies fused, her breasts folded into his chest, and their legs interwoven. Isabella pushed her hands inside Juan Carlos's coat, her fingers sweeping across his chest as she began to loosen the buttons of his waistcoat. He brought his hands down to Isabella's waist, pressing his fingers into her breeches and then up under her blouse, stroking the length of the flesh and muscles along her spine, each movement timed with the rhythm of their kisses.

Isabella drew in another breath, locking her lips onto his before letting her head fall away so she could look into his eyes. *"Mi amor,"* she whispered in a voice so soft only Juan Carlos could sense its meaning.

Juan Carlos looked into her eyes and kissed her cheek. *"Quiero hacer el amor contigo."*

Isabella let another kiss fall onto her lips. "I know. *Mí también.* I remember our last night...in the Wooden Anchor...in Charlotte Amalie."

Juan Carlos pressed Isabella into his body as his lips traced a line from her mouth to her cheek, and she angled her face so they could fall into her neck. "I know. *Yo sé, mi amor. Quiéreme."*

Isabella pulled her hands from the waistcoat and brought them up to cup Juan Carlos's face. "I will."

A thudding knock on the cabin door sent Isabella's forehead into Juan Carlos's chest. *"Mi amor*...my love."

Another, sharper knock separated their ankles and knees, drawing a final kiss from Juan Carlos before Isabella let herself fall onto the edge of her cot. She rolled her eyes before letting them close, savoring the last moment of their touch.

She sighed and kept her focus on the wooden planks beneath her. *"Qui? Est-ce toi,* Jean-Michel?" Isabella turned to look at Juan Carlos, her eyes moist with a glint of remorse.

The latch to the cabin door turned, and Jean-Michel entered the small room, ducking to avoid hitting the crossbeams. He looked at Juan Carlos, registering the folds, creases, and loose buttons marking the captain's dress. "I'm not sure His Most Catholic Majesty would approve."

Juan Carlos shot Jean-Michel a reproaching look.

Jean-Michel unleashed a broad smile. He stepped over to Juan Carlos and patted his shoulder, careful to avoid touching the epaulettes. "Relax, Capítan Santa Ana! You know where my loyalties lie." Jean-Michel turned to Isabella and winked.

"And your crew?"

Jean-Michel gave one shake of his head. "I cannot speak for them all, and I would be lying if I said they were on board with this affair, but they had their opportunity on deck; they stayed loyal to the Pirate of Panther Bay."

Isabella lifted herself from her bed, tucking her blouse back into her breeches. She stepped over to Jean-Michel, touching his shoulder. "I don't know how much longer this can go on."

Jean-Michel patted Isabella's hand and looked over to Juan Carlos. "As long as we claim prizes like *El Cid*, the crew will be fine. Pirates are nothing if not practical and predictable. Isabella brings them riches and that has bought their loyalty."

Juan Carlos reassembled his uniform, unable to control a sheepish peek toward Isabella. "That can't go on for much longer."

Isabella looked at Juan Carlos. "What choice do we have?"

Juan Carlos looked at Jean-Michel. "I don't know, but we don't have much more time. If I don't come back with the Pirate of Panther Bay, I might as well escort myself to the gallows of El Morro and tie the noose around my own neck."

"*Assurément*," Jean-Michel said, nodding before turning to Isabella with a crooked smile. "That creates a problem. I don't think Isabella's ready to meet with your Viceroy."

The trio stood in the small cabin, the heat of the mid-morning sun finally settling into the room. Juan Carlos loosened his collar as Jean-Michel strode past the bed to the windows at the back of the cabin. He peered out the window at the *Santa Mónica*. "Muñoz has been delivered to his charge. I reckon we have an hour before the cutter pulls alongside to take our illustrious captain back to the frigate."

"How long does Muñoz plan to blockade Port-au-Prince?"

Juan Carlos sighed. "As long as it takes, I'm afraid."

Isabella slid to Juan Carlos's side and slipped her arm around his waistcoat. "His arrogance could have killed him on deck before you stepped in."

"Rodriguez is counting on impatience and impulsiveness. He didn't promote Muñoz to admiral even though he gave him command of the squadron."

Jean-Michel turned away from the windows and leaned against them. "An incentive to bring the Pirate of Panther Bay back to the dungeons of El Morro?"

Juan Carlos nodded, pulling Isabella closer. "He won't leave the bay without her."

"I can't allow my men to be slaughtered," Isabella said.

Juan Carlos cocked his head, sending a sideways glance to Jean-Michel. "I thought the *Marée Rouge* carried two hundred pirates."

Jean-Michel sat down on the cot. "We sailed with one hundred fifty from Charlotte Amalie, just barely escaping before a company of marines invaded the town and took control of the Wooden Anchor. We put a score of men on *El Cid* to sail her to Santo Domingo with the prisoners and defend her if she were attacked. They haven't returned, but we've heard they sold the ship and its armaments for a good sum."

"Where are they headed?"

Isabella looked up to Juan Carlos, lifting her hand to touch his face. "Tortuga Bay."

Isabella felt Juan Carlos's body stiffen. "Tortuga Bay?"

She slipped her hand back between his overcoat and his waistcoat. Jean-Michel sent a stern look her way. She smiled but kept her hand flat against his chest, hidden from prying eyes. "It's protected by the French. A haven from your King…at least for a week or two."

Juan Carlos shook his head. "France and Spain have been allies since 1720 and the Treaty of the Hague. We are united now against the British in support of the American rebellion. I'm sure Louis XVI will give you up in short order if asked by my King; His Majesty is enlightened, but he is loyal to his alliances."

"Captain Muñoz isn't going to leave this port without the Pirate of Panther Bay," Jean-Michel said, looking over to Isabella, his eyes softened.

Isabella closed her eyes. "What are our options? I'm not going to sit on this boat and let myself starve."

Jean-Michel looked at Juan Carlos. "We are not going to starve on this vessel."

Juan Carlos pulled Isabella closer under his arm. "I can't stall Muñoz for very long. He already suspects my loyalties."

"And Rodriguez?" Jean-Michel's voice was curious, searching.

"He believes I'm too smart and well trained to have failed so often in my hunt for pirates."

Isabella sighed. "So, we have one choice, *mi amor*. We fight our way to open sea." Isabella's body tightened as she said the words, but relaxed when she felt the calm beneath the tightly woven cotton of Juan Carlos's coat and felt the gentle kiss on the top of her head.

Jean-Michel shook his head. "A twenty-four gun brig against a twenty-six gun frigate, and three sloops of war? I don't like those odds."

Isabella kept her eyes closed. "We faced worse odds off Privateer Pointe."

"And if we had known the odds before we were in the thick of battle we never would have joined the fight!" Jean-Michel turned toward the ceiling. "Besides, we fought to a draw. If Juan Carlos hadn't risked his life then to negotiate a cease fire, the *Marée Rouge* may well have slipped beneath the waves by sundown."

"You see," Isabella said, turning to look up at Juan Carlos. "You've saved us twice on the high seas."

Juan Carlos sighed. "I think twice is all I can muster."

"Then send the cutter back, and stay with me and Jean-Michel. Join our crew and let's fight our way to the open sea. We can die like true warriors. Free warriors. Together."

Juan Carlos didn't look at Isabella. "I am not ready to die."

"I don't want to die either," Isabella said, her voice lowering. "I've faced death, as a slave and as a pirate. I wouldn't be the first to die fighting for others and freedom." Isabella thought of the fires rising above the plantation so many years ago. "Perhaps it's my time." Tears welled up in her eyes as she remembered that no one would know the protective arms of her mother or the love of a boy named Gamba. She looked over to Jean-Michel. "Perhaps it's our time."

Juan Carlos slipped his hands over Isabella's. "Then it's my time as well. I'll fight with you."

"No," said Jean-Michel.

Juan Carlos and Isabella looked over to him.

"No," he repeated, shaking his head. "It's not time."

"Madame Rêve-Cœur foretold my death," said Isabella.

Juan Carlos looked at Isabella then Jean-Michel, his mouth opening as if to ask a question.

Jean-Michel's eyes whipped toward Isabella. "Madame Rêve-Cœur foretold your destiny. You are destined for greatness. She called you 'Binta,' one with God."

Juan Carlos's body stiffened. He turned toward Isabella, holding her shoulders as he looked into her eyes. "Who is Madame Rêve-Cœur?"

Jean-Michel stood up from the cot, an action that put him within a foot of Juan Carlos and Isabella. "A maroon priestess from the mountains of Saint-Domingue. We met her to get supplies after the fight with *El Cid*."

"A priestess, Isabella? You listened to her?"

Isabella lifted her fingers to Juan Carlos's lips. "We didn't go to listen to her fortune telling. We went to get supplies. We were low; our quick escape didn't allow us to stock the *Marée Rouge* properly. After the fight, we needed powder and shot for the cannons. Jean-Michel knew her."

Juan Carlos turned his head to Jean-Michel.

"Relax, Juan," Jean-Michel said, a sparkle in his eyes. "She's an old friend. She knows these hills, who we can trust, who we need to avoid."

Juan Carlos looked across the cabin to the wall. "But a priestess?"

Jean-Michel smiled. "A Catholic objecting to mysticism?"

"You are Catholic," Juan Carlos scolded. "You know pagan beliefs have no place in a true faith."

"I know that my country hunts me down because I am a pirate, and it does not put value in my life. Rêve-Cœur has shown more faith in my life and journey than any priest in my lifetime," said Jean-Michel.

Juan Carlos turned to Isabella. "Do you believe her?"

Isabella closed her eyes. "I'm not sure what to believe." She turned her face up to Juan Carlos. "Is it so hard to believe that I have a destiny to lead others?"

The skepticism in Juan Carlos's voice rattled Isabella. "I believe in you, Isabella. Jean-Michel believes in you. Your crew believes in you. Isn't that enough?"

Isabella lifted her hand to Juan Carlos's cheek. "It means everything to me. But I believe there is more."

"Because of a voodoo priestess hiding in the mountains?"

"No." Isabella's voice was stern and sharp. "Because of a prophecy my mother foretold around the slave quarters on the plantation where I grew up."

"Isabella—"

She brought her fingers to his lips as if to close them. "A death in the Bay of Port-au-Prince, fighting off a squadron of Spanish pirate hunters? Is that my destiny?"

Juan Carlos's eyes began to glisten.

"*Mi amor*, if I let your countryman bring me in alive, they win. Muñoz wins. Rodriguez wins. Slavery wins."

Juan Carlos closed his eyes and breathed in. He lifted his hands to her cheeks. "The cutter will be alongside in fifteen minutes."

"I think we have another way," Jean-Michel said.

17

I sabella would have preferred to trudge to the governor's private hacienda on foot rather than ride behind two horses straining against the weight of his official carriage. The walk would have been harder than a dozen climbs and repels from the highest point on the *Marée Rouge,* but the rhythm and sway of the sea was far easier to navigate than the bumps, lurches, weaves, pitches, and wobbling of the four iron-rimmed wheels of their dressed-up buggy. But Jean-Michel insisted they accept the offer from Governor General Guillaume Léonard de Bellecombe, and the harbor captain's anxious fidgeting wasn't going to stop until she said yes.

The carriage boy seemed much less concerned about the dangers of their trip as he reined the horses around the corners and coaxed them to higher speeds. Warehouses turned into two-story inns with ornate, iron railings wrapping around corner porches. Large numbers of blacks mingled among whites in the streets, all appearing to be focused on purposeful tasks. Many men were dressed in the formal clothes of commerce, while others were in the rough-hewn threads of laborers. The women moved easily, without the deference to Europeans she remembered from her days on the plantation, or at least not the deference a slave would be expected to have.

"I've heard as many as thirty thousand free blacks live in Saint-Domingue," Jean-Michel had said as the harbor captain's crew pulled their launch toward the wharves through the fits and starts of oarsmen. Now, as their carriage left the harbor plains and ascended into the jungle, she had no doubt he was right.

At each turn in the road, the carriage boy cast a quick glance in her direction, as if confirming she was still sitting next to the large, broad-shouldered Frenchman. Once, she caught his wandering eyes, and he snapped his head back toward the road. She touched Jean-Michel's arm. "I wonder if he's seen an African pirate captain before."

Jean-Michel looked at Isabella, a curious look stitched into his expression. She nodded to their driver, no more than eleven years old, she assumed, his eyes focused back on the road. Jean-Michel smiled. "I'm sure he's seen many a free black woman in this town with the number of *gens de couleur* in Saint-Domingue. I doubt he knows your profession, *mon cher*. Although, you are a bit curious with your red bandana for a hat, your saber, and wearing the wools of a sailor."

Isabella straightened her shoulders, pulling the white lapels of her red topcoat together.

"*Voila*," he said, bringing his hand down on her knee for a light tap. "That makes the difference; a half coat to make it official."

Isabella scowled. "I am no ordinary African."

"You are no ordinary woman."

"Do you suppose the boy is free or slave?"

Jean-Michel paused. "I suspect slave, but I do not know. Do you want me to ask?"

Isabella looked forward. "Boy! *Garçon!*"

The second hail was unnecessary because the first call of the word "boy" provoked an immediate response with the turn of his head. "*Oui, mademoiselle?*"

"*Comment s'appelle tu?*"

"*Je m'appelle Louis, mademoiselle.*"

Isabella nodded. "My name is Isabella."

Louis hesitated, stole a glance back to the horses and then turned to face her. He wore the finer clothes of a house servant—pants and clean shirt and even shoes—but he handled the reins with ease as though born and raised in the same stall as the horses he now mastered.

"*Oui, mademoiselle.*"

She touched Jean-Michel's arm. "This is my quartermaster, Jean-Michel."

"*Oui, mademoiselle.*"

Louis turned back to the horses, careful to check their line, before turning to Isabella. His eyes were attentive, but not questioning, as if he expected her to give him an order.

For a moment, Isabella remembered the young, brash slave boy she had met in the sugarcane fields on a plantation hundreds of miles to the east of this town. Gamba was full of life, consumed by spirits and visions of freedom. How could a young slave girl not fall in love with such a strong-willed boy offering himself to the overseer's lashes for his independence? "Louis, are you a slave or free?"

Louis's eyes grew wide as he drew in a breath. "*Comment?*"

"Isabella, that's a bit forward for such a young boy to brave an answer."

Isabella gave Louis an assuring nod. "Are you a slave or *gens de couleur?*"

Panic seemed to overcome Louis, but his gaze remained fixed on Isabella. The carriage jolted as the iron rims crested a large rock in the road. Louis threw a few colorful Creole words at the horses, causing Jean-Michel to chuckle, and turned his head toward the thick palms that lined the road. "Let him do his job, Isabella."

"It's okay, Louis. I won't let anyone know you told us. Slave or free?"

Louis turned back to Isabella. "Slave, mademoiselle."

Isabella sighed. Thirty thousand free blacks on this island, but she was now being taken to see the governor by a slave. Gamba had died in pursuit of his freedom. Would Louis do the same? She rubbed the palms of her hands against her thighs and down to her knees.

Jean-Michel reached over to cover her hand. "In time, Isabella. You will live to see the day Louis is free."

Isabella leaned back, letting the back of her head rest against the edge of the backboard, even more aware of the meaning behind the colonial plumes and the coat of arms of Louis XVI carved into the sides of the coach. A soft breeze created by the collective tug of the horses washed across her neck and under her chin. "If Louis lives."

The horses came to an instant stop in front of the governor's residence as Louis hopped onto the ground and pulled a stepstool out from under the driver's bench. His head popped above the carriage side as the stool's legs lodged into the dirt and the door swung open. Louis looked at Isabella's breeches, turned his head to the ground to look at the stool, and then looked back at Isabella.

"Don't worry," Isabella laughed. "I appreciate your care for my comfort even if I am not wearing a dress elegant enough to meet with your Governor General."

Louis bowed and stepped aside as Jean-Michel descended to the ground. He swiveled to lift his hand to Isabella. She took it with a smile and placed a foot on each step before looking at Louis again. *"Merci, monsieur."* She smiled at Louis. "I feel quite like the lady today, Louis. *Merci."*

Louis couldn't hold back a smile. *"De rien, mademoiselle.* It's nothing. *Merci."*

She must find a way to free Louis.

The thatched palm roof of the governor's mansion was a clever disguise for the well-stitched chairs and ornate benches housed inside. The male servant who opened the door ushered them into the main hall but didn't invite them to sit. The governor would be with them in just a few minutes, he had said. Now, about twenty minutes later, Jean-Michel and Isabella had completed their inspection of the wooden walls and oil paintings of men and women in separate frames, dressed in the formalities of the French court of Louis XVI. While they didn't find a portrait of the monarch who controlled this part of the island, they were sure he was lurking somewhere in the governor's personal office or parlor.

Jean-Michel's pace had quickened from two or three steps before a turn to ten steps in each direction. Isabella wondered if he might just go on a jungle hike. When the servant returned, Jean-Michel slapped his tricorn hat against his leg as he led them down the hall; the clap of the cloth and the sudden movement caused the butler to send a reproachful glance his way. Jean-Michel turned to Isabella with a slight smirk, and Isabella struggled to control a snicker.

The office seemed much grander than the inner hallway or the overwhelming but simple architecture of the two-floor building from the outside. Isabella felt small as they climbed the front steps. The sharp tings of metal pots and skillets on the lower floor identified what was likely the kitchen and food preparation area, as well as the slave quarters, summoning long dormant images from memories interred years ago. The second floor was protected by a wrap-around porch wide enough to keep the monsoon rains at bay and capture whatever breeze might skip along the mountainsides. An iron railing, molded with the colors and lily petals of colonial France, ringed a house held together by thick poles that fixed the walls and ceilings in place. As Isabella touched the smooth wood and railings, her eyes clouded with childhood memories she had learned to accept on the plantation a two-hour wagon ride from Santo Domingo. Now that she was inside, her heart quickened as she envisioned meeting the man who could make the difference between a successful escape or a fiery death at the hands of the Spanish squadron lying in wait.

The man entering the room didn't need an announcement as Isabella and Jean-Michel turned from his portrait on the wall to the sound of the opening door. Isabella's shoulders relaxed as she looked at someone who carried himself with military authority but was both heavier and less regal in his appearance than the image fixed by oils on the wall. His navy-blue half coat was absent the ribbons, sashes, and polished buttons of a governor's formal attire. She smiled to herself as she thought of how Juan Carlos would be insulted by such a pedestrian reception by someone so important.

"Bonjour," the Governor General Guillaume Bellecombe said, giving a nod first to Isabella and then to Jean-Michel. "*Bienvenue a Port-au-Prince.*"

Jean-Michel bowed. "*Merci,* Your Excellency."

Isabella bowed. "The pleasure is ours, Your Excellency."

"I trust your ship weathered the storm well enough." Bellecombe gave a small wave to a house boy who had followed him into the room. The servant, perhaps in his mid-teens, disappeared into the hallway, leaving the door to the expansive study open. Bellecombe strode over to a desk at the end of the room and sat down in an overstuffed chair, its arms and back carved with the three lily petals of the Bourbon monarchy's fleur-de-lis. "Please sit down."

Isabella and Jean-Michel lowered themselves into two chairs positioned two feet from the front edge of Bellecombe's desk. They waited for several minutes, as the governor—the key to their lives—opened drawers as if looking for something and then sat in his chair, hands resting firmly on the neatly kept wooden desk, and looked at them.

"Thank you for taking our request for an audience," Jean-Michel volunteered after a few more moments.

Bellecombe lifted his palms. He brought his fingertips together and looked at Jean-Michel. He raised his eyebrows.

Jean-Michel cleared his throat and leaned back, his hands resting with resolute firmness on the arms of his chair.

Bellecombe shifted his eyes to Isabella. She met his eyes and held his gaze. Bellecombe nodded. "You...your ship...presents a problem for me."

Jean-Michel nodded. "Aye, Your Excellency. We recognize that."

The governor looked at Isabella again, as if expecting her to say something, but she remained silent. "We have strict rules about how we handle pirates."

Isabella's heart quickened, and she forced her fingers to remain relaxed on the arms of the chair. She continued looking at him.

"I hate the British," Bellecombe sneered. "Having to surrender my command of Pondichéry and our territories in India to them, two years after the Americans declared their independence, was a humiliation I have no desire to repeat."

Isabella tried to keep her attention fixed on the governor, but a thin smile from her silent sparring partner revealed he had already sensed her confusion.

"What, you might ask," Bellecombe continued, "does the fall of a distant outpost on the Indian Ocean have to do with the future of Saint-Domingue?"

Isabella's face softened with a curious smile.

"It's simple, really. I've spent my career fighting the British. First in New France, the territories much further north up the Atlantic Coast, and then in India. They treat our people like we are the parasites of Europe." Bellecombe looked at Jean-Michel. "You're a Frenchman."

Jean-Michel nodded.

The governor lifted his hand to his clean-shaven chin and rubbed it. "That helps."

He turned his focus back to Isabella. "You see, France is allied with the Americans, and the Americans are in a fight to the death for their independence from Britain. My predecessor, Jean-Baptiste de

Taste de Lilancour, sent our entire West Indies Fleet—eight ships and five thousand five hundred troops from our colonial regiment—to fight alongside the Americans in Virginia."

Isabella cocked her head. "Our request is much simpler than mustering a regiment of troops and an entire fleet. We would like you to consider granting us a rite of passage through your sovereign waters up the west coast of French-controlled Hispaniola. We would not have to leave sight of land. Our destination is Isle de la Tortue."

Bellecombe turned to Jean-Michel. "Are you fighting the British?"

Isabella felt the muscles in her shoulders and chest tighten. She shifted forward in her chair toward the table. "We are fighting to stay alive." Bellecombe's eyes flicked back toward Isabella even as he faced Jean-Michel, confirming the success of Isabella's interruption.

Jean-Michel turned a scolding look toward Isabella. "Your Excellency, aren't we all allied against the British?"

Bellecombe released a broad smile, *"Exactement."* He turned back to Jean-Michel. "I have been in this position for just a few months. I have few resources. Governor General Lilancourt is a very good administrator—he's served in the post three times—but I am naked in this region without a fleet or an army to speak of."

Isabella straightened her back. "You have the authority of the monarchy, King Louis XVI."

The French general leaned back, restored his fingers to recreate a pointed roof in front of his face, and looked down the ridge toward Isabella as if his fingers had just created a gun sight. "But I don't have an army or a fleet to defend against a British attack. Rather, I have a pirate that the Spanish Crown seems to want very, very badly."

Isabella resisted an urge to shoot a damning look toward Jean-Michel.

"Your Excellency," Jean-Michel said in a deliberate tone. "The Spanish are opportunists. They have not entered this fight because they are committed to the Americans."

Bellecombe's fingers folded together and fell to his waist, elbows resting on the thick cushion of the chair's arm. *"C'est vrai;* you speak the truth. The Spanish are fickle allies."

He leaned forward in his chair and opened a drawer to the side of this desk. He pulled what looked like parchment from the drawer and placed it on the desk. The ivory-colored letter against the dark brown wood made the thin piece of paper appear as if it had become an impenetrable barrier in space.

"This request from Spain's West Indies Vice Admiralty asks for my assistance in capturing and returning the criminal known as the Pirate of Panther Bay to his custody. He has dispatched four warships to escort this pirate, her crew, and her vessel, described as a twenty-four-gun brigantine, back to Puerto Rico to sit in judgment of the Vice Admiralty."

He cast searching glances toward Isabella and Jean-Michel before picking up the letter as if to read it word for word. But he looked over the edge at Jean-Michel. "You are French." He eyes slid over to Isabella. "You are not."

Isabella drew in a breath, pulled her shoulders up, and narrowed her glare.

Bellecombe let the letter drift back to the desk through his fingers. "You are a pirate, a common criminal, a high-seas robber, and murderer."

Jean-Michel raised his hand from the armchair as if to make a point, but Bellecombe lifted his palm to stop him.

Isabella remained resolute. "I was a slave. I captain my ship for only one purpose, to maintain my freedom and that of my crew. I see no other choice."

Jean-Michel began to lift himself from the chair. "Perhaps—"

Bellecombe waved Jean-Michel back to his seat with a determined flick of his hand. "Sit down."

Jean-Michel hesitated in mid-lift, but then fell back into the cushion of the chair. "Your Excellency—"

Bellecombe kept his gaze on Isabella, cutting Jean-Michel's protest off. The governor nodded. "So, I have here before me the Pirate of Panther Bay. I have finally met the pirate who has ravaged our shipping routes to the point where we are lucky to have half the volume of trade from these islands."

The door was open, Isabella remembered, and she could be outside with a fifty-foot sprint. She visualized the position of her saber, secure in the scarlet sash around her waist, and now, lying close to her leg to enable her to sit. She would have to stand before she could pull the blade, eating up critical seconds if the governor pulled a pistol or his servants returned with weapons.

Bellecombe leaned back in his chair with a snicker. "A little nervous?"

"Can you blame us?" Jean-Michel asked. "It sounds like you don't want us here."

"You are right, Jean-Michel, I don't want you here. I don't want any of you in my harbor. I don't want you, or your captain, or your crew, giving the Spanish any reason to violate our sovereignty." He picked up the letter again and shook it. "Especially on a charge so minor. I don't have time to deal with pirates, and I don't want to trigger an international incident between our countries over something so trivial! Anything that provokes a Spanish incursion into our bay would put the monarchy in a precarious position. France can barely afford to finance the Americans as it is, and a Spanish test of our ability to defend ourselves could trigger something much bigger."

"Then don't," Isabella said, rising from her chair. "We'll sail in the morning." She turned to Jean-Michel, who had also risen from his seat.

Bellecombe laughed. "And deprive me of my gesture of goodwill and faith to my country's ally?"

"I'm sorry to have wasted your time," Jean-Michel said. "But I would rather die fighting my way to my ship and freedom than on the gallows after being judged by that buffoon Rodriguez."

Bellecombe stood up from behind his desk, the full stature of his military experience even more evident in the way he commanded the space in the room. "I would be careful how you refer to a high-ranking official in the Spanish monarchy."

Isabella grasped her sword and joined Jean-Michel.

Jean-Michel glared at Bellecombe. "Why does how I address the Spanish colonial administrators matter?"

Bellecombe shook his head. "Sit down! I'm not done with you."

Jean-Michel stepped away from his chair. "Perhaps we are done here. We have a ship to attend to."

"We'll make sure we are underway with the first tide," Isabella said, joining Jean-Michel.

"Sit down!"

Jean-Michel and Isabella didn't turn, but began to back toward the door.

"If you don't sit down," Bellecombe said, his voice softer yet more dogged, "I will call in my guards and have you shot right now."

Isabella looked to Jean-Michel, and he nodded. Jean-Michel let his blade slide back into its sheath. The governor signaled for Isabella and Jean-Michel to resume their seats. "Relax. I'm not ready to let the Spaniards take you." He smiled. "Yet."

The respectful steps of a house boy drew Bellecombe's attention back to the door. "*Oui, Pierre, qu'est-ce qui ne va pas*; what's wrong?"

"Your Excellency, one of the men repairing the roof from the storm's damage discovered a batch of palm leaves was destroyed beyond use. We would like permission to replace them. Would you like to inspect them yourself?"

"No, tell the men we are paying them well, and I expect the quality to reflect their compensation. I want a roof without leaks and repaired with the proper materials." Pierre nodded and left the room. Bellecombe turned to Jean-Michel and Isabella, shaking his head.

"You are paying them?"

Isabella's question seemed to take the governor by surprise.

"We have twenty-five thousand *gens de couleur,* perhaps more, in Saint-Domingue. Certainly, I could find a dozen or so capable of repairing a roof, designed and constructed with their native tools and techniques!"

"Wouldn't slaves from nearby plantations be cheaper?"

Isabella's second question prompted the battle-weary general to harden his expression. "Why would I want to use slaves? A free man will work harder if paid a decent wage!"

Isabella allowed herself to sink back in her chair. "France has not sworn off slavery."

"No, but she should." Bellecombe stood up and walked over to a portrait of a young royal not quite thirty years, his powdered hair curling in two layers up the side of his head even as his hairline had receded to the edge of his sideburns. His cheeks were rounded, having lost the vigor of a teen's youth, but the regal frocks of France's royal house dispelled any whimsy that this might be a common man. Under the portrait were the words Louis XVI, *par la grâce de Dieu, roi de France et de Navarre.* Louis XVI, by the Grace of God, King of France and Navarre.

"His Most Christian Majesty, King Louis XVI, is making changes. This year, His Majesty released the first accounts of the Royal House in history so all could see the State's finances. I understand that his advisors are near agreement in issuing an edict granting religious tolerance in France. I have heard the nobles are concerned that he might eliminate serfdom as well."

"Heartening reforms, indeed." Jean-Michel's voice was solemn.

Bellecombe turned to Jean-Michel. "Reforms deep enough to keep men from turning to a pirating life?"

Jean-Michel smiled.

Bellecombe then turned to Isabella. "And if serfdom and religious freedom are here, can the abolition of slavery be much further behind? Would that be enough to steer the Pirate of Panther Bay onto a legitimate path?"

Isabella's head spun. She drew in a deep breath, trying to calm the rush of images and feelings into her brain. The life of a free woman? "I am free now."

Bellecombe shook his head.

"I can come and go as I please."

"Is that why you and your second in command are sitting in my office, in a governor's hacienda halfway up a mountainside, a stone's throw from a sugar plantation not so different from the one from which you escaped?"

Isabella caught her breath, bringing her hands to her chin and lips. He knew!

"Don't worry, Isabella. If I wanted you dead, you would not have made it up the hillside. I would have had you shot, or arrested, as soon as you were outside the city on the road to this headquarters."

Jean-Michel stood up from his chair, walked over to the governor, and bowed. "*Merci*, Your Excellency."

Bellecombe nodded. "You are still a problem for me. The fact your pirate ship is anchored in my port has created an international incident. While my King has not received word as of yet, I'm sure the Spanish have already sent a request to the ministry in France to clear the way for your arrest and delivery to Rodriguez. As Governor General, I have the authority and obligation to act in a way that furthers my King's interests."

Isabella stood up and stepped over to Jean-Michel, placing her hand on his elbow, looking at Bellecombe. "Will you help us?"

Jean-Michel looked at the portrait of Louis XVI. "He has new ideas about running a country."

Bellecombe nodded. "He has said he must always consult the public because it is never wrong."

"So he is passionate about his support for the Americans?"

"Oui. He has been influenced by many of the new philosophers who have spoken of the dignity of men, all men, in the eyes of God. Alas, he has the mind and heart of a revolutionary, but not the courage or commitment of a field general. Some believe he is moving much too slowly. The nobles are powerful, reluctant to give up their property."

Isabella looked into Bellecombe's eyes. "Do you think he is moving too slowly?"

Bellecombe closed his eyes, a moment of reflection, but when he opened them they reflected determination. "I will not betray my King."

Isabella smiled. "But you hire *gens de couleur*?"

Bellecombe stepped back two paces and turned toward a window that looked out over Port-au-Prince Bay. Amidst the masts of merchantmen moored in the harbor, bales, barrels, and crates of goods were being loaded at a fast pace. The afternoon tide, what little existed, was favorable for leaving, but they had less than an hour to finish loading before the ships would need to cast off. "Slavery is a vile remnant of antiquity." He turned to Isabella, but diverted his eyes to the floor. "No human being deserves the conditions these men, women, and children toil under. Absentee plantation owners, short-sighted overseers." He looked up to Isabella. "This place is a powder keg set to blow. All I can do is hope to manage it and work to abolish these ungodly conditions before the entire island is engulfed in flames."

Isabella's heart pounded. "Is that a warning for us?"

Bellecombe's face brightened. "A warning...or an opportunity. You will have to make that decision. I am only a general, deployed by His Most Christian Majesty to oversee one of his holdings, my last deployment in service to my country before returning permanently to France. I will go where God takes me, but he has not revealed that path to me yet."

Isabella's chest began to tighten. She touched Jean-Michel's elbow and looked into his eyes. Was he remembering the vision? Was the image of Madame Rêve-Cœur levitating in the *bohio* high in the mountains as vivid for him as it was for her, so crisp it could replace Louis XVI in the portrait on Bellecombe's wall? "Binta," Rêve-Cœur had called her: One with God. Isabella felt a sudden pull toward these hills, this port, these people—twenty-five thousand free men and women among five hundred thousand slaves—a cauldron of boiling bitterness, anger, and indignity. The weight of the stew filled her chest, encased her heart. Isabella continued to look at the portrait as a hand slipped into her sash and felt the outlines of a cross and a key.

"Your Excellency, if I may ask, why is the carriage boy still a slave?"

Bellecombe shook his head. "Article 13 of the Code Noir, established by Louis IV, dictates that a child born of a slave mother will be a slave, even if his father is free. Louis's father was a free man who fell in love with a slave woman. They married. He worked for the governor. Unfortunately, he died of the Fever when Louis was just an infant. My predecessor was able to move her to our staff. Let's just say they were less concerned about the lingering inhumanity of this vile institution than I am. I let them live in town. My hope is to have Louis and his mother free by the end of the year."

Jean-Michel stepped past the King's portrait toward another image hanging on the wall, a banner he had noticed when they first entered the governor's office. He could now see its intricate weaves with gold inlays. A second crown adorned the top of the Royal crown of France, the symbol adopted upon Louis XVI's ascension, with two angels acting as heralds, holding staffs and standards representing France and Navarre. Jean-Michel lifted his hand to one of two shields on the crest, the one with the dark blue background and three gold fleur-de-lis. "These lily petals…faith, wisdom, chivalry."

Bellecombe turned with a snap toward Jean-Michel. "Are you of noble stock?"

"My family was well educated in the ways of French nobility."

"And you turned pirate?"

"We all have different paths and journeys. The third son of a landed nobleman has few options in a system where land and peasants form the basis of an economy."

The governor walked over to the royal banner. "And the military was not an option?"

Jean-Michel smiled. "The military was an option, but my family preferred army to navy. I longed for the rush of the open sea. Let's just say my career in the monarchy's navy ran into a few headwinds."

Bellecombe nodded. "You wouldn't be the first to find the pirating life more promising than the poor pay of a naval warship." He turned his attention to the three images of the fleur-de-lis emblazoned on the French coat of arms. "His Catholic Majesty Louis IX—Saint Louis—restored the Church to its authority in France. Faith, wisdom, chivalry. Nobility, honor, allegiance to God. Those values have helped guide France for six hundred years."

"The so-called Saint burned twelve thousand Jewish books and forced conversions to Christianity."

Bellecombe chortled. "You are well schooled in our Catholic history, Jean-Michel. Yes, history is messy, but he also established the presumption of innocence in courts and ended trials by ordeal, requiring the presentation of evidence in court to determine guilt." He turned to Isabella. "That presumption of innocence kept you alive today." He walked over to his desk and picked up the letter from Rodriguez. "Based on this request from the Spanish Vice Admiralty, I should arrest you now and hand you over to the Viceroy. But I think your story is more complicated."

Isabella relaxed. "So where does our story take us?"

Bellecombe let the letter drop back to his desk. "For now, back to your ship. The Spanish will hold off for another couple of days, perhaps a week or more. We'll give you access to Port-au-Prince. Whether you leave is up to you, although the Spanish will likely force our hand before you are ready to depart." He looked at Isabella and Jean-Michel with a serious look. "But be careful in the roads and inns of Port-au-Prince. This town is seething with unrest, and strangers can find themselves in untenable positions without the right support at the right time."

Isabella patted her sword. "We've been in tough spots before. Jean-Michel and I have managed to keep ourselves alive."

"We also need to discuss...professional opportunities...with some of your locals," said Jean-Michel. "If the Spanish are going to force our hand, I would rather meet them with a full crew than a half crew."

Bellecombe looked to Jean-Michel. "You have to do what you must. I understand the need to survive, but I can't support it or condone it. If you are too obvious, I will have to arrest you." He turned to Isabella and bowed. "Mademoiselle, until we meet again. I hope it is soon and under more pleasant circumstances."

Louis was in the seat of a new carriage as the afternoon sun dipped into the western horizon and they emerged from the governor's residence. Jean-Michel extended his hand to Isabella as she stepped inside the closed cab, but she ignored it. As the coach jerked forward for its descent to the town and its alleys below, Isabella slipped her fingers through Jean-Michel's and looked at him. She could see the worry in the dampness of his eyes. He squeezed her hand.

The light faded into brilliant oranges and yellows, dancing between afternoon clouds, but even these colors couldn't penetrate the deepening grays that engulfed their route through the roads, warehouses, docks, and inns below, already seething with characters unsavory and honorable, but most somewhere in between.

18

Each step by the horses leading the covered carriage down the twisting road into port, foreshadowed a lumbering jerk from its frame as Isabella and Jean-Michel considered the next few days. The grand leaves of palm trees arched over the roadway, sending flashes of the fading afternoon light onto the path through the window of their coach. Every one hundred feet or so, Louis ducked his head through a rectangular portal at the head of the cab, as if checking to make sure his passengers were still secure and had not fled into the jungles or ravines.

Isabella looked out into the bay before the thin lines of the masts from the ships disappeared behind the walls and roofs of the port city. "How long do you think Muñoz will wait?"

"We have to trust Juan Carlos." Jean-Michel gave Isabella's hand a gentle squeeze. "But I guess he can't delay Muñoz for too long. Perhaps a week."

"That's not enough time."

Jean-Michel snorted. "How much time is enough? Muñoz has four warships waiting for us. One is a frigate that could blow us out of the water without much trouble if we let her get too close. The schooners are water runts. They couldn't do much damage. But together they make for a tricky noose for us to evade."

"We defeated a larger flotilla off Privateer Pointe last year when we recaptured the *Marée Rouge* from that mutinous scoundrel Stiles and destroyed that rogue, Yellow Jacket."

"We nearly lost everything," Jean-Michel reminded her.

"We defeated Yellow Jacket and the *Wasp*, a frigate-sized ship, and then faced the Spanish frigate *Granada*, two armed sloops, and a schooner. Surely, we can take the *Santa Mónica* and her escorts."

"I've always admired your confidence, Isabella, but we're pushing our luck with half our crew. Plus, the *Santa Mónica* will be expecting us to break out from the bay."

"I've checked the tides. The rise is no more than one or two feet. The speed of the current can't be more than a couple of knots. With a strong night wind, we can slip out before the Spanish know what's happened."

"And what of Juan Carlos?"

Indeed, what of Juan Carlos? Isabella pulled her arms together toward her chest and looked out over the bay as their carriage began its final descent into the plains and eastern reaches of the port. The sun hung over the horizon as the ships' masts disappeared behind the graying alleys and roads of rooming houses, brothels, inns, and stores. The streets were already alive in the dimness of the evening light.

Louis peered through the portal. "Be alert, *mes amis*. Stay with the carriage. The streets are dangerous now that the sun has gone down. Try not to speak to anyone. Ignore them. I will get you to your dock and your ship safely."

Isabella smiled at their young driver's seriousness. She shifted her hands down to the hilt and sheath of her sword, holding it close to her thigh, positioning it in case it were needed. The small clink of metal across from her told her Jean-Michel had done the same.

The pitch of the carriage morphed into steady swaying as the rough-hewn dirt and stones of the road leading to the governor's mansion gave way to cobblestones leading to the quays. Street traffic had clearly picked up, and Isabella took note of the worn woolen pants of dock and warehouse workers. Some wore boots, but many remained barefoot, even on the stones hot from the afternoon sun. Laughing and the occasional blend of native Creole and French spilled from the windows of taverns as tables filled with patrons. French doors began to open behind ornate railings on the second floors as dockhands completed their transition to urban denizens—eating, resting, and frolicking. Isabella wondered how many of them had noticed the seven new masts lurking at the mouth of their bay, just out of reach of the port's cannons, but close enough to pounce on a target if the opportunity arose.

The carriage rolled to a stop.

"*Bonjour*, Louis!"

"*Bonjour*, Dr. D'Poussant."

Isabella shifted her body to give her a few more inches of height, hoping to catch a glimpse of the man who had called out to their driver and brought them to an unscheduled stop. Jean-Michel tapped her thigh, a signal for her to be on guard. Isabella pulled her sword across her lap, lifted the hilt up above her waist, and used her right hand to pull the saber two inches from its sheath to test the ease of its draw.

"Who are your passengers, Mr. Louis?" a strange male voice inquired.

"Visitors of the Governor General." Louis's voice was matter-of-fact. "I told His Excellency that I would have them back at their ship before sunset, Dr. D'Poussant. As you can tell, the sun is almost set. I am late. I don't want to disappoint the governor."

The man laughed. "Not to worry Mr. Louis. You may be a slave, but he won't whip you for being late."

"Yes, sir, but I have orders from His Excellency, the Governor General of Saint-Domingue, to deliver these distinguished guests to their ship."

"Well then, if they are so distinguished, why don't you introduce them to me?"

"Dr. D'Poussant! Please let me pass. They are not prisoners. They have done no harm."

Isabella gripped the hilt of her sword, testing the blade to confirm its release from its scabbard. Hooves clacked against the road masonry, an indication of the horses' eagerness to continue, but the coach stayed put. Isabella looked through the portal behind the driver's seat, hoping to glimpse the man talking to Louis. She noticed several men hovering around the front of the team of horses, holding the reins of one.

Jean-Michel stood in the carriage, careful to lodge his legs against its sides to give him stability while freeing his scabbard and testing the quickness of the metal leaving the leather. "Louis! Is there a problem?" he called in French.

"*Non, monsieur.*"

The pitch to Louis's voice was high, but Isabella couldn't determine if it was nerves or concern.

"*Tout va bien!*" Louis called back. Isabella narrowed her brow, now convinced that everything was definitely not well as the boy had just claimed. He was brave, trying to calm his passengers, but Isabella sensed a situation spinning beyond the realm of their driver's abilities.

Jean-Michel cast a quick look to Isabella, and she slid forward on the seat, her knees bent, ready to spring forward. He looked back toward Louis. "It's okay, Louis. Feel free to introduce us to your friends. I'm sure the governor would not mind."

Jean-Michel had just finished his words when a man rounded the front quarter of the cab and peered into the back seat. "Welcome! *Bienvenue!* We are so pleased to see visitors!"

Isabella sized up the man, dressed neatly in a patrician's coat with gold lace skirting, white lapels framing an open tailcoat with brass buttons, and a white shirt tucked neatly behind the top layer. The man smiled, his teeth unnaturally white against what seemed like ebony skin in the faded street light. Clearly an African, but his diction was too refined to come from a slave. His rounded cheeks and wide nose suggested a man of West African descent. A powdered wig appeared to cover his natural hair beneath a cocked hat with a gold braid pinned along one side. This man must be a *gens de couleur,* she thought.

Jean-Michel nodded to the stranger. "*Bonsoir, monsieur.* We are just returning to our ship, as the boy said. What can we do for you?"

The man put his hands on the side of the carriage door and looked past Jean-Michel, noticing Isabella. "*Excusez-moi, mademoiselle!*" D'Poussant doffed his hat and bowed his eyes. "I didn't realize one of the passengers was a lady!"

Jean-Michel shifted into D'Poussant's sightline, forcing him to look back up at the pirate, who was now using the full advantage of his bulk to overshadow the stranger's view. "As I said, sir, we are on our way to our ship. For what purpose have you detained us?"

The man smiled and shook his head. "For no reason other than saying *hello* to my friend, Louis, and to welcome you to our fair port!" D'Poussant stepped back. "Welcome!" He stepped back again, this time his bow revealing the top of his head. "Allow me to host you for a meal."

Louis faced Jean-Michel and Isabella, concern and worry lining his face. Isabella leaned forward in the coach, reached for Louis's shoulder, and then looked to D'Poussant. "What are you going to do to the boy?"

D'Poussant's expression dampened. "Why nothing, mademoiselle. He is a boy. He can simply go on his way."

Isabella looked at Louis, his eyes wide. He gripped the backboard, pushing the blood from his knuckles. "Louis, what were your orders from Governor General Bellecombe?"

"To make sure you returned to your ship. I was not supposed to leave the docks until I saw your longboat pull up to your ship and both of you were on deck. Then, His Excellency wanted me to report back to the butler."

Isabella gave Louis's shoulder a reassuring squeeze and positioned herself to see a wider swath of the street. "Thank you for your kind offer...Dr. D'Poussant, is it? But we surely don't want Louis to get into trouble. I know he is a slave, and I know from experience that disappointed masters can be harsh."

D'Poussant's face turned serious. He looked at Louis and then to Jean-Michel. He pulled his hands to his hips, and Isabella noticed a sash strapped around his waist, white breeches extending below his knees, and stockings covering his calves to his leather shoes. This man was not a dockworker.

"Are you a medical doctor?" Isabella asked.

D'Poussant smiled. "I'm afraid I can say little about the ailments of the body. I am a doctor of theology and philosophy, and a man of letters. My studies engage the mind and our thoughts."

Jean-Michel huffed. He turned to Louis, whose anxious eyes told him the boy could neither confirm nor deny the man's claims. "Where did you study? You speak Creole, but your dress is more like *les grands blancs*, a free white man with property."

D'Poussant's eyes narrowed. "I am a freedman of mixed race. I'm sure you know, Jean-Michel, that the French are much more accepting of mulatos and *gens de couleur* than your English and Spanish brethren."

Jean-Michel held his hand on the hilt of his sword, not a twitch in his body revealing his surprise that this man knew him. "The English and Spanish are no friends of mine. If you truly know who I am, you know that."

D'Poussant nodded as he looked inside the coach. "I studied in France. Freed men and *gens de couleur* are allowed to own property in our mother country's possessions. I am, as you suspect, a property owner."

Isabella felt a surge of energy run through her chest and arms. She pulled her hand into the carriage and shifted closer to Jean-Michel. "Then what brings you to the port on such a night? Are you overseeing the delivery of goods reaped by slaves?"

D'Poussant nodded his head again. "The Pirate of Panther Bay. I see you more clearly now that the lights from the street have illuminated your face. This is quite fortuitous, indeed."

D'Poussant stepped toward the carriage, his hat lodged under his left arm, and extended his hand to Jean-Michel. Jean-Michel kept his hand on his saber and glared at D'Poussant. The self-described philosopher turned to Isabella, keeping two paces between him and the two pirates, sabers ready, looking down on him. "I am very pleased to meet you. Both of you. Your legends precede you."

The *gens de couleur* sent a sharp look to the driver. "Louis, come down and give us a proper introduction."

Louis hesitated but dropped from the seat and opened the carriage door.

A broad smile turned D'Poussant's cheeks as he stepped up to Louis and reached to touch the boy's back. Isabella watched D'Poussant close in on the boy, and she let go of the scabbard to bring her hand up as Louis let his drop to grab hers. She heard the boy catch his breath and his body stiffen as D'Poussant gave him a gentle pat in the small of his back.

D'Poussant continued to smile as he rubbed the boy's back. "Louis is a good worker. He always does what his employer tells him. I knew he was transporting someone important tonight. The rumors have flooded the streets since yesterday, but I couldn't be sure." D'Poussant looked at their half-drawn sabers. "You can secure those weapons. I assure you I mean no harm to you. Indeed, you are my guests in this town. I believe I can keep you safe, right, Louis?"

Louis didn't look at D'Poussant, his eyes searching, pleading, to Isabella's. "I can take you to your ship, as His Excellency ordered."

"Louis!" D'Poussant's tone was stern. "Let's not be rude to our illustrious guests. I insist that I treat them to good food and wine. My favorite pub is just a few yards from this street. They have freshly plucked game every night. Chicken, perhaps? Duck? Or perhaps something from the sea?"

Louis squeezed Isabella's hand. "*Mademoiselle, s'il vous plaît.* Please. His Excellency would like you back on your ship."

"A good meal for the Pirate of Panther Bay and her esteemed quartermaster!" D'Poussant's hand was no longer patting Louis. He kept it steady in the small of Louis's back as he challenged Isabella with his own stare. "I can guarantee the conversation will be interesting for both of you."

Louis brought both his hands around Isabella's. "Mademoiselle, His Excellency cannot guarantee your safety in Port-au-Prince. He can ensure no one harms you on your ship, but the streets are the province of the mayor, not His Excellency. I cannot ensure your safety."

Isabella smiled at Louis, hoping a more relaxed attitude might calm him.

"Louis is right," D'Poussant said, interrupting their silent conversation. "The Governor General has no authority over domestic law. The Mayor administers the city and its rules." D'Poussant retracted his hand from the boy and looked at Jean-Michel. "But I can guarantee your safety, even if the Governor cannot. I am a man of means and property. The docks respond to me, as do the streets."

Isabella looked at the philosopher turned plantation owner. "How will you guarantee our safety?"

"I have no desire to stake my legacy on the death of someone who is destined for a future much greater than spilling Spanish blood on the high seas or lying lifeless in the sewers of this port."

His legacy? Isabella caught her breath, hopeful the dim light of the streets hid her surprise, but sure D'Poussant had sensed it, like a shark smelling the blood of wounded prey. He knows about the Pirate of Panther Bay and Jean-Michel. Was he hinting at her prophecy? "You sound like a mystic, Dr. D'Poussant."

"Not a mystic," he said in a calm, deliberate tone. "But someone who can read the winds and the spirits of this place, and they are restless. Let me tell you about these winds and what they may foretell for our future, if you choose to believe them."

Isabella couldn't see Jean-Michel's expression, but she knew he would be as eager as she was to investigate this man's understanding of these winds.

"The boy comes with us. You guarantee our safety and then a safe return for Louis to the Governor General."

D'Poussant's smile widened, revealing again a full set of white teeth as his grin chased his cheeks into his sideburns. "Of course!"

Louis's hands grasped Isabella's with a desperation she had not felt since the fires swept away her life and her mother years earlier. But Isabella knew, somehow, the die had been cast.

19

The amber haze blanketing the early evening streets of the port city gave way to teal-blue wisps, cast out from the ends of pipes and cigars, as D'Poussant and his entourage entered le Coq Fantôme. Jean-Michel caught the carved image of a ghostlike rooster hovering over the words on the sign as a thick door exposed the insides of the lodge. Men huddled over benches and tables, filling the air with the clanging of empty and full pewter mugs and impatient patrons ready to devour the first meat to land in front of them.

D'Poussant ushered Isabella through the portal with an extended hand. "*Pardon*, Isabella. But this is a port city, so the clientele is a bit rough."

"Not to worry," Jean-Michel said, tapping the doctor's shoulder with a playful clap. "Isabella's been in worse places than this."

Isabella looked at Louis, missing the quick twitches of D'Poussant's hand as it flicked invisible dirt from the shoulder just touched by her quartermaster. She focused on the boy, keeping her hand on his arm as they shuffled into the room.

The air inside the inn was thick with sweat and braggarts. Isabella used determined, clean steps to thread the arms and legs tossed among the tables and chairs, keeping her gait steady and forward. Louis stumbled, and Isabella used a gentle pull to bring him along as Jean-Michel followed the trio to a table near the back of the room. They ignored the curious stares of men peering behind mugs of ale as the boy and a young, bronze-skinned woman with a saber slung by her side settled onto a bench against the back wall. D'Poussant slid onto a bench across from her. Louis took the outside post of Isabella's seat, and Jean-Michel sat next to D'Poussant.

"I think Jean-Michel is the only European here," Isabella said, surveying the room.

D'Poussant gave Isabella a measured look, turned toward the bar and signaled the barkeep, a muscled African with mahogany skin, thick eyebrows, and close-cropped hair.

"You frequent this establishment quite a lot," Jean-Michel said.

Their host turned back to the pirates and their young charge. "Whether we are European or African is a matter of speculation and debate. What am I? A man of European and African blood. Am I European or African?"

Jean-Michel glanced at Isabella before turning to D'Poussant. "Creole."

D'Poussant lifted his eybrows. "Perhaps, but I have very little in common with the Creole on this island."

Isabella looked down at her hands, resting on the wood of the table. She had noticed her own skin was a smooth brown, not the ebony beauty of her mother or even the shades of mahogany of her friends. She looked up at D'Poussant to see him staring into her eyes. She diverted her gaze to Louis. "Are you hungry?"

"Allow me," D'Poussant said. He turned again to the barkeep and made a circular motion with his hand. "We'll have a seasoned chicken and drumsticks here in just a few minutes."

Isabella followed his hand and saw a young, black woman behind the bar for the first time. She was staring at her, or at least at their group, as she dried a mug. The muscled man responded to D'Poussant with a nod, but the young woman continued her tasks, watching them out of the corners of her eyes and with an occasional glance in their direction. Isabella nodded at her, and the woman turned away from the bar.

She turned back to the table and noticed D'Poussant pulling a pipe from his coat pocket. He tapped the bowl, loosening some ash before taking tobacco from an elegant leather pouch. He tamped the dried leaves, and lit the pipe. Puffs of smoke rose into the air, comingling with the haze and odors of cigars, cigarettes, and pipes enveloping the room. Isabella's mood darkened as she thought of the men, women, and children who worked the fields so D'Poussant could relax in an inn over ale and chicken in Saint-Domingue.

Jean-Michel gave the room a quick scan. "Odd name for an inn."

D'Poussant laughed. "Not so odd if you know the story. The maroons have made the mountains of Hispaniola their home for more than a century, as have the early pirate pioneers, *les flibustiers*. Voodoo ritual calls for the sacrifice of a chicken on many occasions. One time, the story goes, a priest called for a chicken to be sacrificed, but a young boy brought a rooster instead. The loa, the spirit, had already overtaken the priestess and was upset that the fowl was not ready for him, so he refused the sacrifice. The rooster's spirit was not accepted into the afterlife. Its ghost runs through the brush, haunting villages, searching for children, innocents to take his life and expel him from the Nether World."

The taverner brought four mugs to the table, letting them drop with a thud in front of each of his patrons. D'Poussant looked up to him, a smile clearing any worries from his expression. "Thank you, Phillip!"

Phillip gave D'Poussant a small bow. "Anytime, Dr. D'Poussant. Your barbeque will be ready soon."

Isabella raised her eyebrows toward D'Poussant as the taverner returned to the bar. "You are certainly well known."

"D'Poussant lifted a tankard to Isabella. "I know the people I need to know, and I don't worry about the rest. Phillip is a good man, second generation *gens de couleur*. His daughter, Gabrielle—I think you saw her behind the bar when we came in—is a good worker, too. A bit too precocious for my taste, but she follows her father's lead."

Precocious? Isabella smiled. She turned back to the bar. Gabrielle was in a spirited conversation with a patron, a much larger man unhappy with whatever she was or was not giving him at the moment. Phillip returned to the bar and intercepted the man just as he was about to raise his hand to Gabrielle. The young woman didn't flinch. Isabella smiled to herself and turned her attention back to the table.

Louis reached for the tankard in front of him, but Isabella swept it up to her nose before his fingers could touch it. She cast a coy smile to Gabrielle, who turned back to the bar. She put the mug back in front of the boy. Louis gave it a skeptical look before lifting it to his lips and tipping a taste onto his tongue. He scowled and took a long swallow. Isabella laughed, clapping his shoulder. "You're a bit young for a full round of ale or grog. A little wine will do for now!"

Jean-Michel tipped his mug to Louis and took a dutiful swig. "I know about the rituals, Dr. D'Poussant, but it still doesn't explain why this tavern carries the name of a voodoo tale."

D'Poussant lifted his tankard, sweeping it in an arc around the room. "Look around you, Jean-Michel, and tell me what you see."

The inn had become more crowded and rowdy, but nothing further out of the ordinary than the Wooden Anchor in Charlotte Amalie. A few women—entertainment for men later in the evening with more pints of ale in their bellies—showed interest in helping them unload a little more coin. "Looks to me like the same as any tavern in any port. A tad fewer tars, more dockhands, maybe more burghers—bookkeepers, tailors, and dry goods sellers no doubt. No one quite as upscale as you, sir."

"You are too modest, Jean-Michel. I agree, we don't see as many pirates, but you're refusing to acknowledge the most important clue to understanding why this inn is so crowded with a certain type of person." D'Poussant turned to Isabella. "Mademoiselle?"

Isabella had already felt the difference, even if she hadn't articulated it. *"Gens de couleur."*

D'Poussant raised his mug in triumph. "The Pirate of Panther Bay sees more than she admits."

Jean-Michel took another look around the room and inventoried the bodies, clothes, and tones. *Gens de couleur.* Everyone in the inn was a black. Jean-Michel was indeed, the only European in the crowd. He had thought the men were staring at Isabella and the boy when they had entered the bar, but he had not thought that he was just as much a curiosity as the others. "The Nether World," he mumbled.

D'Poussant raised his tankard again, this time connecting his pewter to Jean-Michel's, creating a loud clank before bringing it to his lips.

As Jean-Michel let his mug fall to the table, a knife dug deep into the wood in front of him, forcing him to divert its descent. He snapped his gaze up the arm of the hand affixed to the handle and locked into the sharp glare of its owner, a tall, thin, but muscled, ebony-colored man. His biceps bulged through a cotton shirt, worn thin by months of lifting and toting bales and boxes. "You are not welcome here."

Jean-Michel kept his focus on the intruder. D'Poussant kept a steady fix on Jean-Michel's face but allowed his eyes to dart to Isabella. She had pulled Louis close and brought the hilt of her sword above the table's edge, but she made no move toward her second in command.

"I am here by invitation," Jean-Michel grumbled.

"The Governor General's invitation means nothing in these walls."

The thick smell of rum rolled over Jean-Michel's cheeks and into his nostrils, almost forcing him to cough.

"You are drunk, sir." Jean-Michel's tone was strong and final. "I suggest you go back to your friends and leave us be."

The man leaned over the table, bringing his nose within six inches of Jean-Michel's. "You are not welcome in this tavern. Leave now, or I will filet you in front of everyone, and we will roast you for our dinner!"

"Leaving now, before I have been served my meal, would be rude to my host, Dr. D'Poussant."

Isabella tugged at Louis, pulling him over her lap and into a hole between her body and the wall. She pulled her scabbard across her lap, its tip against the wall as if locking Louis into place on the bench. She gripped the hilt, pulling the blade an inch into the open.

The man's eyebrows narrowed and his eyes hardened. "You answer to me in this tavern, not to a plantation owner."

"I answer to a man's invitation, not a man's threat."

"Come, Aldric, I don't see a need to be rude." D'Poussant's tone was smooth and seductive, absent the measured strength of Jean-Michel's rejoinders.

"You know what I think of your kind, doctor," growled Aldric.

Isabella looked at D'Poussant, saw the sparkle in her host's eyes, and pulled her blade another inch from its sheath.

Jean-Michel didn't unlock his gaze. "I have no quarrel with you, *monsieur*. Please remove your knife."

"*Monsieur*," Isabella interjected, "as you can see, we have a child. Please leave us be so we can go about our business with Dr. D'Poussant."

Aldric's eyes rose to fix his focus on Isabella. "No business with the doctor is worthy of entertainment in this establishment."

"Aldric, Aldric," D'Poussant chided in a gentle voice, "you are out of line. I am afraid you may be stepping into something much deeper than you are aware."

Aldric's forearm bulged as his grip on his knife strengthened. "I suggest you shut up. No woman of any repute should come through those doors." A flick of Aldric's wrist brought the tip out of the wood, the flicker of a candle igniting a flash from the blade as he pushed the tip toward Isabella.

Jean-Michel slipped his arm under Aldric's elbow and pulled it into his chest, deflecting the blade, as he used his other arm to push over the shoulder and slam the drunkard's cheek into the table. Jean-Michel lifted himself from the bench as Aldric's face crashed into the wood and forced his attacker's leg to buckle. "Don't threaten my captain," Jean-Michel snarled into his ear. Aldric tried to pull his arm free, but Jean-Michel clamped down on the elbow, forcing his shoulder into the wood and pinning him to the table.

Isabella swung her leg over the bench and pulled her saber from its scabbard, slicing an arc at an enemy unseen by Jean-Michel. "Stop! *Arrêtez!* Stay back."

Jean-Michel knew by instinct that Isabella may well have just saved his life. Four men with daggers stood a few paces from Jean-Michel's back, well within cutting distance but far enough away the cuts would not be lethal.

A swarthy man, sweat beading down his face, looked as Isabella. "Let our man go."

Isabella shook her head. "He attacked us. We didn't look for this business. Stay back."

A second man, smaller but more muscular with an angled jaw, smiled. "I hope you know how to use that blade, *mademoiselle*. We certainly know how to use ours." He raised his dagger and pointed the tip at her face. "I certainly wouldn't want to damage such a beautiful face."

Isabella brought her tip down to the dagger. "I never start a fight without knowing my enemy."

"You are breaking our rules," the smaller man said. "For that, we will bring you in line."

Isabella kept her tip steady. "Jean-Michel?"

A strong push by Jean-Michel into the back of Aldric's head prompted a painful grunt. "How many are there?"

"Four."

"I'm afraid I would have to run through Mr. Aldric if I came to help you."

"We wouldn't want that to happen. We should try to keep Mr. Aldric alive, even though he's an ass."

"*Mademoiselle*," the shorter man said, "talk means little in le Coq Fantôme. You are in the Nether World of the West Indies."

Isabella brought her right foot forward, a slight bend in her knees, as her body settled into a firm stand. She brought her left hand down and close to her waist, as her right elbow bent, retracting the tip of her blade. She looked at the smaller man and moved the tip as if tapping the end of the man's dagger with air. She moved the tip to the second, leaner man, repeating the same practiced motion, as if part of a pre-battle ritual. The other two men stepped to the side of the first two, daggers in hand, but far enough from her tip so she couldn't do damage. She nodded to each while keeping the first two men in her sight line. "I humbly request that you leave us alone."

The leaner man's face morphed into a scowl. "You will not invade our house. This is where we stand. This is where we are counted."

"*Gens de couleur!*" Isabella called, her voice rising above her attackers and into the clamor of the room. "We mean no harm. Our vessel is moored peacefully in your harbor. All we ask is that you allow us to show our respects to our host and give us safe passage to our ship."

The smaller man with the round face cracked a broad smile, yellowed teeth flinging a ghoulish challenge toward the outsiders and their docile host. The leaner man directed the tip of his dagger toward Isabella, as if lining it along a sight. She lunged at the smaller man, sending her tip deep into his wrist, then twisting so the long side of the blade dug into his forearm. She ducked under his arm, the gash dislodging the dagger as the man buckled from the pain. She let her saber drop as she pushed past him, her edge arcing up under his arm and then pulling an upward cut across the man behind. The slice was not enough to cut into the man's ribs, but a deep red line exploded across his chest and the blade finished its path by carving the second man's knife out of his grip in another spritz of blood.

She now faced the remaining two attackers. The lean man with the angular jaw was unfazed and advanced on Isabella. The fourth man hesitated, frozen in his stance as his eyes tried to catch up to her quick movements. He looked at his two wounded comrades, both brought to their knees as they clasped their bloodied arms and hands to their bodies, wrapping their shirts around the cuts.

141

The lean man brought his dagger up, his eyes blazing with anger and purpose. He was too close to bring her blade into his chest, but her battle-hardened instincts moved her to the side as his blade thrust forward toward her chest. The tip slipped by her torso, and the force of the push propelled his body past her. Isabella took a half step toward him, bumping his leg with her knee, and her attacker spun and flopped to the ground on his back. Isabella angled her body to bring her blade up to the fourth man, who remained standing in the same place, stunned by Isabella's quickness and the chaos. Two men were scrambling to stay alive and another trying to reset his sights on his intended prey. Isabella brought her tip up, hitting the fourth man's knife with a force that jettisoned it from his hands. The dagger clattered across the floor. He stepped back, palms in the air, eyes wide with fear. She pushed him back with short thrusts of her saber.

Isabella turned back to the lean man, who was now on his knees, his knife in his hand, ready for another attack. She shook her head.

The man stood, his defiant knife pointed at her face.

Isabella steadied herself, her saber extended toward what now appeared to be the leader of the four men. "You still have a chance to live."

She could see the man's teeth grind with anger.

"Even with short blades, your men could have beaten my one long blade," she said. "Two of your men have been taken out of the fight, and a third has wisely recognized he is beaten. I should run you through right now. That would be the smart decision for me, but I will let you decide whether to live or die. If you attack me again, I will assume you want to kill me, if not now, then in the future. For that I will kill you. For me, it's a matter of simple self-preservation. If you secure your blade, I will show you grace. I will still believe you will try to kill me, at some point, but I will let you live...for now."

The man looked at Isabella's blade, its tip steady and her voice sure.

"Bruno," a raspy voice called from the tabletop. "Don't be stupid. We can't afford another corpse."

Bruno closed his eyes and let his blade fall to his side.

"Bruno, is it?" Jean-Michel had turned to look at their attacker even as he kept Aldric's head pinned to the table. "You've seen what

142

the Pirate of Panther Bay can do. I would make sure that dagger is secure—right now."

Bruno's eyes snapped open. He looked at Isabella, then Jean-Michel, as if he were seeing them both for the first time. He peered past Jean-Michel to D'Poussant. His jaw tightened and his lips pursed. His grip on the knife handle tightened as his free hand balled into a fist, as if his piercing glare alone would label D'Poussant a traitor. Bruno straightened his shoulders, tucked his dagger in his waist, and showed his hands free of weapons.

Isabella let her sword drop toward the floor, but kept its blade free of its scabbard, her grip firm and the tip ready. She kept her focus on Bruno. "What did Aldric mean when he said you could not 'afford' another corpse?"

20

D'Poussant raised his mug, tilting the rim toward Isabella. "Welcome to *Libérté Noire*."

Jean-Michel pulled Aldric up by his collar and pushed him away from the table. Isabella stepped back to the table but stayed standing, as if blocking Louis from leaving. The excitement had drawn Louis to the end of the bench, so she nudged him back toward the wall.

"Relax," Aldric said, swiping his shirtsleeves as if dislodging dirt caked into the fibers. "We aren't going to attack you."

Jean-Michel patted the hilt of his sword, still secure in its scabbard. "Excuse me if it takes a little more than your word for us to believe you. If either one of you makes another move, Isabella won't be the only one to have fun in this fine establishment."

Bruno stared at Isabella, his look softened by the reality that two of his men were now with doctors tending to wounds that may well result in their deaths, and another cowered by the agility and skill of an expert swordsman...who was a woman. "You are the Pirate of Panther Bay?"

D'Poussant laughed. "Isabella warned you. Never start a fight without knowing your enemy. Your crew has suffered from your ignorance. Isabella is none other than the Pirate of Panther Bay!"

Bruno's eyes widened as he drew in a deep breath. His eyes pierced the air separating him from D'Poussant with the quickness of an expert knife thrower.

D'Poussant rolled his eyes. "Please, Bruno. You are quick to the fight, but you need to be more nimble in the attack. We've discussed this. You are a good strategist, but you must assume your enemy is as quick and smart as you are."

"You could have warned me."

D'Poussant shook his head. "You know a warning would serve no purpose. Our movement has to fight from the trees and alleys and commit to the final solution. You must fight as if each attack is a new one, from an unknown enemy."

Jean-Michel, sensing the tension was now between comrades and no longer between strangers, leaned against the bench. "What do you mean 'final solution'?"

D'Poussant diverted his eyes back to his mug and then to Louis. "We are in a fight for our lives on this island. My home."

"What fight?" Jean-Michel asked, looking around the tavern. "I see men drinking after a long day on the docks. I doubt there are many slaves among this crowd, but right now, they seem to see strangers as the subject of their sport, not men of the island. Or France, for that matter."

Bruno continued to glare at D'Poussant. "You should have warned me. I've got two men down and another I can't trust. You let me walk into a trap."

"Not at all," D'Poussant said, his voice absent the aloof patrician tone that had kept Bruno and his men at an invisible distance minutes earlier. "You know that we have to test every stranger that comes in these doors."

"But you brought a European. You knew as well as we did that he had only one way to survive."

"And you didn't count on Isabella."

Bruno looked at Isabella, his eyes more measured and calm. "If I had known this was the Pirate of Panther Bay, we would have handled this differently."

"Precisely. You assumed she was a slave, or a concubine, and that the white man was her master."

"She had the boy."

D'Poussant looked at Louis. "Yes, a clever twist on the story, I think."

Isabella reached toward Louis's shoulder and squeezed it. "How can you involve him in whatever plot you are devising, here? He's just a boy. He's a slave. Any dispute he witnesses puts his life at risk."

Louis looked at Isabella, his eyes pleading. "I want to go home."

D'Poussant shook his head. "I'm afraid we can't let you go now, Louis."

Louis caught his breath, his eyes glistening. "Please, Dr. D'Poussant, please let me go home. My mama will want to know where I am."

"I know your mother, and I'll send her word that you are safe." D'Poussant looked at Isabella. "He's the perfect cover for you. You are a woman with a young child." He looked over to Jean-Michel. "And you are the plantation owner returned to his mistress and son."

Isabella shook her head. "D'Poussant, what is going on?"

A broad smile crossed the doctor's face. "Why, Isabella, *Liberté Noire*. We are going to set this island free of the chains of slavery. Welcome to the revolution!"

21

"I did not sign up for a revolution!" Jean-Michel's statement had a finality that would have shaken timbers loose on the *Marée Rouge* but generated little more than a thud in the cobbled back streets of Port-au-Prince.

"My mama wants me home," said Louis, sidling up to Isabella's leg. He grabbed her hand and tugged. "I want to go home. I'm hungry. I've got to get the horses to bed. Sun'll be up before too long, too."

Isabella let her hands slip around Louis's shoulder and she pulled him closer. "It's not fair to keep the boy. He shouldn't be part of this."

Jean-Michel shot a look toward Isabella, locking his eyes on her and cocking his head, as if saying: You aren't seriously thinking about joining this revolution, are you? "I'll have no part of this. I'll have Louis take me back to the ship. If you want to abandon your crew and follow this madman, that's your choice."

D'Poussant watched Jean-Michel, keeping his hands clasped around his mug of ale as he watched.

Isabella looked at Louis and then turned to the man that had protected and comforted her since Jacob's death. "Perhaps this is it."

"You have a crew waiting for you to return. You know how fickle pirates are. If I return without you, they will assume the worst. They will probably call an election for a new captain. It's in the pirate's Articles. I can't guarantee they'll elect me, and I can't guarantee you, a woman, will be welcome back on board."

D'Poussant looked past Jean-Michel and Isabella. "Bruno?"

Bruno stepped toward Isabella. "She's good. When my man backed down, rather than close in on her, he knew he had experienced something different. She may be The One."

Jean-Michel's expression became serious. "What do you mean 'The One'?"

D'Poussant raised his cane to the table, twisted the gold-bladed handle, and pulled a square-shaped rapier several inches out of what was now a scabbard. "I know a little bit about you, too, Jean-Michel. You know the legends of these hills. You hear the talk of the spirits, even if your Catholic heart won't let you believe it. The slaves in this colony are ready to change their lives. They want something better for their children and their grandchildren, even if it means sacrificing what they have now. We have thousands of *gens de couleur* ready to take their rightful place as full citizens in a democracy, out from under the shackles of an empire and king a world away. They have been waiting for the right time…and the right person."

The din of the tavern seemed to ramp down several decibels. Jean-Michel lowered his voice. "You have been plotting this conspiracy for a long time."

Bruno and Aldric stepped closer to the table. Isabella extended her blade to the point that it almost touched their shins, as if creating a wall that stopped their advance.

"It's a revolution, Jean-Michel." D'Poussant's voice was serious and steady, his gaze unwavering. "Slavery is a tumor on society, and it must be eradicated."

"By your own admission, you own slaves."

D'Poussant nodded. "I own a plantation. Bruno is my overseer. Aldric is a foreman. You see, my plantation is really an army."

Isabella brought her scabbard across her waist and straightened her shoulders.

Jean-Michel put a hand down on the table, turning his body so he could face Isabella. "Tortuga Bay. We need to stay focused. Muñoz has a frigate and three warships blockading this port. One hundred men—your men, Jacob's men—are trapped on that ship, sitting ducks if Muñoz comes into the port. This is Jacob's legacy."

"You heard Madame Rêve-Cœur," Isabella said, her face cast to the table as her hand drew to her chin in thought.

"We heard many strange things that night."

Isabella thought of the cross and key secured in her sash. "Lasiren and Papa Legba. They are both calling me. My calling is to more than one spirit, one god. I am supposed to be part of something larger than the *Marée Rouge*. Binta."

"Binta?" D'Poussant had pulled himself closer to the edge of the table. "Who were you speaking with? Which mountains? The Black Mountains to the north? Or the Chaîne de la Selle?"

"It doesn't matter," Jean-Michel said, avoiding eye contact with D'Poussant. "Isabella, remember the ship, its crew, Tortuga Bay."

Isabella lifted her hand to Jean-Michel's arm and held it in a soft grip. She raised her other hand to his chest. "Jean-Michel, the prophecy. You know I have been haunted by it since my mother's death, since the slave revolt set the plantation on fire and sent me on this journey."

"Yes, Isabella, but the flames of the revolt sent you into the arms of Jacob, onto the decks of the *Marée Rouge*, and into the arms of Juan Carlos. Don't give into these spirits. Stay true to your course. Let's escape and sail north to Tortuga Bay. We can regroup there."

Isabella closed her eyes, letting her breathing calm her nerves and settle her brain.

"Four hundred thousand slaves work the fields, hillsides, groves, and ports of this colony." D'Poussant's voice was soft, even soothing. "They are looking for a spark of hope, a leader to forge their destinies into one."

"That is your role," Jean-Michel snapped at D'Poussant. "You are building your army." He lifted his hand, with a thumb pointed to the room now full of drunken dockhands and the thugs that had attacked him. "That's your army. You have the means to finance this revolution of yours. You do not need Isabella."

"On the contrary, Jean-Michel, our revolution needs Isabella. That's what this little incident in the le Coq Fantôme demonstrated so clearly, not just to me, but to Bruno and Aldric. To all in this room. A plantation owner, a slave owner, can't lead this revolution. I have been educated in France. For many, I am the colonial master. We need an independent spirit to lead us."

Isabella closed her eyes.

Louis tugged on Isabella's sleeve. "Can you take me home, Mademoiselle Isabella? I want to go home."

D'Poussant looked down at Louis and patted him on his shoulder. "Louis, you will have to stay with us right now. I will keep you safe. I will tell your mother that you are safe. I will take you and your mother back to my plantation, and I will give you good work, and you can help me with my army."

Louis began to breathe harder. "I want to work for His Excellency. I like the horses. I like driving his carriages. I like living with Mama."

"Governor Bellecombe hates slavery," Jean-Michel pointed out. "He will bring it to an end. Revolutionary forces are building in France as well, and that will change everything in the colonies. They are inspired by the same philosophers as the Americans, and the Americans are showing the rest of the world the way. Louis XVI sees this, and he is already trying to make changes in France, including listening to the people."

"The men and women suffering as chattel on this island will not wait. They are ready to seize their own destinies, to forge their own identities. We have been building our stores. We have been training our armies. We need leadership."

Isabella turned her attention to Louis. His eyes glistened with fear, his hands holding to the fabric of her shirt. "Louis, I don't think it's safe for you to stay in Port-au-Prince right now. Can you go with Jean-Michel to my ship?"

Louis's eyes widened, and he brought both of his hands to hers. "*Mademoiselle, mademoiselle*, I can't leave Mama. Please let me go home."

Isabella sat down on the bench and held his hands in hers. "Go with Jean-Michel. Get your mother. You can both go to my ship, where you will be safe."

"Isabella!" Jean-Michel said in a horse whisper. "Muñoz! We can't have a boy and his civilian mother—another woman—on board."

"Juan Carlos will keep Muñoz at bay for at least two weeks. Maybe three." Isabella stood up, using a gentle pull to bring Louis off the bench. "I am going to see what D'Poussant has prepared and planned." She looked at D'Poussant. "If I don't like what I see, I'll be back on board the *Marée Rouge* before you can say 'booty'!" She turned to Jean-Michel, looked into his eyes, and brought her hands to his cheeks. "Jean-Michel, *mon ami*, my best friend, my protector. I have to do this. I have to see for myself if Madame Rêve-Cœur is right. I have to see if this fulfills the destiny foretold by my mother. I have to discover if Binta is my true calling."

150

22

Jean-Michel fumed as he climbed through the gangway of the *Marée Rouge,* pulling Louis so hard his feet left the ground.

"I thought you were taking me home!"

Jean-Michel pulled the boy onto the deck, prompting gasps from the few crewmen that remained on the deck as darkness invaded. He looked at the boy and shook his head. "I couldn't leave you in port after what happened in the tavern."

"Why not? Mama will be angry. What will His Excellency think?"

"We'll send for your mother."

A weathered, older sailor trotted up to the pirate quartermaster and his reluctant charge. "What've we got here, meat for the stew?" he cackled.

Jean-Michel shot a stern look his way. "I don't have much use for the boy, Smoothy, but I wasn't left with much choice."

Smoothy reached to touch Louis's head. Louis turned to avoid the strange hand. The pirate laughed. "Feisty bugger. I was thinking he'd be a good powder monkey, but you might be better off making him your cabin boy. Keep 'm under your thumb rather than worry about running powder to my guns during a fight."

Louis's expression became hard as he glared at the old pirate.

Jean-Michel put a hand on the boy's shoulder. "I don't know what we'll do with him, but we need to get his mother first."

Smoothy hurled a sharp look toward Jean-Michel. "His mother? The crew's not going to like that. A young'un like him is good for doing grunt work. But his mother? Last thing we need is another woman on this ship. Pirates don't take to women at sea. She'll doom us all. It's been tough enough keepin' the crew together under Isabella. If it wasn't for her reputation and Jacob's record takin' prizes, we wouldn't have a tar anywhere close to these decks."

Smoothy looked around and cocked his head. "Where is our esteemed cap'n?"

Jean-Michel expelled a huff of air. "Assemble the crew."

Jean-Michel stood at the helm, the tiller idle and bound by rope, as one hundred pirates filled the weather deck and crammed in openings among the cannons, ropes, and hatches. Little chatter disturbed the darkness, but the curious expressions of the tars were clear even under the pulsating flames of torches and makeshift lanterns. Smoothy stood nearby, along with his mate Herrera.

Jean-Michel stepped forward, positioning himself under a torch so that he could be seen. "Isabella and I met with the Governor General Bellecombe of Saint-Domingue this afternoon. Something's come up, and we need to discuss our next course of action." He pointed to the mouth of the bay. "A Spanish frigate sits out there with three sloops of war, waiting for us to leave this harbor. We have a choice. We can make a run for the open water or we can stay here in the harbor. Bellecombe says we can stay here if we want, but if the dagoes try to press their hand, he won't be able to do much to protect us, seeing now that France and Spain are allies fighting with the Americans against the British."

A lanky, barefooted sailor stepped forward, just enough to be noticed. "From what the dago captain said yesterday on this deck, he'll let us go if we give up Isabella."

"Aye," said Smoothy, "but do ya really believe Rodriguez'll just let us hand her over and be done with us?"

Herrera shook his head. "I was master gunner on a sixteen-gun schooner in Charles III's navy before being captured by the British and imprisoned in Pensacola. *Mis amigos*, Spanish captains carry much pride. You saw that when Muñoz boarded the *Marée Rouge*. I did not like this capitán at all, *para nada*, when he demanded our surrender. He wants more than Isabella to take back to Puerto Rico. Mark my word."

"Where is Isabella?"

The question emerged from within the group, defying attempts to identify its owner.

Jean-Michel reached for a rope to hold himself steady. "She's on shore, in Port-au-Prince."

Murmurs rolled through the pirate crew. A cool gust of wind swept over the deck, agitating the flickering light.

"What's her plan?" Another unowned question.

"We met up with a local planter." More murmurs. "Something's afoot on land, but I don't know what yet."

A seaman stepped forward from the crowd. He was tall and thin, with a round face and long forehead. "Is that why the boy is with you?"

Jean-Michel nodded. "He needs to be kept safe."

The seaman looked at the boy and shook his head. "Children on a pirate ship?"

Jean-Michel shifted his weight against the rope. "I don't like it any more than you, Sarhaan. We were in a tavern and events…took an unexpected turn. We decided it was no place for the boy."

Sarhaan turned to the pirates and then back to Jean-Michel. "Jean-Michel, where is Isabella?"

Jean-Michel looked past Sarhaan to the legion of hardened sea warriors. "I told you, she's still in the port. She's talking to the planter and others on land."

Sarhaan's jaws tightened. "She would not abandon us that easily. You would not have left her side. Why is the boy on board our ship? Did she bargain for him?"

Jean-Michel hesitated then pulled Louis closer to his side. "This is Louis. He's the carriage driver for the governor. She didn't want to leave him alone in the streets of Port-au-Prince."

Louis looked up at Jean-Michel. "I would've been fine! I drive the streets at night all the time."

Jean-Michel sent a scolding glance to Louis and gave him a tap on the back of the head.

Sarhaan shook his head. "You need to be honest with us, Jean-Michel. We have given you and Isabella much discretion. You know we have every right, according to the Articles, to elect a new captain and quartermaster."

The pirate crowd seemed to pull together as individuals blurred into a solid mass. Jean-Michel straightened his back and brought his shoulders up, giving his stature several more inches. He focused his gaze on the body of sailors. "Most of you have been crew under

Isabella's leadership for more than a year. You stayed loyal after the mutiny. You helped us regain the *Marée Rouge* and defeat Yellow Jacket at Privateer Pointe. You have helped us stop the trade of slaves and stolen riches that feed Europe. The Pirate of Panther Bay is known as the scourge of these seas. Now is not the time to doubt her or our task."

Sarhaan shook his head. "It is not Isabella that I doubt. But I am beginning to wonder about you, Jean-Michel. You have returned without her, and in her place, you have brought a boy."

Herrera looked over to Jean-Michel. "Sarhaan has a point. Rodriguez is not going to stop with Isabella, and Capitán Muñoz is not going to let you—or any of us—go. Have you seen Juan Carlos?"

"Is Juan Carlos with us or his King?" another unowned voice interjected.

Jean-Michel paused. "Juan Carlos is with us; he is with Isabella."

"Aye," Herrera said. "Juan Carlos is with Isabella, but is he with us?"

Alarmed mutterings buzzed through the crew.

Another tar stepped forward, this time a swarthy man with a thick mass of hair, broad shoulders toned by scaling masts and setting sails, and a scar streaking down his cheek. "Something's not right. Is Isabella alive?"

"Yes!" Jean-Michel's response was forceful and strident. "She is alive. She is, as I've told you, discussing the conditions of Port-au-Prince with men, free and slave."

The word "slave" prompted Sarhaan's eyes to harden. "The rumors are true."

"What rumors?" Jean-Michel's response was so fast, its sincerity seemed to tamp down the discontented muttering.

Sarhaan turned to the crowd. Even in the pulsating yellows of the torches, he could tell that many, but not quite half, the faces were African. "A slave revolution! *Liberté Noire!*"

The voices converged into a rising buzz rolling in waves through the crowd.

Smoothy stood up from his perch on the breech of one of the long guns. "Is that true? The slaves are revoltin' in Saint-Domingue?"

Jean-Michel raised his hands and motioned downward. "I saw no sign of a revolt, slave or otherwise, when I was on shore."

Sarhaan turned back to Jean-Michel. "You do not need to see guns and knives, or cannons, to see a revolution. You may not have seen it," Sarhaan nodded, "but Isabella has. She has seen the future of the West Indies."

A pulse of mutterings filtered through the crowd as pirates conferred with each other. "Is that why she's abandoned us?"

Jean-Michel kept his hands raised. "No, Isabella has not abandoned us. She has not abandoned the *Marée Rouge*. That is why Louis is with us."

"Louis is an innocent," Sarhaan said, his voice loud enough to carry across the deck and pierce the crowd. "She has sent Louis to us, so she can save the innocent. She is committed to the slave revolution. It starts here, in Port-au-Prince!"

"Hold on, mates!" Smoothy's voice carried a seasoned tenor that disrupted the pulsing murmurs sweeping the deck. "We know that Isabella's called to do much more than pillage ships in these sea trading routes. None of you would've signed under her flag if you were interested in just gold, coin, and silk. Many of you signed on after being freed from the slavers."

"We didn't sign up to be part of a revolution!"

Sarhaan faced the crowd. "Perhaps, my friends, this is where we part ways! I am going to join Isabella on land. I will join the revolution. It is my right to leave this ship and forego my shares. Those who are not with me—stay with the *Marée Rouge* and continue your journey."

"Sarhaan!" Jean-Michel's voice boomed over the deck, silencing the most trivial mumblings. "Don't rush into this! I was with Isabella as we negotiated our safe harbor despite the Spanish blockading our exit. I was at the table with Isabella as she heard the plans for the revolution. We cannot commit to this action yet. They are not ready! Joining their movement now would mean certain death for any African aboard this ship or any white man who chooses to join them. The Governor General is sympathetic to ending slavery in the colonies, but he has not committed to seeing that happen. Joining Isabella now would be certain death!"

Sarhaan advanced on Jean-Michel and locked with his eyes. He lifted his hands to his shoulders. "Jean-Michel, *mon ami*, you have been a great friend. You have led us through dark times and kept us alive.

155

For that, I am grateful, but I believe the time has come to be part of something bigger."

Sarhaan turned to the pirates and raised his hands, palms toward himself as if beckoning them to join him. "Fellow warriors, comrades, *compañeros*! This is not just Isabella's fight. This is our fight. This is our destiny. We heard in Charlotte Amalie that the French West Indies were near eruption, ready to cast off the torture and brutality of the slave system that drives the trade for indigo, cocoa, and sugarcane in those hills and mountains. We have taken up pirating because we have no other choice! But Isabella has found her place, a new path. Join me. Join Isabella! This is our time!"

The mutterings ascended to a cacophony as discord clashed among the voices and urgent tones punctured the night air. The mass began to dissipate, as clusters split into smaller groups, and the unity of their voices collapsed.

"Wait!" The urgency of Jean-Michel's warning ushered a silence across the deck. Jean-Michel stepped up to Sarhaan and clasped his shoulder. "Sarhaan, Isabella may have found her place, but it's too soon. The slaves are not ready to revolt. They will be slaughtered. I have met the men who say they will lead this revolution, and I have no confidence they will achieve the justice they seek."

"But it's time, Jean-Michel. Africans across the colonies are waiting for this moment!"

"Perhaps." Jean-Michel squeezed Sarhaan's shoulder. "You know where I stand. I am with you, but I don't have good feelings about this effort in Port-au-Prince."

Smoothy lifted his eyes, his brows furrowed, lifting his arm to wipe a band of sweat that covered a grimace. "Sarhaan, I've sailed with Jean-Michel for many years. I sailed with him under Jacob the Red. I have sailed with him under Isabella, the Pirate of Panther Bay. I've learned 'is feel for men is right more often than not."

Sarhaan closed his eyes, letting his face dip. "I can't let Isabella do this alone. I have to join her."

"Sarhaan, *mon ami*, I agree. We can't let Isabella stay in Port-au-Prince. This place is very dangerous right now. I am afraid she is with men who do not have her best interests at heart. She may have a calling, as you say, but I need more before I am willing to let her go."

Sarhaan lifted his eyes to Jean-Michel. "Then show me. Take me into the port. Let me meet these men. I have been betrayed before. That betrayal led to Isabella's capture on St. John and her torture in El Morro. I can see their betrayal in their faces if you show them to me."

Jean-Michel nodded. "I'll take you to her." He turned to Smoothy and then to the pirates gathered in what was now, thoughtful silence. "With your agreement, we will put Smoothy in charge of the *Marée Rouge*. Nobody better than a master gunner to run a pirate crew while the captain and quartermaster are away! I will return to shore with Sarhaan to determine Isabella's intentions. I will take Herrera and three other volunteers. We will return, with or without Isabella, and we can decide our future course then!"

The crew grumbled assent.

Jean-Michel turned to Smoothy. "Keep the boy safe."

23

The warmth from Isabella's kiss had lingered longer than usual when Juan Carlos returned to the *Santa Mónica*. He had to push that touch as far from his mind as possible now that Muñoz had summoned him to the captain's cabin. The gentle sweeps of aspiring waves under the frigate's keel veiled what, he was sure, would be turbulent breakers now that their spies had returned from the back alleys of Port-au-Prince. The two towering masts of the *Marée Rouge* remained undisturbed since anchoring three days earlier, but Jean-Michel's plan could turn those sticks into billowed canvas runners in minutes. While his heart would cheer, his head knew the pirate's run would trigger death. He had to find a better way.

The captain was leaning over a map on a table in the officer's mess, his palms holding his body up as he inspected the bay and crude lines marking the roads, alleys, warehouses, and inns. Four of the ship's lieutenants and two other men in civilian clothes circled the tabletop and map. The gunner's mate and quartermaster had stepped back, letting the officers direct the conversation.

A lieutenant with a thick mustache that turned up at the ends of his mouth seemed to catch the army captain's shadow as he approached what was now a crowded stateroom. "*Buenos dias, Capitán Santa Ana.*"

Juan Carlos bowed and stopped two paces from the table.

"I'm pleased you could make our briefing," Muñoz said without looking up. "Our rogues have made our lives interesting, it seems."

Juan Carlos remained standing.

Muñoz motioned for Juan Carlos to approach the table. "According to Sanchez and Torres, our pirates made landfall about mid-morning yesterday. They were met by a coach and carried to the governor's hacienda in the hills." He turned his head to look at Juan Carlos. "An interesting choice, don't you agree? A formal reception in the palace in the city would have been more appropriate for dignitaries."

Juan Carlos nodded. "Sí, Capitán. Apparently, the governor does not want to be seen with pirates."

The naval fleet captain returned to the map. "After several hours, they returned to the city but didn't go back to their vessel. Instead, they entered a tavern called le Coq Fantôme." He leaned further over the map and dropped his index finger on a building two roads in from the eastern edge of the city, a block at the intersection of Rue de Bretagne and Rue de Dauphines. "They had a fine dinner of barbecue chicken, rice, and ale."

Juan Carlos looked at each of the officers around the table, as well as gunner's mate Sanchez, who was holding a round-brimmed hat in both hands in front him, and quartermaster Torres, a larger man who looked like he could handle stores and supplies of all sizes and types.

Muñoz cast a sideways glance toward Juan Carlos. "You seem surprised."

"I wouldn't expect the governor to entertain them, unless he intended to arrest them, but he let them go."

Sanchez kept his attention focused on the frigate's captain. "We saw them come down from the mansion in the governor's official carriage. They stopped just as they returned to the city and went into the tavern after they met with an African. We think he is a *gens de couleur*."

Juan Carlos looked at the map and then turned to the gunner's mate. "How did you find them? That tavern looks like it's off the main roads."

Sanchez dipped his head and his hands traced the rim of his hat. "Sí, Capitán Santa Ana. We spent most of the morning and afternoon searching the wharves and quays. We could not find anyone who had seen them."

Juan Carlos shook his head. "Why didn't you ask the harbor captain?"

Torres perked up, bringing his eyes up to meet Juan Carlos. "Our orders were to find information without raising suspicions. If we had gone to the harbor captain, he would have known we were looking for the pirates."

"Good work, Torres," Muñoz said. "Our interests are best served by staying low and invisible." The frigate captain turned back to Juan Carlos. "Do you have any relevant questions for Sanchez or Torres?"

Juan Carlos felt his cheeks flood with warmth and his chest tighten. "Capitán Muñoz, I did not mean to be disrespectful, but I was not included in their briefing before they were sent on shore."

Muñoz let a few silent moments pass, allowing Juan Carlos's admission of exclusion settle into the mood around the map table. He looked past Juan Carlos to Torres. "Continue with your report. What happened after they fed themselves?"

Torres nodded. "The male pirate, a Frenchman we believe, left the tavern. The carriage boy drove him back to the quay. We were on foot, so it took us a few more minutes to get to the quay, but we saw the launch pull up to their ship."

Juan Carlos resisted the instinct to draw in a deep breath. He felt his heart skip as he turned the image of Jean-Michel leaving a tavern at night by himself over in his head. "The female was nowhere to be seen?"

"Non, Capitán. But we followed the carriage back to the bay."

Juan Carlos snapped a look toward Torres. "You didn't split up? Have one person watch the tavern and the other follow the carriage?"

The silence of the two sailors was answer enough. Juan Carlos drew in a breath, and he let the air out in a quick huff, making his frustration clear.

The lieutenant with the mustache looked over to Muñoz. "Capitán, she can't be far. The jungles of Hispaniola are not kind to strangers. She would not last long."

Juan Carlos brought his shoulders back, but he kept his head bent to avoid hitting the beams over their heads. "She is at home in those jungles. She survived days in the forest of St. John after her crew mutinied and she was gravely wounded. I would not underestimate her ability to survive."

Muñoz nodded. "She is a survivor. We should not underestimate her." He turned toward Torres. "Is she still in the port?"

Torres nodded agreement. "She did not leave in the carriage, and she could not have made it to their launch in time to be taken back to her ship. She must still be in port."

"Bueno," Muñoz said. "She is separated from her crew."

The lieutenant looked over to Muñoz. "Do you want to send a landing party to capture her?"

Muñoz turned to Juan Carlos. "What is your opinion, Capitán?"

Juan Carlos knew by his tone that Muñoz was testing him, and a quick glance at the expectant faces around the table confirmed it. "I have no doubt a landing party led by Señor Torres would be effective, and Rodriguez is most interested in capturing Isabella alive." Muñoz's eyes narrowed. Juan Carlos locked his sight on Muñoz. "But I think it would be premature."

Muñoz's expression didn't change, as if he were waiting for a response from one of his other officers. More silent moments created a fog of expectation that pulled at Juan Carlos, but the lieutenant succumbed first.

"If the Viceroy wants the pirate wench," he said, turning away from Juan Carlos, "we should send a landing party into the city and capture her. Then we should surround her vessel and destroy it before it leaves port."

Juan Carlos tamped down an urge to snicker. Muñoz was too seasoned to be that reckless. The Capitán de Navio ticked a sharp glance toward the lieutenant before executing a quick shake of the head, sending the lieutenant's eyes back to the map.

Juan Carlos dropped a hand to the table and tapped the top with his forefinger. "I admire your aggressiveness, Lieutenant, but that would provoke an international incident."

Muñoz gave a reluctant nod of his head, ceding the discussion to the army captain.

"I believe, using his formal authority as Capitán de Navio," Juan Carlos said, "our captain can send a second letter to the Governor General requesting that he turn over the pirate to Spain for transport and trial in Puerto Rico. This formally puts the decision about how to dispose of Isabella and Jean-Michel in his hands. If we send our squadron in to destroy the *Marée Rouge* in their port, we would indeed provoke an international incident."

The lieutenant lifted his hands to his mustache and began to twist the ends. "We are allies."

Juan Carlos nodded. "Against the British. While pirates are a common enemy, our diplomatic protocols determine how we handle individual threats like pirates. If we were on the open sea, France

161

would have no objection to us blowing them out of the water. But they are anchored in their harbor, and apparently, they haven't seen any need to force them out."

"Surely they see the need to purge the seas of pirates!"

"If it were only that simple," Juan Carlos said. "With the Americans in revolt against the British and the French aligned with the Americans and Spain, a single action on our part could complicate relations between our countries in ways we can't anticipate."

Muñoz heaved a sigh into the circle of officers and spies. "I am afraid Capitán Santa Ana is correct. We can't attack their ship while it lies in the harbor at anchor."

Torres lifted his head to look at the captain. "But the pirates' captain is on land."

Muñoz nodded his head.

Juan Carlos's head began to spin. Muñoz was thinking of ignoring the *Marée Rouge* and going on shore to capture Isabella!

The lieutenant's mood brightened. "We could capture the wench on land, and perhaps draw their crew out of the bay to rescue her. We could send the schooners off, putting word on the wharves that we have dispatched them for more supplies, or perhaps to return to Puerto Rico for support now that we've found the *Marée Rouge*. We would have them lie just off the horizon so the pirates will think we are a lone frigate."

Muñoz cocked his head. "Good thinking, Lieutenant Guerrero. Pirates run from trouble. Why would they come after a fully armed frigate?"

"Because they defeated one before," said Juan Carlos.

Muñoz's surprised look was just what Juan Carlos wanted to see.

Juan Carlos looked at the other officers. "Isabella defeated three larger ships less than a year ago. She destroyed a thirty-two-gun frigate, the *Ana Maria*. She destroyed the pirate frigate the *Wasp* in a duel of broadsides, and she disabled the *Granada* at Privateer Pointe. I'm sure they are confident enough to think they could defeat another unescorted frigate!"

Juan Carlos concealed the deep breath he had taken in to calm his nerves with his decision to change Muñoz's strategy.

Muñoz continued to nod his head with a steady rhythm that encouraged Juan Carlos. "She was very arrogant when we confronted her on her brigantine," Muñoz said. "She must have known she was outgunned, but she showed no signs of recognizing the uselessness of her situation." He sighed. "I don't like the idea of sending my schooners out of sight. This operation will have to be precisely timed and executed."

Juan Carlos nodded. "We will have to capture her on land first, while she is alone and away from her crew. We will need to move quickly."

A hard glare from Muñoz settled on Juan Carlos. "You will lead the landing party, Capitán Santa Ana. You will take Torres and Sanchez, as well as Lieutenant Guerrero and five marines. You will not be in uniform, and you will be armed with one pistol and one knife each. Your mission is to find the rogue, Isabella, this so-called Pirate of Panther Bay, and bring her back to this ship alive. You are not to engage the French in any way. Do not let the harbor captain know you are on the ground."

Juan Carlos forced a smile onto his face and executed a deep, respectful bow. *"Gracias, mi capitán.* I will not disappoint you."

Lieutenant Guerrero's face brightened, the prospect of a clandestine land operation invigorating him. Torres and Sanchez remained quiet, observing the officers. Juan Carlos watched their silence from the corner of his eye. He was sure they knew more than they were telling. Whether that boded well for keeping Isabella free and alive, he had no way of telling, but he would find out soon.

24

Isabella could feel D'Poussant watching her as she crossed the room in le Coq Fantôme, and she struggled to keep her focus on the bar a few paces away. The day had plodded along as he moved her from a warehouse in the morning, to a cobbler's shop tucked in back around noon, and a sailmaker's loft in the late afternoon, before settling into the tavern for the evening. She reckoned they hadn't traveled more than four blocks the entire day, but she felt like she had hiked up a mountain.

D'Poussant's attitude seemed to change, too. His gentlemanly manner gave way to a curt, brusque style soon after they topped off a sampling of a Creole blend of rice-honey mead. By the time the afternoon sun had begun to stalk the western horizon, Isabella was thinking of Jean-Michel, the *Marée Rouge*, and the return of the prize crew from Santo Domingo. She hoped Louis and his mother were safe on her faithful, well-armed brig.

"I guess you've had a busy day."

Isabella looked up to Gabrielle, her serious face trained on hers as she was stowing a clean mug. Isabella gave her a half-hearted smile. "D'Poussant has kept me running."

Gabrielle brought a towel to her face and wiped the sweat that had beaded across her forehead, reminding Isabella of the humidity that had descended from the jungles. Her shirt felt heavy, sticking to her back, and the sleeves caught on the perspiration rising from her arms as she brought her hands to the bar, sliding her palms along the smooth juniper. "I would think pine would be easier to work with."

Gabrielle smiled. "Pine has to be brought in from the northern mountains. Juniper is easier to get locally, and Papa has a fondness for its look. Besides, the juniper berries are great medicines. I've used the leaves to stop infections from cuts. I think juniper could flush any poison from your body."

Gabrielle looked over to D'Poussant, sitting in the back of the room at the same table where the blood of two patrons had spilled the night before. "Be careful, *mon cher*."

Isabella followed her gaze and noted D'Poussant's easy smile and comfortable conversation with two black men near his table. "He has a vision for the future of this people and this land."

Gabrielle slipped a tankard into her hand, and Isabella returned her focus to the bar. "Mmm, honey mead. The Spanish were good for one thing right? Bringing bees to ferment my favorite beverage."

Gabrielle laughed. "Yes, *mon cher*. That's why they brought it over here. They knew that one day freedom would be secured on a pint of alcohol."

Isabella tipped her tankard. "Much better than the watered down rum in our mugs at sea."

Gabrielle reached across the bar and placed her hand over Isabella's. "I'm serious, Isabella. D'Poussant is not someone you treat lightly."

"He has a vision for the freedom of all blacks and Creole." Isabella thought of her vision in the hut, the call of Lasiren and Papa Legba. Madame Rêve-Cœur had seen her future, as her mother had before. "He needs a leader."

Gabrielle brought her head closer to Isabella. "Dr. D'Poussant has spent many nights in this tavern. You are the first woman he has invited to his table. Most, including me, do nothing but serve him. Don't be fooled." Gabrielle put a glass of wine, D'Poussant's favorite brand, in front of Isabella. "He serves himself."

Isabella turned her attention back to the table. Two new men had joined D'Poussant at his table. She slowed her gait as an image of another Aldric took shape in her mind. The two men seemed to apparate, as if transported by some magical spell from the mountains, and they were now immersed in an intense conversation.

As she approached, a bald-headed man in a billowing cotton shirt pointed his finger at D'Poussant, letting his hand chop the air with each point. The second man, heavier set and with a beard and a full head of hair, poked the arm of the bald man. He turned, noticed Isabella's approach, dropped his hand to the table, and sat back with straightened shoulders.

"Isabella, I would like you to meet two very important people, Paul and Henri."

The bearded man looked at her and dropped his eyes to acknowledge her. The bald man looked at her with fierce condemnation. Isabella moved her hand to the hilt of her sword. She nodded to both of them with her eyes focused on their expressions.

"Please, Isabella, sit down." D'Poussant patted a spot on the table that would put her next to him. She hesitated, unsure of whether she should be more wary of the two strangers or her new best friend, Dr. D'Poussant. She lowered herself to the bench.

"*Bonjour*," she said.

"Good," D'Poussant said with a sincere trace of glee. "*Trés bien.* Henri and Paul are a bit impatient, but I told them a little more time would increase our odds of success significantly."

Isabella's eyes darted around the room, noting a few more patrons lumbering around the tables and up against the bar, and she settled on the two men across from her. She could see the bald one was clearly a field hand. At least, the soil on his shirt and crusted hands was consistent with long hours in fields, hacking at the stalks of sugarcane. She resisted a shudder as she remembered hauling bundles of the cane shafts, each longer than she was tall, to the mill for processing. A hint of an ache created years earlier seeped into her shoulders.

"She shouldn't be here," the bearded man said, looking directly at Isabella. "She can't do anything but bring bad luck." The bearded man, perhaps a few years older than the field hand, but much younger than her well-educated advocate, also wore the clothes of a man consumed by hard labor while making his living.

D'Poussant wasn't giving in. "Did you talk to Aldric?"

"Pfft," the field hand scoffed. "He's an idiot."

Isabella watched the bearded man for a moment. "You work on the quays, loading and unloading ships." Isabella's statement seemed to punch him back an inch on the bench.

D'Poussant laughed. "You see, Henri? She observes."

Henri reached for his beard and tugged. "You told her we were coming."

"I've never seen you before in my life."

D'Poussant shook his head, letting his grin dip into a measured smile. "Why would I jeopardize your identity? Whose interest does that serve? Not mine."

Isabella turned to the bald field hand. "And Paul, why does a girl have you worried? Don't you have an army waiting for you at the plantation?"

D'Poussant nodded and drew both men to him with the seriousness of his expression. "She's The One."

Paul drew in a deep breath. "The men won't believe it. They won't follow a girl."

Isabella leaned over the table, reaching for Paul's hands, but her fingers seemed to chase them toward the table's edge. She shot her fingers forward and grabbed his palm, keeping her eyes trained on Paul's face. His startled eyes glistened with a momentary fear before they hardened again, letting her hold the top of his hand in place. She let her fingers slip under his palm. Their tips registered the hard layers of callused skin that coated his grip.

Paul's expression remained hard as she gave his hand a slight squeeze. She closed her eyes and turned her hand, palms up, in one continuous and deliberate motion, letting the back of his hand rest in one of her palms. Paul's hand relaxed, and she placed her other hand over his. Her fingers traced the curves and depressions and then dodged islands of layered, stiff skin.

She found a depression at the base of a callus under his thumb and followed it from the thumb to the center of the palm. She smiled, but kept her eyes closed. "You are a man of action. I see why Dr. D'Poussant has you at the plantation. Your lifeline is short, but that's exactly who he needs to keep the army in check: someone he can trust...a man who will lead them when the time is right."

She opened her eyes, looked at Paul, and pulled her hand back. "You've been waiting for a long time, and you are ready."

Paul's eyes softened, but he pulled his fingers together and clenched his hand into a fist. "My men won't wait much longer. This life is a living hell."

Henri gave D'Poussant a sharp look. "She's toying with us. Why did you bring this devil into our midst?"

D'Poussant's smile faded into earnestness. "Henri, I think you are judging too quickly."

Henri turned to Isabella. "She's a devil. You're a doctor. You don't believe in this mountain magic."

"Why don't you show her your hand?" D'Poussant's tone was more of an order than a request.

Henri pulled his hand back.

Isabella put both of her hands flat on the table. "It's okay, Dr. D'Poussant. I don't need to read his hands. Henri is a man of action, just like Paul. I have many Henris and many Pauls on my ship. They keep our vessel afloat, our holds full of riches and gold, and our freedom alive."

D'Poussant tapped his finger down on the table. "You see? She doesn't have to read your palms. She can read your spirit. She can read your soul!"

Henri's expression weakened, and he pulled his hands into his lap. "We don't need her. We can do this without her."

Isabella looked at the two men who had spewed vengeful energy at D'Poussant. Now, they seemed pliable and moldable. She turned her eyes down to the table and crossed one hand over the other. "Perhaps you are right. Maybe I should go back to my ship. Back to my crew." She looked over to D'Poussant who was still watching, even studying Henri and Paul. "I think Jean-Michel was right. My place is on my ship. We should make a run for the straits and to Tortuga Bay."

D'Poussant didn't look at Isabella. "Look at Henri's palm."

Isabella cast a quick glance to Henri, his hands back below the table. "He doesn't want me to read his palm."

D'Poussant sent a gentle nod to Henri. "Let her see it, Henri. Let's see if she's right about you."

Henri pulled his shoulders up. His jaws tightened.

D'Poussant gave a more insistent nod.

Henri lifted his hand and placed it palm up on the table. Isabella looked at D'Poussant who was still glaring at Henri. She turned to Paul. He diverted his eyes to the wall, almost as if his spirit had departed from the conversation.

Isabella breathed in and took Henri's hand in hers. She closed her eyes and let her fingertips dance on his fingers and then his palm, feeling for the telltale ridges. Eyes closed, she released a silent exhale, allowing the tips of her fingers to fall into Henri's palm as his muscles relaxed. Each tip seemed to have its own brain, its own sense of what

Henri's hand would tell her. She found the line crossing under the base of his fingers and stopping just between the middle and index finger.

"Your heart line," she whispered. "As I thought. You are a man of action—but few words. You care passionately about your freedom."

Isabella's fingers then traveled to the base of his thumb and stopped. She curled all her fingers into a ball except the index finger and traced a deep ridge from the center of his wrist as it curved toward the flesh between his thumb and index finger.

"I'm sorry," she said, her voice soft. She traced the line again, stopping three times, as if to check her reading. "You have experienced trauma in your life. Your lifeline is long, but broken." She felt tears gather, and she struggled to keep her voice steady. She swallowed. "You lost your wife, perhaps a child."

Isabella opened her eyes just as a tear crested the top of Henri's cheek and dropped into his shirt. "You've lost more than one child."

D'Poussant lifted his hand to cup Isabella's forearm. "His wife and children; an illegal sale to a plantation overseer in the north. He raped her and then found an excuse to have her executed. His daughter became sick with the Fever, and the overseer refused to help her."

Isabella closed her eyes. "Henri, I'm sorry."

"But you know his story," D'Poussant said in a soft voice. "After all, your mother kept you alive long enough for you to escape."

Isabella's breath stuttered as she inhaled and exhaled to keep her tears inside, as the flames lashed at the night sky in her memories. The screams, the crack of whips, the reports of pistols, the fires consuming their slave *bohios* and fields. "Not soon enough to keep her alive. Or Gamba. I was lost."

D'Poussant squeezed her arm, lifting his lips to her ear. "But you are here. Listen to your heart. Tell Henri more."

Isabella nodded. She used her index finger and middle finger to find his heartline. She suppressed a gasp. She opened her eyes and locked onto Henri's vacant gaze, knowing she could do nothing to offset his sadness and hurt.

Isabella let Henri's hand rest on the table, and she lifted herself from the bench. She looked for the front door to le Coq Fantôme and stepped forward, then turned toward Henri. He sat in a trancelike state. Paul continued to stare at the wall, as if held by a spell. D'Poussant seemed unfazed, treating the men like they were subjects in a medical laboratory. Isabella lifted her hand to her forehead, her breathing shortened. She felt her heart beat faster and the blood rush into her chest and head.

"My God," she muttered. "I know what you are doing."

Isabella turned toward the door and almost broke into a run, not even registering Gabrielle's stunned stare.

Isabella sucked in as much air as she could the moment the door slapped closed behind her. She stepped over to a light post. The flames flickered and mixed with the dull light from the building to create an early evening glow that blanketed the streets bordering le Coq Fantôme. She breathed in, holding the air for a few seconds, then exhaled with slow deliberation. The process was now instinctive since she calmed herself this way before opening a broadside at sea. She leaned her forearm against the post.

"I confess; I'm surprised."

Isabella shook her head at the sound of D'Poussant's voice.

"You should understand," he continued, walking to the side of the raised wooden sidewalk and looking out over the cobblestone road.

The streets were coming alive now that the warehouses had shut down for the evening, and the ships were moored safely in the harbor. Isabella didn't look around, although her instincts told her to shut down her feelings and pay more attention to the movements of the street.

"I know what you are doing." Isabella straightened her back and cast a distrustful look toward him. Gabrielle's warning blazed through her head.

D'Poussant fetched his pipe from his coat pocket and lit it from a the flames of a streetlamp. "They understand the stakes."

"Do they understand the risks?"

D'Poussant pivoted toward Isabella. "What risks do they need to know?" He shook his head. "What risks did you need to know before you left that night the plantation went up in flames?"

"You don't know anything about that night." Isabella could feel the breadth of D'Poussant's smile, even if she couldn't see it in the haze of the evening light.

"Oh, you underestimate me, Isabella." He let a light chuckle escape into the alley. "You are the Pirate of Panther Bay, the protégé of Jacob the Red, the most notorious pirate of the Caribbean Sea since the death of Blackbeard."

"You know nothing about Jacob."

"Oh, I know much more than you think. Don't underestimate your enemies."

"Are you my enemy?"

D'Poussant looked out to the alley again. "That is your decision, not mine. Aldric...Henri...Paul. They should be your allies. They are essential to our success."

"Our success?"

"Of course. I can't do this without you, Isabella."

Isabella surveyed the street, now thick with a mottled assortment of drab and bright colors, broadcasting the trades of dockworkers, sailors, slaves, and merchants, and more than a few women casting for economic opportunities that might present themselves. She knew the Code Noir ensured the slaves were toothless threats in a revolution, but by law, the *gens de couleur* had all the rights and freedoms of French citizens, including the tools of defense and offense. She let her hand drop to her blade, pressing it against her thigh.

"Henri has already lost so much," she said.

D'Poussant snickered. "I gambled on that. Your legend goes well beyond Jacob the Red. The revolt in Spanish Hispaniola, your success on the trade routes—they add up to quite a reputation."

"Legends."

D'Poussant shook his head. "No, Isabella, there is much more truth than you admit. Your escape from El Morro, the victory off Privateer Pointe—"

"Privateer Pointe was not a victory. It was a draw."

"Anytime a pirate draws on the high seas, it is a victory for the pirate." He let a column of smoke flow from his lips. "And a victory for blacks, slave and *gens de couleur*."

"I think you are overestimating my influence and my abilities."

"No, Isabella. *Au contraire.* I know your abilities very well. Your palm-reading skills are quite advanced."

Isabella shook her head as she smiled. "My mother taught me many things around the fires after the overseer had gone to bed."

171

"She knew you were destined for more than a slave girl's life."

Isabella drew in her breath. The prophecy. The words swirled in her mind as she remembered her mother looking over the fire at her, telling her she was destined for something great. "Binta. One with God." She remembered looking at her mother as tears streamed down her face. She knew, even then, their time together was short; but at thirteen, she was too young to know, or to care, or to understand. Tears welled up in her eyes, and they began to trickle down her face as she tried to sniff them back.

"It's okay to cry," D'Poussant said. His voice was tender, understanding, and he stayed by her side looking up the street. "You won't have time to cry, soon. The time is upon us."

"It's not fair to Henri and Paul."

D'Poussant looked at Isabella again, taking his pipe from his mouth and lifting it to the sky. "What's not fair? Their lives were stolen from them by the French. Even we *gens de couleur* know that is wrong, but too many of us stay in the comfort of our property and the laws. Nothing will change unless we make it change, unless we carve out our own future."

"You don't know what you are doing," Isabella said, looking down at her feet. "The fires. The death. The torture."

"Oh, Isabella, I know all too well. I know what I am doing."

Isabella nodded. Yes, she corrected herself. D'Poussant knew what he was doing. Henri and Paul had lost everything to slavery and the ugly reality of second-class citizenship in a French colony. Henri, a man who savored freedom, had lost those who meant the most to him, to the masters and overseers and the Code Noir. What life was worth living without them? "Bellecombe will bring it to an end."

"Another French Governor General? Please, don't patronize me. No governor can free us."

"Louis XVI is making changes."

"He is weak. He won't go up against the nobles."

"Bellecombe hates slavery."

"There is nothing he can do."

Isabella turned to lean against the lamppost. She looked up at the sign and the rooster peering over their boardwalk. "The phantom chicken."

"Everything must come into alignment."

"And you are the person to bring that alignment?"

D'Poussant puffed on his pipe. "Every movement needs a leader."

"Every revolution needs a leader."

"The Americans are showing us the way. They are fighting against the world's greatest empire."

Isabella laughed. "You don't sound French."

"I'm not. I'm a man who understands the abomination of this system and who is committed to doing something about it. Surely you understand that."

Isabella brought her sword up and rested her chin on the hilt. "Aye, I understand." She turned to D'Poussant. "I don't think you do."

D'Poussant stood, looking at Isabella, his expression calm and relaxed. "I know I will do what needs to be done. For freedom. For equality. *Liberté, egalité.*"

"And you will lead this revolution?"

D'Poussant shook his head. "I am a doctor of letters, a planter, and a slave owner. A reluctant slave owner, but a slave owner like all the others. I can't lead from moral authority." He turned to look at Isabella. "We need a leader."

Isabella shifted her weight and looked down at the dirt. "I have trouble seeing you follow anyone else."

"I will support whoever takes the lead on our moral quest. I can make kings even if I cannot be king."

"With men like Henri, Paul, and Aldric?"

D'Poussant took another puff from his pipe. "Who else? You need men of action. Men who understand the stakes. Men who are committed to changing the system, whatever it takes."

"Men who have lost everything."

"And men who will not back down," D'Poussant said, pointing the end of the pipe at Isabella. "No matter how tough things get."

That was Paul. His lifeline ended at the center of the palm. Isabella sighed. "Paul feels safe when he is active, when he is doing something. In the fields, under the whip, he can't act. He has no volition. A revolution gives him purpose."

D'Poussant let another plume of smoke escape from his mouth.

"Henri has lost everything he cares about," she continued. "But he is passionate. He can't let this life stand. He wants others to be free. He can see them. He can feel their pain, their suffering. He wants to stop it."

D'Poussant pulled his pipe from his mouth and rested his hands on Isabella's shoulder. "You understand what motivates them. Your legend precedes you, in truth and in their minds. They resist now because they don't accept what has been foretold. That can change. That changed inside. I knew as soon as you took Paul's hand that I no longer needed to lead them, even if I thought I could. This is your revolution, Isabella, not mine anymore."

25

Juan Carlos felt the ground beneath his boots and relaxed. The roll and pitch of ships was disquieting, even on a frigate anchored at the mouth of a bay. Loose gravel and dirt were the veneer of hard soil, and he knew he could almost always find his ground with the right angle of the boot, a heel, and sometimes a toe. The fact the landing party had made it unchallenged to the hard, wagon-packed muck of the streets of Port-au-Prince settled his nerves, allowing him to focus. Juan Carlos looked back at the bay. The wooden wharves seemed to create an invisible wall, locking his small group of pirate hunters into a game of cat-and-mouse in which no one really understood the rules.

He walked to the end of the wharf and looked out into the bay. The two masts of the *Marée Rouge* stood stark and uncluttered, a ship at rest with no intent to flee. Bright yellow flecks twinkled from its deck, an unusual sight at dusk. Jean-Michel was overcautious, ensuring that Spanish marauders would be unable to take the vessel by surprise.

Juan Carlos squatted at the bay's edge and closed his eyes. Isabella was somewhere in this town, meeting with men, plotting. Tightness gripped his chest as he remembered how she talked of her mother and her life on the plantation. He remembered the blood-soaked linens after that brute from the *Ana Maria* had flogged her in the dungeon of El Morro. He clenched his fist at the image of her cleaved flesh and muscles left bare and nicked by a whip. Her survival was a miracle. Tears welled as he remembered the first time he felt the scars on her back as they lay together in Charlotte Amalie. He tried to ignore the thickened skin, layered over the cuts, closing his eyes so he could focus on his touch, hoping his lips would somehow absolve the pain his brethren had inflicted. She accepted his embrace, his kiss, seeing beyond the ribbons, lace, and epaulettes that secured his royal status and rank. She saw something in him he didn't see in himself. And now, he was tasked with tracking her down and arresting her. Again. What trick could he muster this time to keep her alive and free? Juan Carlos's chest stiffened further, and he reached up to grab his shoulders as he dipped his head into his forearms, making sure his back remained turned away from the men he would lead—men who wanted to ensure the demise of a woman who had fully accepted him and shown him grace, despite his prejudices.

Six other Spaniards, all dressed in the clothes of commoners, stood in the dimming light of the port's streets, warehouses looming over them as laborers, merchantmen, and tradesmen finished their tasks before the sun set. Dusk was a useful mask in a busy port town.

Juan Carlos stood up and walked up to the *Santa Mónica's* gunner's mate turned spy, Torres. "How much longer before Sanchez reports back?"

Torres lifted his hand to his chin as he paused, his faced darkened by the smooth-brimmed hat perched on his head. "Not much longer. He landed an hour before us."

"I'll give him thirty minutes. Then, we'll have to move on our own."

The marines huddled, double-checking the pistols hidden in their coats, inventorying their powder and ball bullets and pulling their daggers every few minutes. Standing watch on a frigate was one thing; standing in a foreign port out of uniform with a clandestine mission to find and detain a pirate was new for all of them. Juan Carlos watched their movements, but didn't say anything. The longer they stayed at the spot, the more likely someone would ask questions and jeopardize the entire plan.

"Guerrero," Juan Carlos said in a low voice, knowing that any mention of title or rank would invite suspicious looks from passersby and court disaster.

Guerrero stepped away from the teetering cluster, giving it some stability. The dusty fog of early evening hid much of his mustache, but the darkened line around his mouth gave telltale signs to those who looked. He touched his hat instead of providing the customary salute of removing it.

"We've been at this spot for too long. Having eight men assembled in one spot creates suspicion, particularly in a city run by slaves as this one is."

The lieutenant tipped his head, turned to the marines, pulled three of them out of the huddle. He directed them to a new location one block down but within sight. None in the landing party thought to search the upper floors of the warehouses along the quay for prying eyes leery of a group of dallying foreigners with no apparent interest in nightlife.

Juan Carlos scurried down the alley skirting the north side of Rue Royale de Grande Rue, his faith in Sanchez waning with each step. The streets were dark, and their band was stumbling through the muck of unfamiliar streets. More than one trip had drawn curious looks, a confirmation of the awkward progress of strangers. The stench rising from the ditches had dulled his senses, but the odor of rotting food, human waste, and pooling water in the humid, tropical climate still overwhelmed him every hundred paces or so, forcing him to bury his mouth and nose in the linen covering his arms. He followed Sanchez's back, not daring to look behind him, wondering if the others would see the tears that the fetid smells conjured from his eyes.

Sanchez stopped at a crossroad and signaled for the others to halt. Sanchez turned back to the group, careful to remain in the shadows, and stood next to Juan Carlos. "Across the street is the cemetery. Two streets beyond the cemetery is another block of buildings on the southern edge of the city. The pirates are in a tavern called le Coq Fantôme."

Juan Carlos nodded, his mind spinning. He remembered the time he and Isabella were almost caught by Spanish marines raiding Charlotte Amalie on St. Thomas despite Dutch colonial objections. He'd left her side early enough to avoid the raid, but Isabella and Jean-Michel were forced to take to the rooftops and rejoin their crew on the weather side of the island. At least that's the story he gathered from his spies in port.

He looked at the two-story buildings across the street. Their pitches were too steep to consider clambering over, and few connected in a way that would create a true path. They would have to remain on the ground, weaving between buildings and through alleys.

He turned to Sanchez. "What do you know of this tavern?"

"It's a central place for free blacks in the port. I was warned that foreigners…Europeans in particular…are not welcome."

Juan Carlos pulled his hat from his head and worked the rim with his hands before looking back to his guide. "You know the streets. What do you suggest?"

Sanchez lifted his hand to his chin and rubbed it. "We've got nine in our party. That's a big group, makes us suspicious. We haven't seen whites in groups of more than two or three. We're all heavily armed; the law says the free blacks can't carry their guns or knives in public. So, no long guns."

"How many entrances to the tavern?"

"Just one that I could see. It fronts the road, Rue de Bretagne."

"This should be a straightforward operation," Lieutenant Guerrero said.

Juan Carlos sent a wary look toward Guerrero, but the darkness hid his skepticism. What choice did he have at this point? He looked at each of the men. "We will split up. One party take up positions on each end of the street. That way we can capture her whether she heads into the hills or to the sea. Torres, Sanchez, each of you will be in a group to serve as a guide. Lieutenant Guerrero, take Torres and three marines and take up positions east of the tavern to prevent escape into the jungles. Sanchez, you join me and the others at the west side to capture her if she heads back to the bay and her ship."

Juan Carlos warned each man to be careful and keep his visibility as low as possible. The soldiers stood, and two groups walked into the hazy, yellow glow lighting up the evening streets, unaware of the gathered eyes watching their every move from other shadows.

Cedric thumbed the blade on his knife as he watched from the doorway of the cobbler's shop. The streets around the cemetery were sparsely populated this early in the evening, with most laborers choosing less odious routes that avoided the spirits he found comforting. He looked over to another *gens de couleur,* a short, swarthy man with a stoic expression, and cupped his shoulder with a reassuring grip. "These whites are up to no good, comrade. They are headed directly to le Coq Fantôme."

The man nodded, shadows hiding the full breadth of his figure. "They are Spanish."

"It doesn't matter if their tongues speak in Spanish or French; the whites are one. They will not let slavery fall. Spain is allied with France. The Code Noir means nothing to our brethren in the fields, and the laws on us—free blacks—have become worse." Cedric lifted his blade. "We cannot even show these in public, while the whites can walk with guns in plain sight."

The swarthy man nodded again and turned to five others waiting for orders behind Cedric. He ran down the line, checking their tools—rods, knives, and machetes.

Cedric looked at the Spaniards as they headed west on the street and turned south to skirt the cemetery. "We saw them land, and they waited. They are Spanish navy in the clothes of regular workers and merchants, on a mission to spy on Dr. D'Poussant, the right hand of Bellecombe. Tonight, we will rise, and the whites will die."

The five pirates were barely noticeable to passersby just one block from le Coq Fantôme. Anyone who had bothered to stop them might have wondered why two white men seemed to be hanging casually around five Africans, but the bustling activity, at the end of the day in a busy port, created many strange pairings and activities. As the light faded and night invaded the streets, few questioned the entertainments hidden behind doors and windows in pubs, inns, and taverns, particularly in the southern reaches of the city's alleys along Rue de Bretagne and Rue D'Orleans just a few blocks from the French army's munitions depot. The harbor captain needed little explanation for a return visit, and the small band made quick work, weaving their way past the artillery batteries on the quay overlooking the bay and to the cemetery at Rue Dauphine. Now, they made their way to the inn where Jean-Michel hoped he would find his captain and not a revolutionary intoxicated by the dim prospects of an improbable victory. This would also give his party time to reposition their escape boat, a cutter, on the southern side of the city and well out of sight of the harbor captain and French garrison.

26

Isabella thought le Coq Fantôme was filling up faster than in previous nights, but D'Poussant didn't seem to notice. Aldric had returned with two new sidekicks, but neither seemed to carry any more bravado or walk with any more confidence than the two she had dispatched earlier in the week. Henri and Paul had settled in toward the back of the inn. Isabella watched from her table with D'Poussant as he stopped sailors passing by. Others delayed to catch a few words with the doctor. Isabella curled her fingers around her mug and smelled the mead, savoring the sweet aroma and wondering if this would be her standard drink if she decided to stay with D'Poussant.

She looked across the table at the doctor, his bicorn hat by his side as he smiled across the room. She lifted her mug and tilted it toward D'Pousssant. "A busy night!"

D'Poussant nodded and pointed toward the bar. A large man with a soiled cotton shirt leaned over the wood, his head steady as he chatted to Gabrielle's father who never seemed to stop scanning the room. Gabrielle busied herself clearing and cleaning tankards and mugs, tossing hopeful glances toward Isabella. The air was close even with the breeze coming across the mountain, cooling off the roads leading into the bay. A breeze steady enough to slip the *Marée Rouge* out of the bay under the noses of the Spaniards, Isabella thought.

She drew in a deep breath and thought of Jean-Michel as the fermented liquid drained into her belly. He had tried to convince her that her place was with her crew of pirates on the *Marée Rouge*. They had captured many prizes. *El Cid* likely brought a pretty set of coin even though she was a lightly armed schooner by naval standards. That should be enough to satisfy her tars for their last voyage.

But what did she care, anyway? Jean-Michel was a pirate before she met Jacob and took to the waves. He'll be a pirate afterwards. His reputation would raise another crew and finance another excursion. Without her, he and Smoothy would be free to roam the trade routes and pillage the Spanish, French, Portuguese, Dutch, and anyone else they thought ripe for the picking.

Her tour of the warehouses along Rue de St. Claire, right in front of the French colonial regiments, told her enough. Every black they passed stole a glance toward D'Poussant as if looking for a sign. The sail makers talked in hushed tones about when the revolution would happen, not if. The port was ripe for a revolt. She looked over her mug at D'Poussant. "You have been planning for a long time."

D'Poussant conducted a quick search of the room before nodding his head. "I was the son of a slave, a child born of two races. My master freed me, but only after my mother died from the Fever. He educated me, allowed me to become one of the *gens de couleur,* but we have nearly a half million slaves on this side of the island, while my people, the free blacks, number just twenty-five thousand. It's not me that wants the revolution. It's the mass of blacks that now call our colony home and yearn for their freedom."

"A noblemen among the commoners?" Isabella asked.

"Equality," D'Poussant said, lifting his cup. "It's what the Americans are fighting for. The right to be their own men. It's the right of men, of all men, our natural God-given right."

Isabella shook her head. "Growing up…on the plantation…we had no rights, except what the overseer chose to give us. On that day. At that time." The wet air had begun to lay heavy into her shirt, the wool clamping to her back. She adjusted her spine, as if trying to loosen the cloth, but knew immediately the ridges would not straighten. The scars from the whip would hold the cloth along those lines for the rest of her life. She gripped her tankard with great strength, wondering if she could break its pewter mold and send the beer across the table.

"Soon," D'Poussant said as if reading her mind. "Very soon."

D'Poussant rose from the table and lifted his mug above his head. Within seconds, the clatter and clamor of the evening meals and drinking disappeared. More than fifty men looked toward D'Poussant. Isabella's heart raced as she realized each man, each face, looked to the doctor with an expectant expression. A bead of sweat broke out over her eyebrow as she looked down at the table and pulled her mead closer to her chest. She focused on her thoughts, sensing she would soon be thrust into a series of events she would have to ride like the storm that had blown them into Port-au-Prince.

D'Poussant traced a wide arc with his mug from one side of the room to the other. "The time has come."

Mutterings broke out among the crowd as men looked at each other, some with surprised expressions while others nodded their heads, and still others released broad smiles.

D'Poussant surveyed the room with a broad smile. He lifted his hand to the end of his bicorn hat and removed it from his head, letting it drop to the tabletop. "The time has come. We have heard rumblings among our brothers on the continent as peasants rise against the noblemen." D'Poussant put his hands inside his topcoat, hesitated to take advantage of the thickening anticipation within the room, and removed a bright, red felt cap. He lifted it above his head, revealing a cone shape to the top. "*Le bonnet rouge*," he called to the crowd. "A symbol of our struggle for freedom!"

Cheers erupted in waves, interspersed with "here, heres," as D'Poussant presented the cap to different sections of the room before placing it on his head.

"What about Bellecombe?" called a voice from the crowd.

Paul stepped over to D'Poussant and turned to the crowd. "The French are sleeping in their barracks under guns pointing out to the bay, not into the street of our homes and shops. We must secure the city tonight, before they waken."

As if in a cue, Henri joined Paul and also turned to the throng. "Once the flames of Port-au-Prince reach into the night, the armies will rise from the fields. The colonists will reap what they have sown for three hundred years. They will seize the plantations and finally profit from what they have labored to create. They wait, not for their masters, but for their liberators!"

Voices rumbled through the crowd as heads nodded. D'Poussant seemed to identify each man with an affirming nod, as if keeping count of his assurance that he has joined him. The doctor's determination hardened his gaze with each deliberate tick of the head. "We have already sent a party to seize the powder magazine. The French will soon be starved for ammunition and powder. We have the advantage!"

Isabella looked around the room and noticed that Aldric had disappeared. Whether he had taken additional men, she couldn't be sure, but his destination was clear enough now.

Mutterings turned to shouts, and questions crested the rumblings of excited revolutionaries. How many men do we have? Will the whites accept their fate? Where can I get a gun? Will the slaves join with the *gens de couleur* or stay with the givers of their special status? No one asked who would lead them.

D'Poussant lifted his walking stick. "Tonight, comrades! This is our time! Tonight, we cleanse our city of the injustice of slavery, of rule by elites. Tonight, we begin our own rule, without interference by a King or another army. Tonight, we send the signal to our brethren that it is time to rise and unite, to cast off our shackles!"

"D'Poussant!" The challenge came from within the throng as a tall African emerged, his eyes fixed on the revolutionary at the front of the crowd. He held a round, smooth-brimmed planter's hat under his arm. A topcoat projected an air far more distinguished than the dock workers and warehouse hands that made up most of this crowd. "We aren't ready."

"Ahh, Thomas, I am so glad you could come to our gathering tonight." D'Poussant raised his cap from his head and swept it in a circle above his head. Cheers erupted from the crowd. "I think some in this room disagree." A smile opened across the doctor's cheeks, bearing white teeth, but the ivory enamel couldn't hide the intensity of the doctor's look as it sliced into the man who dared disrupt his rally.

Thomas shook his head and raised his hand. "My fellow *gens de couleur,* we are not ready for the fight Dr. D'Poussant is calling forth! The French will not buckle under this threat to their colony. We need more time…to prepare…to rally…to train. We need patience!"

D'Poussant shook his head. "Comrades! The time is now. We have been planning this for years. You have seen my men come from the fields, and you have heard them tell their stories of brutality, of disgrace, of humiliation. Their fields are ready to erupt, but they need you to give them the signal! The need to see the pyres explode in the flames of revolution, to see their tormentors tremble in fear of the power they have ground into the soil for so long. But they will not move; they will not rise until you tell them it is time! They need to see Port-au-Prince burn!"

Thomas raised his hat. "My fellow citizens! You have the rights of the colonists. Let's work to end this system without sacrificing the lives of our families, the livelihoods of our children. Governor General Bellecombe works on our behalf! Hasn't our lot improved since he has come to Saint-Domingue? Don't we have more freedom?"

"No!" chanted the crowd.

Another voice rose from the bobbing throng: "We can no longer work under the oppression of these laws! The French care nothing about our welfare. They kill us, our brethren, our sisters, our families! Death to the French!"

The crowd erupted in a roar. D'Poussant lifted both his hands to the sky, and the crowd cheered. Then he turned his palms outward, as if pressing against the anger enveloping the thick air of the tavern, and brought them down. The shouts ebbed, flowing into rumblings and then mutterings and then silence.

"Comrades," D'Poussant said, his voice just loud enough to skim the tops of the heads in the pack of rebels. "Thomas is right. We must proceed with care. The French will not give up their control of our lives or our livelihoods. We must expect resistance from the authorities, from the monarchy, from those loyal to their king. Our fight will be long and against superior odds."

The energy in the room seemed to go dormant, but it did not evaporate. Isabella brought her hands to her thighs, ready to bring one up under her shirt to grab a knife, the other ready to pull her saber from its scabbard. She had seen this energy, this look among men before, and it had cost her dearly. Their injustice was a hibernating bear, awakening and ready to hunt for sustenance. And D'Poussant knew it.

185

27

Jean-Michel pushed himself away from the wood-paneled walls of the building and looked down the street toward the sound of muffled cracks in the night air.

Herrera was at his side in an instant. "I do not like those sounds."

"Aye, sounds like gunshots."

"Small arms. I would say pistols." Herrera stepped closer to the noise, looked around the streets and lifted his index finger to his nose as he thought.

Jean-Michel turned up the other side of the road and nodded to Sarhaan. The African pirate's gaze in his direction told him he had heard the shots as well. Jean-Michel raised his hand in a short wave and then pointed back to le Coq Fantôme.

He hadn't thought about it during the meeting on the *Marée Rouge*, but bringing three Africans as part of their landing party helped them avoid a lot of unwanted attention. Most travelers along Rue Dauphine passed the two white men and three blacks without a glance. An occasional *gens de couleur* would give a tip of the hat or cast a smile toward Sarhaan and the other two African pirates, but Jean-Michel and Herrera could have just as easily been another plank of wood affixed to the walls of the storefronts.

Herrera rubbed his hand against his leg. "I do not like it."

"It's a port city, Herrera. Some sailor's going to get sideways with some dock worker and do something stupid."

Herrera flicked his thumb across the street. "We've been outside the tavern for a while. I have not seen a drunk or trigger-happy sailor on these streets yet. Now, I've heard four shots. Not enough for a battle, I agree, but more than enough for a skirmish."

Jean-Michel pulled a knife from behind his back and rubbed the blade against his breeches. "We know Isabella's in there. We can't go in too fast. That inn must have fifty men packed in there, all full of grog, ale, and mead. Last time I was in there, I was an outsider, and they let me know it right away."

Herrera looked over to the tavern. "I wish I had packed a few more pistols, or maybe a musket."

Jean-Michel chuckled. "I'm sure you would rather light the fuse on a twelve pounder aimed right at those doors."

"Aye," Herrera laughed. "The Spanish navy trained me well before sending me into the arms of the British in Pensacola. They get rusty stuck in port...or in chains!"

The clatter of men drinking and arguing cascaded into the street, and the pirates looked to a square of light that was the open door to le Coq Fantôme. Jean-Michel stepped closer to the end of the boardwalk and watched a man stand for several seconds. He was soon joined by five others, two from inside the tavern and others from the shadows of the building. Three men each appeared to carry long rods draped in canvas. "Those are long guns," Jean-Michel said to no one in particular.

"They didn't come from inside," Herrera said as the small party of men scouted the road and then turned west on Rue de Bretagne.

"I don't like the look of this," Jean-Michel said, turning to Herrera. He looked toward Sarhaan and motioned with his hands to join him. "I'm pretty sure that was Aldric, the guy that tried to kill me the other night."

28

The mug of mead clunked down on the table in front of Isabella like a warning. Isabella followed the hand as it retreated to the shape of Gabrielle. The barmaid looked down at Isabella, brows drawn together in concern, and turned back toward the front of the tavern. Isabella wrapped her fingers around the pewter and stared into the liquid as the last of the tiny bubbles disappeared. Gabrielle's words hung with her as D'Poussant's voice lifted itself over the crowd of men, the urgency of his words creating fists from outstretched hands and sending fingers curling around knives. It all seemed wrong. Where was Thomas?

"Isabella! Isabella! Isabella!"

The chant wrenched Isabella's head up to look into the crowd and then back to D'Poussant. The doctor looked out over the faces, expectant and energized, as he straddled a bench and the tabletop. "We have with us someone who understands the need to fight to the death for liberty. She has led this fight every night since her escape from slavery, with every trigger that she pulled, for every axe that she swung, for every knife she thrust at the heart of our tormentors. She knows the difference between freedom and eternal damnation on these plantations under the whips of evil built over hundreds of years. Men! *Gens de couleur*! Our duty, our obligation, is to rescue our brothers and sisters in the fields and orchards of this territory, to free them so they will own their destiny, not ones defined by masters in far off lands or by overseers, black or white, on the slopes of these hills."

D'Poussant paused, and the horde erupted in cheers. D'Poussant looked down to Isabella and put his hand on her shoulder.

"Men! My army! Our army! The army of our brothers and sisters! This is our leader!" D'Poussant kneeled just low enough to find Isabella's forearm and lift it into the air, letting his hand slip into hers.

He pulled, and Isabella seemed to elevate from her bench upright onto the table. Another round of discordant cheers swept across the crowd.

Isabella looked out at the men. All were ready to march, to stomp into the streets of Port-au-Prince. But to where? Would they go to the quays? Attack the fortress? Or would they turn toward the hills, burning the plantations?

She inhaled as she felt D'Poussant tug at her arm again, enough to unleash another round of fervor. She exhaled, letting the collapse of her lungs draw her muscles into a more relaxed state. D'Poussant must have sensed the release of tension because his next words were only heard by her. "Well done, Isabella. A true warrior. You fear nothing. We will bring these colonists to their knees. We will show them the full meaning of their brutality. We will rise up to create a new land, a new place, where our people, through our leadership, can flourish and build and create!"

Isabella heard the words, but they weren't navigable points in the bitterness and anger seething before her on the faces of the mob. "Dr. D'Poussant, these men are ready to explode. They are tinder, waiting for the flame."

"Oui, Isabella. They need a leader. Lead these men: *conduit ces hommes*! They need you! Light the fire!"

Isabella's eyes searched the expressions of the throbbing bodies before her. Another wave of fists, knives, and now rods carved the air above their heads. Her lungs heaved with the dark energy subsuming the room. Their faces flicked in and out of shadows cast by the candles lighting the tavern.

As she rose, the mob transformed into a makeshift army led by torches as they marched toward a Spanish plantation mansion as a teenage-slave girl looked on. The evening sky was already overwhelmed by the pulsating oranges and yellows of burning fields, and a strong, determined young boy led an ill-fated legion toward freedom. "Go, Binta," her mother had said. "Your destiny is in the fires, as was prophesied at your birth. Follow Gamba like the others." Isabella felt her mother's push against her shoulder, her chest consumed by the smoke and fires of her injustices and those endured by so many thousands before her.

Another push against her body and the scene dissolved, replaced by the pulsating faces, hands, arms, and anger of the tavern's horde.

She stood on the table, erect, Her hand pulled her sword from its scabbard, its tip lifting into the rafters. The crowd cheered.

"Wait! *Arrêtez!*"

The mob's protests dulled to a steady whirring of confused words and talk. Isabella refocused on the front of the crowd, searching for the source of the warning.

Thomas stepped from the front of the crowd and turned to face them. "My friends, we are moving too quickly for such a strong action." Arms fell from the air as anger turned to indecision. "Let's wait for Aldric to report on the munitions depot and the state of the French garrison. We need to remain calm to avoid starting something we cannot finish on our terms!"

Thomas's body crumbled in front of Isabella almost as soon as her ears registered the report from a pistol. The crowd roared, protesting fists flying again.

"Traitor!"

"Coward!"

"Turncoat!"

"Judas!"

Isabella's head whirled as she brought her saber down to a ready position. She scanned the crowd but all seemed to focus on the lifeless body of Thomas. She looked toward the door, expecting a squad of soldiers to burst into the inn and start shooting, but the door remained shut. Gabrielle was at the entrance, her eyes fixed on Isabella. What was she trying to say? If only she were closer; she could read her expression even if she couldn't hear the words coming from her lips.

The heavy thud of boots next to her brought her attention back to the front of the crowd. D'Poussant's voice boomed by her ear. "Now, my brothers, it's time for us to put turncoats behind us and step into the winds that will secure our liberty!" Isabella felt the tension leave her chest and the confidence of a field-tested warrior return. She looked back at Gabrielle, still standing by the tavern's door. Isabella lifted her saber toward the crowd. Another cheer erupted from the mob.

"We will seize our freedom," D'Poussant called over the crowd. He raised a pistol into the air, its hammer lodged against the flint in the steel, a wisp of blue smoke trailing its muzzle. "We will use blades. We will use guns. We will use whatever means available to seek our rightful place in society and community!"

190

The sight of the spent flintlock pistol jarred Isabella, and she looked at the collapsed body of Thomas. She looked back toward Gabrielle, when the door opened with a loud crack and a jumble of men tumbled into the tavern. The chaos calmed the crowd as anxious eyes and faces turned toward the entrance. Several black men pulled and tugged three other men whose unsuccessful resistance appeared to anger their captors even more. Several rods came down on the heads of the apparent prisoners as the crowd created a channel toward D'Poussant and Isabella. As the group pressed forward, the captives were pushed to the floor, and they sprawled over Thomas's corpse.

"We saw these whites on the docks and captured them at the cemetery," said one of the captors. "They were heading here."

D'Poussant stepped over the table and down to the floor. "Thank you, Cedric." D'Poussant grabbed the hair of one of the men and pulled his face into the light, revealing a man with a distinctive mustache but little recognizable beyond that. His eyes were bloodied and bruised, and dark red streaks dripped over his cheeks and into his clothing. His shirt was ripped, and dark lines crossed his torso as if carved by a knife. "What is your name?" The man's eyes were visible through the slits of swollen flesh, but his lips remained closed. D'Poussant kneeled down so he could look into his eyes. "Who are you? Where are you from?" The man remained silent.

"We found this on one of the men." Cedric handed D'Poussant a medallion with the royal crest of Spain.

D'Poussant picked up the button and smiled. "Only those with official business for the King of Spain carry these." He pulled back the hammer of the pistol, lowered the muzzle, and rested it against the lieutenant's cheek. "What are you doing in Port-au-Prince? The King of Spain would have no official business in this port." He looked at the man's clothing. "These are not the clothes of an official visit. You are here for reasons that are not connected to official business with France. Why is your travel on our shores a secret?" D'Poussant pushed the muzzle up against the Spaniard's face. "Perhaps we can help you. What is your mission?"

The man wavered, then lifted his eyes to D'Poussant. "We're looking for a seaman who abandoned our ship."

"Which ship?"

"The *Santa Mónica*. A frigate anchored at the entrance to the bay."

Isabella's heart seemed to skip to a stop as her body felt like it would tumble forward into the captive. She gave the man before her a more intent look. Then she turned her eyes to the second and third men. One man was clearly a stranger, but the man in the middle—his frame, his arms, his hair…Juan Carlos! She was sure her heart had stopped, and now it fell into her stomach. She tried to gasp for breath, but her lungs refused to function. Her knees weakened. Was he alive? She lifted her eyes to the throng, its fury on the cusp of a release that would kill everything in its path. She had to remain calm. She kept her saber ready, its tip now wavering before the prisoner with the mustache as she inventoried the fallen figure of her lover—breeches, deck boots, woolen shirt, dark streaks across his front and down one leg.

Cedric stepped up to the limp body of Juan Carlos and grabbed a mass of hair. He yanked his face up for D'Poussant to see. The army captain's eyes were mere slits, but open enough to confirm enough life to feel whatever pain Dr. D'Poussant was about to inflict. Blood streaked down the side of his face from a wound over his left eye while dark spots over the right side of his face provided evidence of a thorough beating.

"This one here was in charge." He pulled harder on the hair of his captive. "Didn't say anything." He jerked Juan Carlos's eyes to the side so he could see D'Poussant. "Didn't know if you would want to cut out his tongue or slit his throat or do something else to him."

Isabella stood on the table, struggling to collect her thoughts. Her chest tightened, from fear or anger, she couldn't tell, but her arm swung her blade in an arcing cut through the air. "What is he doing here?"

Cedric looked up at Isabella, back to D'Poussant, and then smiled. "Why don't you ask him, Captain?"

Isabella drove the tip of her saber into the top of the table. "Where are the others? How do you know he was the leader?"

Cedric lifted his cap, tipping it to Isabella. "*Mon commandant*! Six others are filling the sewers of Port-au-Prince. Two were spies that I discovered two days ago. Spaniards." Cedric bowed. "They were looking for you, *madame*."

A ribbon of sweat emerged over Isabella's forehead as she fought to breathe. Nine marines and officers looking for her! "Why were they looking for me?"

Cedric laughed. He turned to the crowd and lifted his hands. "Your army, *mon commandant!* They know we stand ready for your command." A cheer erupted from the crowd as Cedric turned back to Isabella. "This is Lieutenant Guerrero," he said as he pulled a knife from his waist. "He is the first officer on His Most Catholic Majesty's frigate *Santa Mónica.*" Before Isabella could register the movement, Cedric cut a wide slit across Guerrero's throat and pushed him to the ground in a rapidly expanding pool of his own blood. "Spanish filth! They don't give a damn about our Hell. They ally with the French to defeat the British, not to give us our rights or the freedom we deserve under colonial decree, nor to enforce the Code Noir."

Isabella watched the knife blade sway in Cedric's hand. She stepped down to the bench, closer to the prisoners, pulling her saber from the wood but keeping its tip at rest behind her. She kept her focus on Cedric, hoping a stray glance toward the battered face of Juan Carlos wouldn't trigger a suspicious reaction that would lead to her own death. "Why, Cedric, were they looking for me?"

Cedric's eyes became unfocused as he watched Isabella descend toward him. "They don't want us to take our rightful places as citizens of the colony any more than Bellecombe does. The Spaniards know we are ready to rise and claim our rights, now that the truth of the prophecy is revealed."

Isabella stood in front of Cedric. "What prophecy?"

Cedric removed his hat and bowed. "The prophecy that a leader, a woman, close to God, would lead us to freedom."

Isabella caught her breath and asked the question even though she knew the answer. "Who told you of this prophecy?"

Cedric looked to D'Poussant. Thoughts began to flood her mind as she realized the full depth of the doctor's conspiracy.

D'Poussant stepped down onto the floor and walked over to the man Isabella did not recognize. He was on his knees, too tired and worn to lift a hand in protest, arms hanging limp by his side. D'Poussant pulled a second pistol from an overcoat pocket, lifted it to the man's forehead, and pulled the trigger. The man's body lurched backward as he fell, another pool of blood spreading across the floor. "We will let the Spaniards know that this is our revolution, and we don't need a European to secure our rights."

D'Poussant moved the muzzle of the pistol over to Juan Carlos's cheek and pushed his face to the side. A reddened circle appeared at contact, as the heat of the muzzle burned his flesh. Isabella's stomach seized.

D'Poussant turned to Cedric and gave him his pistol. "Take this man back to the quay. Put him on a boat back to his precious frigate so the Spanish can hear his story."

Isabella's heart began a steadier beat, as she thought of Juan Carlos hurt, but alive, being lifted to the safety of the *Santa Mónica*.

"But first," D'Poussant said, turning to Isabella. He put his hand inside his sash and pulled out a knife with a long, straight blade. He kneeled before her, lifting the blade as it crossed both palms to present the handle to Isabella. "*Mon commandant*, I humbly request that you leave the mark on this man that leaves no doubt about our intentions or expectations of victory."

Isabella froze, the image of D'Poussant's red felt cap, *le bonnet rouge*, and its cone-shaped top draped over a cannon's barrel flashed before her. She lifted the knife from the doctor's outstretched hands and looked at the blade. She shuddered at the vision of the tip carving into Juan Carlos's skin as she sculpted a crude outline of D'Poussant's revolutionary symbol, branding him as her mortal enemy. If he was lucky, the wounds would heal and scar. Or perhaps he would be luckier if an infection embedded itself into his flesh and killed him. She looked over to Juan Carlos.

"*Mon commandant*," D'Poussant said in a low, insistent voice, "we are ready for your leadership. We must show no quarter if we are to succeed."

Isabella turned to look at Thomas, the reluctant revolutionary, shot down for his caution, now obscured by the corpse of a Spanish naval lieutenant, dispatched because he was loyal to his King. The third man, one of three who made it into the tavern, also lay splayed on his back. A bullet had shattered his skull because he was on the wrong side. And now Juan Carlos, the man she had come to love, was to become the messenger of the Angel of Death in a noble revolution.

She closed her eyes, remembering Juan Carlos's gentle kiss on her cheek, his lips making their way to her neck. She could feel his hands on her breasts as she caught her breath and pulled herself close to feel his body and draw in his scent. His hands had wrapped around her

194

waist, pulling her close as they kissed, and she felt every touch of their embrace. Now, she was to sacrifice the man she loved for the liberty of a half million souls trapped in the chained hell of slavery in Saint-Domingue.

Isabella opened her eyes and turned to D'Poussant. She stepped back from him, turning the knife's tip away from Juan Carlos, and transferred it to her left hand as she seized her saber with the right. "No!"

A shocked murmur passed through the crowd. Cedric looked at D'Poussant. Henri and Paul stepped off the table, making their way toward D'Poussant as they watched Isabella with a murderous intensity.

D'Poussant stepped back. "Isabella...*mon commandant*! Your prophecy. It must be fulfilled. It was foretold by the priestess of the southern mountains, la Chaîne de la Selle. You heard her! You must fulfill your destiny, for the sake of your brothers and sisters who toil in the fields, and orchards, and plantations."

The room fell silent as D'Poussant rotated to face Isabella, putting his body between Henri and Paul. He raised his hand toward Isabella, a priest casting a spell.

Isabella raised her saber and moved it slowly in front of her, carving out space above Juan Carlos with each pass of the tip. She stepped closer to his body until it rested on her boots and legs. "I will not scar this man. I will not leave him with the same marks that plague my body because of an overseer's whip. I did not escape from slavery to assume the mantle of my masters."

D'Poussant's expression darkened, the whites of his eyes appeared to disappear into ever-widening black pupils. He lifted a hand, a new pistol leveled at Isabella's head.

29

The barrel of D'Poussant's pistol looked big enough to shoot a cannonball through her head, but Isabella didn't budge. "Don't come any closer, D'Poussant."

"Isabella, be reasonable. These men are willing to take up arms against our masters to seize their own destiny, as you did years ago in Santo Domingo. They are merely asking you to lead them as you did the slaves on your own plantation."

"And I saw the result—death, destruction, failure. These men don't know what lies ahead of them if they pursue this course. I have lived it."

D'Poussant shook his head. "I thought you would see. This is different. We have prepared. We have munitions. We have guns. We have an army. The revolution starts here, in this tavern, but it will spread throughout the city and countryside. You can lead it, Isabella! You can be their commander. They are waiting for you. They see the signs. Binta: One with God. Madame Rêve-Cœur prophesied your coming, the combined spirits of Lasiren and Papa Legba. They are ready for you to lead."

"I will lead them, D'Poussant, but not in this way. Not by murdering and committing the same brutality that scarred me and my African brothers and sisters. These men—Thomas, the Spanish lieutenant, the other man lying here—what grace did you give them?"

D'Poussant shook his head. "They deserve no grace. They serve their King before they serve their God, and their King has no place for us except under the lashes of his overseer's whips."

Isabella nudged the sagging body of Juan Carlos. "This man is not like his King, or his administrators. This man understands our purpose, our life."

D'Poussant's expression registered a hesitation as he processed Isabella's confession. "You know this man?"

"He is the senior advisor to Viceroy Rodriguez in Puerto Rico."

"Hah, then he is no better than the French colonists!" D'Poussant turned his pistol toward Juan Carlos.

"No, D'Poussant," she said in a stern, full voice. "This man saved my life as I lay near death in the dungeons of El Morro. He risked his station and his life to free me."

"He is a slaver, just like the traders that bring our people from Africa to this cauldron of sweat and misery. He landed with the others, on a mission from the Spanish Crown, in alliance with our tormentors—oppressors who showed no respect for our dignity or place in this world as free men. One act cannot redeem centuries of torture and murder." D'Poussant spat on Juan Carlos's body and lifted the muzzle toward his temple.

Isabella lunged, thrusting the tip of her saber between the wooden stock and the metal barrel, sending the weapon into the crowd. D'Poussant lifted his head in rage. "You are one of them!"

The murmur from the crowd escalated into a steady buzz, just as the front door burst open again. Aldric barreled into the room, forcing his way through the crowd. "It's taken," he yelled. "We have the armory!"

Isabella reached down to grab the collar of Juan Carlos's shirt and pulled him away from the boots and legs of the crowd, creating another yard of distance between her, D'Poussant, Henri, and Paul.

"You see, Isabella? We are poised for victory."

D'Poussant turned to the crowd, raising his fist into the air. "We will be free!"

The crowd roared, fists and weapons pulsating into the air again.

The doctor turned to Isabella. "Your last chance—join us or perish with the slavers."

Isabella pulled at Juan Carlos's collar, dragging him another foot. "I will not join this murderous movement. I will not sacrifice the lives of the honest and sincere for the bloodlust of revenge and retribution."

D'Poussant advanced toward Isabella, signaling Henri and Paul to join him. "Then you have chosen your lot, and you will die along with these traitors and slavers."

A shot rang through the tavern. "All of you, out of this inn." The men turned to see Gabrielle elbowing her way through the crowd. "Take your killing into the streets, where it belongs!"

"Gabrielle, you have no place in this fight."

"I have every right to be in this fight. You have used my family's establishment to plot your revolution, but I won't put up with more killing. We have three bodies, one black and two white. How many will be enough?"

"A last warning, Gabrielle. Let our rebellion take its course. We can't allow traitors in our midst. If the Pirate of Panther Bay would rather side with the slavers and colonists, then she is a poison that must be expelled from the body. Anyone who sides with her will experience the same fate."

Heads bobbed up and down as D'Poussant spoke. Isabella looked toward the back of the room and could not see through the mass of human bodies. She pulled at Juan Carlos's body, inching it toward the door. Several men turned to watch her, their glare burning away any thoughts of escape. She looked over to Gabrielle, who still watched D'Poussant. Isabella stepped in front of Juan Carlos's body and pulled her saber.

"Isabella is not with the slavers or the colonists," said another voice from the crowd. A tall, lean African with a long forehead pushed his way through the crowd. Only Isabella seemed to recognize that his rough-patched clothing with a maroon sash was more suited to a pirate than a warehouse laborer.

D'Poussant wheeled toward the new voice, a fire in his stare challenging the man as he walked toward the table.

He stepped up to square himself in front of D'Poussant. "I escaped a sugar plantation on St. John, and I proudly serve under her flag. I have boarded slavers and merchant ships under her orders and committed myself, like her crew, to destroy anything that can be connected to those dark places."

"Do not interfere with our destiny," growled D'Poussant. "Be aware of our numbers."

"My name is Sarhaan, and I am here to escort the Pirate of Panther Bay back to her ship, where she belongs." Sarhaan pulled a pistol from his sash.

Aldric appeared next to D'Poussant. "We can't afford to wait any longer. The garrison is surely waking. Kill these traitors now."

Sarhaan lifted his pistol, pointing it at D'Poussant's head. "I will shoot anyone who tries to stop me."

D'Poussant laughed. "I have fifty men in this tavern right now. One good shot still leaves forty-nine to finish the task."

"Then I will take as many with me as I can," he said, using his free hand to pull a knife from his sash.

"Sarhaan is not alone," said another voice. Two more men, both African, stepped forward next to Sarhaan.

The fury in D'Poussant's face seemed to overwhelm the flickering candles. "How many traitors are in this room?" he roared.

Sarhaan pulled the hammer back from the pistol's flint. "Let us go, and you can carry on with your revolution. We'll continue with ours…on the sea."

D'Poussant looked out over the crowd and then down at the bodies of Thomas and the two Spaniards. "Make a path!"

The crowd growled its discontent. D'Poussant looked to Henri and swept his hand toward the crowd. He pointed to Aldric, and with a twitch of his finger, the two revolutionaries cleared an opening for Isabella and her pirates.

Isabella pulled Juan Carlos upright, lodging a shoulder under his arm. Gabrielle joined her, and they dragged his near-unconscious body toward the door.

As they passed D'Poussant, he stepped in their path, blocking their exit. "You are traitors, protecting slavers over the security of your own freedoms. Once that door is closed, I will show you no mercy."

Isabella looked at D'Poussant. "I will expect none. May God have mercy on your soul, because my pirate crew will show none if you threaten us any further."

Isabella and Gabrielle hauled Juan Carlos to the front door of le Coq Fantôme as Sarhaan and two other pirates protected their backs until the doors closed behind them.

30

Isabella knew their lives were in just as much danger outside the den of murderous revolutionaries in le Coq Fantôme as they were when inside. They now had to worry about a garrison of French soldiers roused to quell a revolution, not just avoid becoming the targets of a band of bloodthirsty rebels.

Sarhaan and the other two pirates grabbed Juan Carlos and pulled him across the street with lightning speed. He motioned for Isabella and Gabrielle to follow as one-by-one the rescue party disappeared into a pitch black crack between two buildings. Once Isabella had slipped into the darkness, Sarhaan followed, leaving nothing visible from the streets outside the tavern.

"What are we doing?" she hissed.

Sarhaan grabbed her arm and squeezed. "Shhhh."

The door to le Coq Fantôme burst open as bodies poured into the streets, shouts and calls jumbled together as a mob took form to march west toward the ammunition depot. The street brightened as lamps ignited torches and men separated into smaller groups.

D'Poussant's solid, elegant frame took up a position on the raised boardwalk in front of the tavern, Henri and Paul at his sides. "Track down those pirates! We'll string them up along with the French colonists to answer any questions about who's in charge in Saint-Domingue!"

Sarhaan grabbed Isabella's arm, keeping her body pinned against the side of the building. His breath was even and paced while Isabella's frantic heart fought against her attempts to stay calm. She felt the heavy, uneven breathing of someone else next to her. Gabrielle? she wondered, based on the lightness of the puffs of air. The street was difficult to see from the narrow gap between the buildings, but the heavy march of boots on the cobblestones told her a small army of men was looking for them. Sarhaan's grip became stronger, quickening the pace of her heart. She tried to find the hilt of her sword with her free hand, even though any attempt to use it would be useless in the tight space.

Isabella closed her eyes and let her head lean against the boarded walls. She breathed in and slowly let the air out, feeling a calm overtake her as her shoulders drooped and her body relaxed around her spine. Her heart slowed. Her ears picked up the sounds of several people breathing near her. Her mind pictured the battered, weak body of Juan Carlos. Some of those breaths were his. Were they becoming weaker? Or stronger?

A tug on her arm brought her back into the blackness of the crack. A hand had grabbed her arm and was pulling her away from the street and le Coq Fantôme. Another started pushing her, and she side-stepped her way deeper into the blackness.

Isabella stood in a moonlit courtyard, surrounded by the dark gray walls of buildings on all sides. She figured at least six people made up their group, and a body slouched at the feet of two men—Juan Carlos. She kneeled and reached to feel his face with her palms. She touched the crusted blood along one cheek and the puffed flesh around his eyes as she cradled his jaws and caressed his eyelids with her thumbs. She brought her forehead to his, and their noses touched. "Stay with us," she whispered in as gentle a tone as she could muster. "Stay with me." She leaned forward and kissed his lips. "I will protect you."

"Isabella, we have to go."

Isabella drew in a deep breath. She should have been surprised to hear Jean-Michel's voice, but knew in her heart she would have been disappointed if it were someone else. "We have to help him."

"Aye, we will. If we leave him, he's a dead man. If we stay, we'll all be dead."

Isabella stepped back. The moon didn't illuminate their features, but she could tell by their bodies and attitudes that Jean-Michel had come ashore with the some of the most hardened crew of the *Marée Rouge*. "You chose well, *mon ami*."

201

Jean-Michel chuckled. "Well it wasn't like we were walking into a picnic."

Isabella smiled in the darkness. "No, I suppose not."

A seaman stepped up to Sarhaan and Jean-Michel and pulled them a few feet away. He conferred with them in a low voice. Sarhaan's head nodded. Jean-Michel's body seemed to lose some of its form when the pirate leaned over to help the others gather Juan Carlos.

"What is it?" Isabella asked.

"We need to move." Sarhaan's disembodied voice carried an urgent warning. "The entire town will be burning before the night is over."

"But—"

"D'Poussant is the Angel of Death," Jean-Michel's voice said, "and *l'ange de la mort* will stop at nothing to obtain the grail."

Sarhaan's body moved toward a wider alley at the back of the courtyard. His hand signaled other pirates to bring Juan Carlos.

A smaller-framed figure moved closer to Isabella. "*L'ange de la mort* has now made us a symbol of his power," said Gabrielle. "He will stop at nothing to keep us from returning to your ship."

"I'm assuming this young woman is one of us," Jean-Michel said as he nudged Isabella toward the alley.

Isabella nodded. "She saved my life in that tavern. This is Gabrielle. She makes a wicked honey mead."

"She was strong," Sarhaan whispered as the group picked up speed. "She will make a good pirate."

Yellow bulges of heat pulsated above the rooftops of the port city, waiting to become the next round of tinder in the flames of revolution. The band of pirates and their wounded human cargo skirted the southern edge of the city, moving along Rue de Normandie. They hoped to avoid the marauding rebels and outrun the fires that marched toward the sea. Musket fire popped in the night air behind them, but it didn't seem to chase them or lead them. Men and women, some pulling wide-eyed children, fled in the streets, all headed into the jungles and fields among excited shouts and yells of "La Révolution!" and

"Liberté!" The chaos created convenient cover for the group as it made its way to the bay, few noticing, let alone caring about the fact they seemed to be moving into conflict rather than away.

Jean-Michel raised his hand and brought the group to a rest before entering the next intersection. The early morning hours kept the quay—their key to escape—under a dark shroud, but he knew they would be outside the city once they crossed the Rue Saint Claire. Just a few hundred feet of waterlogged plots of land lay between them and a cutter that would ferry their group back to the *Marée Rouge.* Jean-Michel stepped into the intersection, using his eyes to scout for any signs of danger.

"Révolutionnaires! Shoot them; *leur tirer dessus!"*

The cry from down the street had just reached his ears when the sharp reports of muskets followed. A crushing pain in his upper arm overwhelmed him as he jumped back into the shadows of the building, failing to suppress a grunt as he reached for the wound.

"Are you hurt?" Herrera's voice was direct and without emotion, sounding more like a bookkeeper than a doctor. He stepped in front of Jean-Michel to position himself at the corner of the building, dipping his head just enough to see down the street. "It looks like they are not ready to let us leave. They are coming toward us at a fast pace."

Jean-Michel grunted again as he explored the wound with his fingers. "They've got some ground to cover, based on this wound." He felt the cut cloth around the flesh and his fingers passed over the smooth curve of a ball lodged in his arm. "Didn't get far enough to hit the bone." He wiped the blood from his fingers before pulling a knife from his sash and thrusting its tip into the wound. Once he felt the blade lodge against the bullet, he pinched the ball against the blade with his thumb and levered it. He winced as the pain seared through his upper body. "Ugh!" The ball popped into the open and tumbled into the dirt.

Gabrielle ripped a length of her sleeve with the help of another knife, creating a strip long enough to wrap around Jean-Michel's arm. "This won't last long, but when we get on the boat I can do more."

"They are two hundred feet away," Herrera said with gunner's mate precision, looking back toward the advancing soldiers.

"Aye," Jean-Michel acknowledged, checking his pistol and dagger. "How many?"

"I think I see about twelve. More than a squad."

"Seems like fair odds to me," Isabella chuckled. She pulled her sword in front of her and conducted a quick inventory: Gabrielle, Herrera, Sarhaan, two other pirates, plus Juan Carlos. She turned to Gabrielle. "I don't know how well you fight, but if your courage in the tavern tells me anything, it's that you are up to this skirmish!"

Gabrielle smiled. "I can handle a blade, but I've shot only a couple of times while hunting with my papa."

Jean-Michel looked at one of the pirates. "Give her a dagger."

Herrera inspected his pistol. "We've got four pistols. Four shots. They have to count."

"Keep low," Jean-Michel said. "Stay still, deep in the shadows. Sight a pistol on a man, but don't fire until you see the flash of Herrera's flint. Herrera won't give the signal until they are close enough to rush with our blades. As soon as you've fired, drop your weapons and attack with blades. We'll have to cut our way out of this mess."

Isabella's mouth went dry at the thought of Juan Carlos lying near death as she fought to save herself and her crew.

"Leave Juan Carlos here, for now," Jean-Michel said, putting his hand on Isabella's shoulder. "He'll be safer. If we lose this fight, we won't be able to help him anyway, and the French may see fit to show him some compassion given his state."

Isabella crouched next to Juan Carlos and stroked his head as she gave him a light kiss on the forehead. *I won't give you up. You will be with me on the* Marée Rouge *soon.*

A hand grabbed Isabella's arm and pulled her back toward the Rue Saint Claire. Isabella focused on the road.

The shadows of men, soldiers in service to their king, oscillated from a flame-driven backdrop of a city in revolutionary turmoil. She saw the bayonets first as they broke the plane of sight, four spaced across the street as the French guard advanced. A bayonet turned in their direction as the muzzles of the others came into full view. The pirates pressed against the wall, hoping the shadows would darken their images even more. A second bayonet turned up the street in their direction as the hands and bodies of soldiers materialized at once. They had to wait until all the pistols flared—four flashes—before she could rush into the skirmish. One second. Two seconds.

Despite her anticipation of the flash and pop of Herrera's pistol, Isabella still had to catch her breath before throwing herself into the melee. She sensed the discharge of the other guns as she jumped into the crossroads, her sword protruding forward. The pirates' volley had taken the Frenchmen by surprise. While a few triggers were pulled, the surprise of the coordinated strike was enough to scatter the French musket balls and send them into walls rather than flesh.

She brought her saber's blade down on the first soldier in her path, but he lifted his spent musket in a defensive parry that kept his body intact even though his rifle now sported a deep gash and his terror-filled eyes revealed a man already beaten. She shoved forward, her elbow driving into his chest as he fell backward, the stock of his rifle providing a fortunate if temporary shield.

Isabella sensed movement beside her and pulled her saber back in an arc as she twisted, deflecting a bayonet as it snagged her shirt. Her blade cut under the soldier's arm, unleashing a gush of dark splatter across his ribs as he tumbled forward. She lifted her sword in another cut to his back, and the soldier screamed as he fell to the dirt road.

Isabella dropped into a crouch, her battle-hardened instincts telling her to make herself small. She scanned the street, trying to feel movement in the air, not trusting her sight in the grayed streets. Her win wasn't a lonely one: the pirates had taken control, using surprise to their advantage. Six Frenchman lay on the ground, dead or unable to move from their wounds. Four others were on their knees, their weapons at their feet, hands up. Their commanding officer and one other soldier appeared to be still standing and ready to continue the fight.

"The tables have turned," Jean-Michel said, pointing his saber at the young officer. "Lay your weapons down and let us pass. We have no dispute with soldiers under the command of His Excellency Governor General Bellecombe."

"My orders are to put down the rebellion," the officer said, his voice sure, even if his expression doubted success now that he was surrounded by pirates.

"I won't interfere with that, either," Jean-Michel said. "We are not part of the rebellion. We just want safe passage to our ship moored in the bay."

The officer looked at Jean-Michel and then to the others. His eyes turned to Gabrielle and to Isabella. "What is your ship?"

"The *Marée Rouge*," she said.

"You are the Pirate of Panther Bay?"

"Oui."

"Your cunning and daring are legendary."

"*Merci*. All we are asking is one hundred yards of safe passage. Can you give us that; *pouvez-vous nous donner cela?* Is that too much to ask in exchange for your life?"

The officer, a lieutenant, bowed to Isabella. "My orders are to quell the rebellion, not arrest pirates."

Isabella signaled to Herrera and two others. "Get Juan Carlos and prepare the cutter." As they disappeared into darkness, she turned to the French officer. "This rebellion has no place for individual lives in the quest for justice. Your blind loyalty may well lead to all of your deaths."

"I serve my King and Country."

Sarhaan, Jean-Michel, and Isabella advanced on the captives. The four men on their knees bent their heads, as if offering their necks to the clean slice of the beheader's axe. The lone standing soldier raised his flintlock firearm, bayonet at the ready, and stepped in front of the officer.

Isabella pointed the tip of her saber at the soldier. "Your men are loyal."

The young officer looked at Isabella, his expression stoic and immovable.

"As soon as my men have cleared Rue Saint Claire, we'll leave you." She positioned herself in front of each of the soldiers and used her foot to push their firearms away. Sarhaan collected the guns and disappeared at a quick clip into the blackness toward the quay. Isabella turned back to the soldiers and officer. "I'll leave you with your blades, so you can defend yourselves. If you follow us, I can't guarantee your safety or your lives."

Isabella lifted her saber in such a fast action that the soldier did not have time to see how it dislodged his musket from his hands and drove the bayonet into the ground. She shot her leg forward, using her knee to whip the stock away from the soldier, at the same time using the force of her body to push him into the officer. Both tumbled backward. Before they could regain their balance, Isabella had the musket under her arm. She pulled the hammer back and spat onto the flint, soaking it with her saliva. Then she disengaged the bayonet, secured it in her sash, and handed the firearm back to the soldier. "This should give us enough time to return to our ship."

The soldier nodded.

She turned to the officer. "Take your men back to the battery and engage the real enemy."

The officer looked at Isabella and nodded.

Jean-Michel placed his hand on Isabella's shoulder and began to pull her back toward the Rue de Normandie.

A pop drew Isabella's attention down the street as she saw another French soldier fall. Two more pops and the soldiers were no longer watching the retreating pirates and instead focused toward the center of town. More guns cracked, and yells grew louder.

Isabella looked down the street. An unordered assortment of men was making its way toward the group of soldiers and pirates, flashes and bursts from ignited gunpowder, filling the streets. The French soldiers ducked, dropping to the ground even as their commanding officer remained standing.

As the mob closed its distance, the distempered looks of two dozen rebels with knives, axes, cutlasses, machetes, and an occasional firearm appeared. Isabella recognized some of the men from the tavern, but the only face that really stood out was that of the large African whom D'Poussant had lured into attacking Jean-Michel the first night in the tavern: Aldric.

"We have to move," Jean-Michel murmured. "The cutter should be just about ready by now."

She glanced over to the French soldiers and shook her head. "They'll die if we run."

"D'Poussant will make sure they die sometime tonight whether we stay or leave."

Isabella refocused on the advancing mob. "D'Poussant has them chasing a false God."

Jean-Michel nodded. "D'Poussant has them chasing him."

Isabella eyed the quay. "No sight of Sarhaan." She looked over to Jean-Michel. "Leave. Return to the *Marée Rouge*. Get her ready to sail."

"Isabella, you have to come now."

"I can't leave these men without defense to be tortured by Aldric and his thugs. I have been there. We have been there, in the dungeons of El Morro. They should at least die defending themselves rather than meet that fate."

Isabella lunged toward the French soldiers on the ground, grabbing their collars and lifting them to their feet. "Get up!" She pushed their hands onto the handles of daggers, and she shoved a musket with a bayonet at another's body. She marched in front of the French officer, whispering an apology for leaving him as she passed.

"I will die honorably, fighting for my King," he said.

Isabella turned to the Frenchman. "You will be tortured if you allow them to capture you or your men alive."

The horde's advance slowed to a processional pace as Isabella moved toward them with a determined gait. "Stop, Aldric! *Arrêtez!*"

Aldric's steps quickened even as Isabella's determined voice slowed the group.

His faced opened into a wide, sinister smile. "We have won! Le Batterie Saint Claire is under siege by our main forces. We control the armory, and the city is burning!"

Isabella extended her sword toward Aldric. "Then there is no need to harm these men."

"All Frenchmen are poison in this land." He raised a machete to the French officer and pulled a dagger from behind his back. He turned toward the mob and raised the weapons above his head. "We must remove the venom by cutting it out from the flesh!"

The crowd roared, "Death to the slavers! *Mort aux négriers!*"

Aldric turned back to Isabella and Jean-Michel. "Anyone who defends a slaver is a slaver!"

"*Mort aux négriers!*"

"Down with the king!"

The French officer stepped up to Isabella. "We have a garrison of two thousand men on this island. You may win today, but tomorrow you will all be dead or under arrest. Lay down your weapons, and I will speak on your behalf, in the name of King Louis XVI!"

The crack of a pistol sounded in the crowd as a bullet pierced the officer's shoulder, pushing his body backward.

Isabella raised her hand and pushed forward. "No more bloodshed, Aldric! If what you say is true, then you have no need to kill anyone else. Let these soldiers go. They are not armed with anything other than spent muskets and blades. They will not harm you."

"*Mort aux négriers!*"

"*La mort du roi!*"

Aldric advanced, one hand holding his machete to strike, and the other hand holding a double-edged dagger so that the tip would rip into her body with a downward thrust. "Liberty for all; *la liberté pour tous!* Even in death!"

The crowd echoed Aldric's cries and moved forward, weapons undulating as heads bobbed and weaved.

Isabella's heart quickened. Four untested French soldiers, a brash, unseasoned junior officer, and two pirates...against two dozen undisciplined, angry, and bitter rogues, emboldened by a leader who cared little about any life but his own. She mentally mapped the distance to the quay. She and Jean-Michel could make it as the mob feasted on the remains of the French squad. Juan Carlos was safe. She should join him, nurse his wounds and bring him back to health. Live to fight another day.

Binta.

Isabella's lungs heaved as she recalled Madame Rêve-Cœur's revelation. How had she known? And D'Poussant knew. He knew her past. He knew of her prophecy. He knew Madame Rêve-Cœur. He had called her to her destiny through the prophecy. The revolution. *La révolution.* Liberty from the slavers. Freedom for the slaves. Freedom for all men. Freedom for all people. *La liberté pour tous les gens.* That was her destiny. That was God's purpose. Binta. One with God. Liberty for all people, not just those favored by those with power.

Blood coursed through her veins and arteries, shooting flashes of heat into her mind. Her senses exploded as she soaked up the fear, anger, frustration, and bitterness flooding toward her from the mob. She looked at Aldric as he advanced on her, dagger and machete rotating to strike as he sought death. D'Poussant had chosen Aldric for this purpose, the sole purpose of destroying everything in his path. No mercy could be found in the rage igniting his eyes as he descended upon her.

Isabella sprang forward, raising her saber in a parry that deflected the arc of Aldric's machete into a useless void by her side. She darted past him, twirling to bring the dagger sweeping around his back. She ducked, dodging a blade as it swished over her, meeting nothing but air. She thrust her head into his ribs and toppled him onto the ground. Aldric rolled with no physical sign of the cracked ribs her hit must have created. She charged, but he swiveled on his knee, raising his blade in time to halt the arc of her saber. Sensing the power in his parry, Isabella whirled. She felt a thin slice break through her shirt as the dagger crossed her side.

Isabella followed the arc of the cut with her blade. Aldric's scream almost froze her in place as she reset her stance to inspect her enemy. Aldric had fallen, his knife resting in the packed gravel of the road as he stared at the stub of an arm that once included his hand. He still controlled his machete, and his eyes seemed to shoot flaming darts into her skull. He shifted his weight so that he was on his knees. "Kill her!"

Isabella kept her focus on Aldric, waiting for his next attack. The crowd held steady, its parts unbound and loosely tied together.

"Kill her! In the name of liberty, kill this woman who defends your French masters!"

Aldric raised his machete in an effort that pulled him from his knees onto his feet. The crowd tightened as its mutterings became more defined and pointed. "*Mort aux négriers!*" "*La mort du roi!*"

Isabella raised her sword. "Stop this madness!"

The crowd's shouts waxed into waves of rumbling roars. Metal clanged against metal. Wooden handles knocked against the dirt.

Aldric turned to the rebellious gang. "Exorcise our bodies of these devils! *Pour liberté!*"

He raised his machete and swung toward Isabella's head. A shot rang down the road and Aldric's body stumbled toward the mob. He lifted a weakened arm, pointed his machete toward Isabella, and crumbled to the ground.

Another crack signaled another shot, and another revolutionary at the front of the angry crowd fell.

Isabella turned toward the shots. "Stop! *Arrêtez!*"

"Isabella, let us get out of here!" The body sending the voice out into night was still unseen, but Sarhaan's accent was distinctive enough.

A flash from one of the soldiers' muskets stirred the mob, and the horde advanced toward the motley band of pirates and Frenchmen.

Isabella felt a grab on one of her arms and a wrenching tug toward the Rue de Normandie. A deafening crack ejected all sound from her consciousness, and she stumbled. A hand pulled her, and she felt the weight lifted from her feet as she continued to clutch her sword. The buildings lining the road spun around her as her body kept falling, images swirling in a cocoon of silence. She tumbled backward but was saved from the ground by another tug on her shoulder. She saw more flashes and smoke rise over the crowd, the pulsating axes, rods, and blades puncturing the glow created by fires throughout the city.

The tugs and pulls continued, over and over, as the street gave way to a pitch-black wall that shielded them from the fires consuming the city. Across the street, hedges of vegetation obscured crops soaking up nutrients from an unbuildable marsh. Between jerks, she would steal a glance behind her, hoping to gauge how many yards, if any, they had before turning to fight again. But each time her eyes seemed to find the path of their retreat, the grip would haul her forward, and she would lose her focus.

After what seemed like a mile of being dragged, snippets of sound began to resound through her eardrums. First, she heard the scratching of leather soles on dirt. Then she heard the clumping of boots on the road, followed by muffled shouts. With each new sound, her steps became more sure, her body more settled, and the grip on her sword more firm. As their feet crossed onto the stone-laid wharf, she could hear the yells and shouts of the mob behind her. She leapt forward, creating slack in the grip of her savior, and wrenched her arm from his hands.

Jean-Michel turned, alarmed, but his expression eased when he saw Isabella's determined and focused look. He turned back to the wharf's edge, only a dark, narrow line projecting from the hull of the cutter in the water below, despite what must be high tide or near it.

"Cast off!" he yelled at the mast.

A head poked up from above the edge.

"Cast off!" The second call sent the head out of sight, and the line began to sway from side to side.

Jean-Michel turned to Isabella and pulled her toward the edge. "Go. *Aller!*"

"Where are the others?"

"Go, Isabella! The tides are shallow, and the winds are light."

Isabella turned toward the pursuing mob. Their yells had faded and the throng had slowed as they marched toward their prey. A musket cracked behind her, and another one of the leaders fell. Another crack and a second rebel was on the ground. The pack began to close ranks and push forward faster.

Isabella turned back toward the boat, and she felt a force push her over the edge of the wharf. She flopped in mid-air, her arms and legs flailing, landing in the arms of a seaman...or two. They all fell backward, and Isabella heard the break of the water under the keel as the hull pushed away from the quay.

"Jean-Michel!" Isabella sent a frantic look around the inside of the boat as tars hoisted a sail on the mast.

A muzzle flash at the stern illuminated the swarthy frame of Jean-Michel. "Pull at those oars! The tides need our help!"

Isabella felt the jerk of the hull pushing against water as the bow tipped up from the force of oars pulling the boat into the bay. She could see the outlines of two seamen, one on each side of the boat, pulling at the heavy wooden rods that were the handles of large oars.

Flashes along the edge of the quay were just enough warning for Isabella to duck as balls of lead socked into the gunwales and deck around her. She rolled over the hardwood planks and fumbled along the edges for a rifle she figured her crew would have stored for the escape. Her hand fell on a long metal rod, and she curled her fingers around the metal until she felt the smooth wood securing the barrel. She let her hands slide down the barrel to the flint, lock plate, and trigger, and pulled the musket to her shoulder.

Herrera's laugh broke through the darkness. "I've got something for those irreverent scum." The hot end of a fuse made its way to a long barrel cylinder, not more than three feet long. A swivel gun. Isabella smiled as she pictured Herrera's glee in rigging the cutter to allow the fast movement of these weapons. The muzzle flashed with a boom that sent a shudder through the boat's deck and narrow gunwales.

Screams erupted from the human mass on land as small metal balls plowed into the horde. Several heads disappeared in the blackness. She shifted her attention back to the sight of the musket, keeping her mind away from the image of the grapeshot dicing the flesh, muscle, and bones of the men leading their pursuit.

The cutter had already pulled several dozen yards from shore, pushed a few feet more by the recoil from the small cannon, but the mob still had clear sight of the retreating pirates. Isabella aimed at a taller figure silhouetted against the glow of the burning city, and squeezed the trigger. The spark from the flint triggered a wrenching kick as the gunpowder ignited and sent its ball toward the pack of revolutionaries. She recovered just in time to see the figure disappear into the ragged line of shadows on the shore.

Another frenzied round of muzzle flashes from the quay sent metal projectiles across the bay. The balls landed with fragile thuds against rails or masts, or splashes near the hull. Isabella leaned back on her heels and put the musket aside, taking a deep breath and bringing her hands to her face as if wiping away the soot from spent gunpowder. They were safe. For now.

The cutter fell silent as the yells and taunts from the horde on land receded, overtaken by the steady, urgent rhythm of oars that pulled the pirates closer to the safety of the *Marée Rouge* with each sweep. The sound of wood scraping against wood rose above the fading din as the main sail caught what little wind meandered through the harbor in these early morning hours.

Isabella felt her brain ease, her shoulders slumping as the muscles relaxed and her hands fell to her knees. She lifted her face to the sky. Stars were emerging against the rich, deep blue of the night, the glow of the fires in the city unable to extinguish them. She had cheated death once again, thanks to Jean-Michel and Sarhaan.

A sharp pain returned to her side, and she lifted a hand to the moist slit created by Aldric's machete. She felt a thin flap of skin below the woolen fabric and let out a small huff of air at the realization that the wound was superficial. The cut did not go below the skin. No scar was

213

likely to appear, unlike the ridges of hardened tissue marking her back that reminded her of the lashes of the plantation overseer and her tormentors in El Morro.

She reached up to her shoulder, letting her fingers find the folds of callused skin created by her ravaged body. She closed her eyes, and her mind slipped back to the dungeon of El Morro. The revenge whipping by the boatswain from the *Ana Maria*—her first defeat of a Spanish man o' war—had left her clinging to her last thread of life. Juan Carlos and Rosa brought her back to life. Isabella's chest and arms became heavy. Juan Carlos should have left her to die, but he enlisted the help of Rosa to keep her alive, and she was sure—even though she couldn't prove it—that Juan Carlos had organized her escape from the prison fortress as she was being taken to the gallows.

She turned toward the bow of the cutter. Three vague shapes gave the front of the boat a lumpy look. A few more seconds revealed three figures, one lying down, one sitting, and another on its knees. The one on its knees was tending to the figure lying on the deck, like a doctor to a patient.

Isabella lifted herself to her feet and was grateful for the calm waters. With tides of less than two feet this time of year, the sea's ebb wouldn't interfere with navigation. A light wind kept the sails full enough to demote the oarsmen to a supporting role but not enough to give the deck an awkward pitch or force her to duck under the boom. She made her way to the bow.

"He'll be okay, Cap'n."

Isabella couldn't attach a name to the voice at the moment, but it was a familiar sound that comforted her. "Thank you."

She kneeled down beside the body, the head now positioned at the front of the deck. Her hands fell to Juan Carlos's leg. She felt the smooth, firm leather of his boots. Her fingers searched the cotton of his breeches for any sign of an injury. Her hand continued to his shirt and stopped. "Have you found any injuries?"

"Nothing below the belt as we could see," said the seaman. "Above the belt's another story, Cap'n. Sometimes it's good what the night hides."

Isabella drew in a short, deep breath and held it. Her hands hovered over his waist, the fold of his cotton shirt skimming off the back of her fingers. She let her hands descend onto his body, trying to feel his skin beneath his shirt and the warmth of his body.

"We'll get Doc to look at 'm when we're back aboard the *Marée Rouge*."

Isabella nodded, unsure of whether her two crewmen could see her. "Check with Jean-Michel at the stern to make sure everything is secure."

The tar paused before replying, "Aye, Cap'n."

Both men stood, and she could hear the pad of four bare feet dwindle as they made their way to the back of the boat.

Isabella pressed her hands against the living but unconscious form of the man who had saved her from the vengeful whippings of a Spanish mariner not more than a year ago. She moved her palm up from his waist and onto his belly, letting her cheeks dip to his stomach, letting his scent invade her head. She sighed, hoping the deep breath might stop the tears welling in her eyes. The image of Aldric dragging his near lifeless body into le Coq Fantôme. The hatred D'Poussant directed at Juan Carlos—nothing more than a Spaniard, a slaver—sent a shiver up her spine and into the back of her head. The doctor of letters, the rebel, the leader of the masses couldn't see...or didn't want to see...this nobleman's kindness, his sense of justice, and his love for a rogue pirate and escaped slave.

Isabella shuddered. "I'm sorry," she whispered.

She brought her hands inside his shirt, the heat of his skin warming her, her touch triggering a small moan. She let her nose touch his chest, and kissed his ribs, letting her hands fold around him in a gentle hug. "At least you're alive. God has shown mercy. *Merci, mon Dieu.*"

She pictured the cuts on his broken face as she pulled him from the mob at the tavern. Her right hand glided over his chest until she could feel his neck. She turned to face him, the outline of his jaw visible in the darkness. Her thumb explored his chin and lips as her fingers touched his cheek and ears. The men had washed his face of the dried blood, but she could feel the tenderness of bruised skin and the dampness of cuts and open wounds. "I am so sorry. I will not let this happen again."

She rested her head on his chest, feeling it rise and fall with labored breathing, and tears burst from her eyes. She pulled his body close, praying her tears would become the ointment that would heal him faster and make him stronger. *"Te quiero, mi amor;* I love you."

Capitán de Navio Muñoz stared into the pulsating glow created by the fires rising from the city across the bay and tapped his spyglass.

"The flag of Louis XVI still flies above the batteries of St. Claire," said the lieutenant standing beside him.

Muñoz stood, a silent witness to something historic. He turned to walk the rails of his command, pacing several dozen steps before turning. He looked at the position of the *Santa Mónica*, her bow almost completing its turn as the tide began its ebb. He turned his cheek to feel the breeze against his face and looked up at the furled sails. "The blood will run deep in the sewers of Port-au-Prince tonight. The pirates will run. Prepare the squadron for battle."

The lieutenant hesitated, but Muñoz sent him a sharp look. He bowed. "Sí, Capitán Muñoz." The officer turned to sound the beat to quarters.

31

Isabella cringed with each pull of the hoist as Juan Carlos's crippled body made its way to the top of the gunwales, through the gangway, and onto the deck.

A man dressed in breeches, boots, and a blue waistcoat kneeled beside the erstwhile Spanish army captain stretched on his back before the crowd of pirates. Sarhaan positioned a lantern over his head. The man used a gentle but capable touch to turn Juan Carlos's face from one side to the other, examining cuts, bruises, and swollen tissue. "Anyone else hurt?"

"No," Sarhaan said. He looked at Jean-Michel. "We were lucky."

"Many more would have died if Jean-Michel and Herrera had entered the tavern." The voice of a confident woman turned heads, most of whom hadn't noticed Gabrielle when she made her way onto the pirate vessel. Murmurs surged through the pirates.

Jean-Michel stepped forward, lifting his hand to the pirates. "None of us might have gotten out of that city alive if it weren't for Gabrielle."

"Aye," Sarhaan said, stepping over to Jean-Michel. "She is one of us. Her words were strong with that devil who is burning the port, and she knew the back alleys and roads like the back of her hand."

A tall, barrel-shaped tar advanced from the group. "I don't like this at all. We already had the Spaniards sending their fleet after us. We barely made it into this bay alive. Now, we got to deal with a dago army captain and another woman?"

Jean-Michel shook his head. "If you…or anyone else…objected to Isabella as captain of this vessel, the time to make your voice known was in Charlotte Amalie, not here or now."

"I signed up to join the Pirate of Panther Bay and loot the merchant ships along these trade routes. I didn't sign up for any revolution. Pirates don't like women on board their ships; they get in the way, and

I don't want no smell of a dago prisoner to draw those dogs at the mouth of the bay into our business."

Isabella moved out of the shadows. "I know you didn't sign up for this. We didn't plan on any of this happening, but I am also sure that Port-au-Prince is burning for reasons other than me. No one is safe in the city right now, and all ships moored in this port are in danger. If the revolutionaries are successful, they will loot every vessel they can reach. If the French put down the rebellion, they will assume our crew was part of the plot."

"Isabella's right," Jean-Michel said. "This port holds nothing for us but death. Prepare to make sail for Tortuga Bay! We'll run with the tide and slip out under the cover of darkness."

32

An early morning breeze filled sails that unfurled from the masts of the *Marée Rouge,* and she turned toward the open sea. The wind pulled the hull against reluctant water, and the deck leaned forward as the brigantine gained headway, its cannons and crew primed for a fight.

Jean-Michel shook his head. "Three knots, maybe four. Not enough to outrun a frigate."

Isabella peered out over the bay in the direction of the Spanish warship now absent at least one army captain, a navy lieutenant, and seven other warriors. "Enough for us to maneuver. That's all we can hope for. We're lucky we are not completely calmed."

Jean-Michel huffed. "At least our crew is. They would be hauling us out of the bay using oars on a launch."

Isabella turned her attention back to the city, flames shooting into the sky, feeding great black billows that threatened to blot out all the stars. She gripped the railing and dipped her head. The waves unfolded away from the boat as it settled into its slow but steady pace. White foam lined the ridges as they rolled toward shore.

"He'll recover," Jean-Michel said as he joined her.

"I know." She dipped her head closer to the rails. "It's just that he seems so broken."

"He is broken. He's lost everything. As far as he knows, he's even lost you."

Isabella closed her eyes, picturing her last moments with him in the cutter. "He knows I'm here, by his side."

"Then he has hope. That's all he needs."

She reached to lay her hand on Jean-Michel's. "I hope you're right. He no longer has King and country."

"He may still have his God."

Jean-Michel's words caught Isabella in mid-breath. "I thought my destiny was in that port, in that town, with D'Poussant."

Jean-Michel turned to Isabella and cupped her face with his hands. "That's what I was afraid of, *mon cher*. That's why we returned for you."

Isabella brought her hands up to rest on his wrists, "I know, I was stupid."

"No, Isabella, you were following the prophecy, a promise that was made to you many years ago when you were a slave girl in Santo Domingo."

"A prophecy is not a promise."

"To a girl, with nothing to live for, whose world consists of links between brutalities, a prophecy becomes a promise."

Isabella turned back to the port, the glow of the fires consuming everything made by man. "A promise of something bigger than yourself."

"Every child needs that promise."

"But what of an adult? Do we need the same promise?"

The quartermaster looked down the length of the warship. A half dozen pirates kneeled at each stations, ready at a moment's notice to unleash the fury of their guns. The quiet on the gun deck was eerie, as if the silence of each stare was gathering to coax demons into the open and a fair challenge for the open sea.

"I suppose we do," Jean-Michel said after a few minutes. "Some are on this ship because they want a hand in destroying the Spanish and French. Some are here because they think our loot and plunder will make them something bigger than themselves. And some, like Louis, are here because we gave them no choice."

Isabella's heart fell at the mention of the boy's name. "Where is Louis?"

"In the stateroom where Doc has set up shop. He's going to learn a lot about fixing wounds and bones by the end of the day, I think."

"It's not fair to Louis."

"Was slavery fair to you? Or your mother? You make do with what you have. And move on."

Isabella nodded in the darkness. "I guess Madame Rêve-Cœur was wrong."

"How so?"

"She said I was destined to lead. I was 'One with God'."

"How was she wrong?"

Isabella pointed to the blob of pulsating yellow that was once Port-au-Prince. "I could not lead the revolution. I could not stop the revolution. I am back where I was before, a lone pirate, prowling the seas in search of revenge."

The clucks from Jean-Michel surprised Isabella. She turned to him with a curious look.

"Isabella, you are no longer seeking revenge. Sarhaan told me what happened in the tavern. You could have let them take Juan Carlos. That would have been the easy path, the path to revolution, the path to leadership that had been established by D'Poussant; but you didn't. You turned your back on the Devil and embraced the love of a man who should have been your sworn enemy."

"Juan Carlos is different."

"I don't think so, *mon cher*. Juan Carlos showed you grace in the dungeons of El Morro. He risked his own station with his King by negotiating the stalemate off Privateer Pointe. He accepted you for who you were. You have done the same for him."

"I couldn't let more innocents die."

"Few would claim Juan Carlos, emissary to the Viceroy of the West Indies, decorated captain in His Most Catholic Majesty Charles III's army, an innocent. If anything, he is an example of all that is wrong in our world."

Isabella sighed. "But he is a man."

"As you are a woman."

"Where do we go from here?"

She reached for Jean-Michel's hand. The report of the cannons drowned out anything that Jean-Michel was about to say. A ball burst onto the deck and plowed its way into a hatch. Jean-Michel and Isabella braced against the nearest ropes and blocks as another cannonball tore through the main sail and landed in the water across the beam.

"Report!" Jean-Michel's voice boomed over the deck.

"Just saw her with the light from the first cannon," came a call from on top of the main mast. "On our port bow. Appears to be chasers, but she might be turning."

Isabella swore. She peered into the night, toward the opening to the bay, unable to see. Another bright flash and she ducked as another ball landed just short of the gun deck.

Anger built inside her body. How did the ship get so close? "Smoothy!"

"Aye, Cap'n."

"How far off is she?"

"From the overshoot, I would say she's about a quarter mile out. Too far for our big long guns."

"What about the nine-pounder bow chasers?"

Smoothy looked out over the bay as another shot was released from the Spanish ship. He didn't flinch as the ball sailed five feet above the deck before arcing inches above the gunwale and falling into the water. "Can't be sure. We could turn into her and see what happens."

Isabella turned to Jean-Michel. He nodded. "Right now, we'll be broadside within the next thirty minutes. I'd rather put Smoothy on the chasers in the bow and pick at her rigging than face that dago ship in an attack."

"Set the course," Isabella said as she looked at the helmsman. "But keep us just a few points to the north so we can run upwind of her." She wheeled toward Smoothy, who was already in the bow, setting the sights on the chasers with another three seamen running balls and powder.

As the *Marée Rouge* turned toward her attacker, another shot fell harmlessly off her bow. A sharp crack chased the silence off the deck as the first of Smoothy's shots sailed across the bay. The horizon was beginning to trickle through the early morning light. Isabella could make out the distant shape of the warship but couldn't see its details.

Jean-Michel swore. "She must have been tracking us all night. Muñoz must have plotted our position in the bay, saw our masts against the fires in the background, and decided this was his opportunity."

"If that's true," Isabella said, "he's a much better seaman than we thought. We underestimated our enemy."

"He's still a Spaniard—"

"Who caught us asleep in port."

Isabella could now make out the sails pulling the two ships together. Three masts. "We've fought a frigate before. We'll fight another one. This time, we won't settle for a draw." Isabella turned toward the helmsman again. "Once we have closed to a quarter mile, wheel hard right. We'll rake her across her bow."

The next fifteen minutes passed like three hours for Isabella as she watched the *Santa Mónica* close in. She looked into the sky and noted the light cushion holding in the peaks on land and other larger puffs of clouds hanging in the sky. She didn't relish the thought of a nighttime fight, but she had no choice. Each flash, each spark from a flint, each shot ignited would telescope the position of her ship, crew, and armament.

"Is it always this quiet before a fight?"

Isabella shifted her eyes toward Gabrielle's voice but kept her body facing the approaching ship. "Is Doc ready?"

Gabrielle followed Isabella's gaze out to the *Santa Mónica*. "Is that a big ship?"

Isabella smiled. "You live in a port. Don't you see ships?"

"Only from land. Girls aren't allowed on ships."

"That ship is a frigate. It should have thirty-two cannons as its main armament."

"How many cannon does your ship have?"

"Twenty-two."

Gabrielle turned to face Isabella, her eyes widened with concern. Isabella smiled. "I've faced worse odds."

Gabrielle opened her mouth as if to say something but held her breath instead.

"Gabrielle, go back down below. Help tend to Juan Carlos. Take care of Louis. He's alone right now, and I don't think a crew of pirates ready for battle is going to comfort him."

Gabrielle turned toward the hatch leading below deck and looked back to Isabella.

"Go, Gabrielle. Help Doc. Take care of Louis." She spread her arms and lifted them toward the masts. "This is my ship, my crew." She looked back toward Gabrielle. "This is where I belong."

The *Santa Mónica*'s gunners opened a half dozen more holes in her sails by the time Isabella ordered the helmsmen to turn the *Marée*

Rouge, but they failed to damage rigging or land a shot close enough to damage her armament seriously. Smoothy's experience, on the other hand, had disabled one of their enemy's chasers and stays in the bowsprit.

The turn of the tiller evened the deck's pitch as the *Marée Rouge* curved north. The first forward cannon thundered and a flash lit up the deck, and the first shot from a larger caliber gun flew toward the target. Thirty seconds later, another boom from the forward cannon sent another ball of iron toward the *Santa Mónica*.

Two flashes and distant booms from across the water announced the arrival of two cannonballs crashing through the gunwale between two gun ports. Screams pierced the night as wounded pirates reeled in the darkness, the first injuries a jarring reminder of what the next thirty minutes might bring in their quest for the open sea. Another flash illuminated the weather deck of the *Marée Rouge* as Isabella's crew responded. Seconds later, another cannon flared sending a second shot at their Spanish pursuer.

A flare from the *Santa Mónica* prompted Isabella to flinch, and iron whistled through the air just a few feet above her. She fumbled with her sword as her blood began to course through her veins. Her cheeks flushed with warmth as she found herself longing for the opportunity to board the frigate. Could the *Marée Rouge* withstand this pounding?

Another flash from the boat's midship lit up the gun deck, and Isabella could see Jean-Michel watching the duel from the bow. She dashed down the deck just as another cannonball from the Spanish frigate sent a shudder through the vessel when it hit the *Marée Rouge*'s hull. Moments later, she was at Jean-Michel's side, and she pulled him into the bow where Smoothy was crouching next to one of the chasers. He lit the fuse, and the cannon barked as another ball flew toward the Spanish warship.

She grabbed Smoothy's arm and turned him toward her. "Run down the line and sight each gun. Our crew can't work as quickly as you. Each ball has to count. Aim for her rigging. We can't disable her guns, but we can keep her from chasing us!"

Another flash in the night gave Isabella a glimpse of the carnage that was about to befall her pirates—two men were sprawled across the deck, no signs of life, and another carriage was manned by just one crewman. Another shot and she saw two more pirates at the gun. She felt the bulk of Smoothy's figure pass her, and she followed it as she sprinted toward the helmsman.

The crack of splitting wood and the swish of cut rope sent Isabella scrambling to the deck as block and rope fell around her. She tripped and rolled forward but pulled herself out of a mess of tangled hemp and continued running toward the rear of the boat. Two more cannons roared as she passed too close to the path of the recoil, but she cleared the carriages by inches.

The *Marée Rouge* heaved to the left just as Isabella reached the helm, and three separate flashes revealed the helmsman's body draped over the tiller, blood soaked through his shirt. She rushed to the tiller and heaved the lifeless body to the deck, seized the tiller, and pulled. The keel turned, and the deck pitched as the sails refilled with the morning wind. More balls hurtled through the air, but the sudden turn of the vessel had thrown the Spanish sights off, and their projectiles landed in the bay without connecting with the *Marée Rouge*. The unexpected repositioning of the hull gave the gunners time to recharge their cannons. As the *Marée Rouge* came back on course, each cannon flashed as it found a target. When the last cannon discharged, the first cannon had been reloaded and another string of shots fired across the bay into the *Santa Mónica*.

As the last cannon flared, Isabella turned her attention back to their target while keeping the vessel on course. "Yes!" she yelled as she saw three fires burning on the deck of the frigate, two midships and one toward the stern. The flames leapt into the rigging, igniting canvas, rigging, and ropes, creating a beacon in the night. She smiled as she realized each growing flicker of the flame illuminated another target for Smoothy and his gunners.

Isabella turned her attention back to the gun deck and struggled to make out the shapes of the hatches, gun carriages, and crew. Somehow, the *Marée Rouge* had avoided devastation—no fires revealed targets to the Spanish crew.

The *Marée Rouge* was now cruising north of the frigate as the day's winds picked up and the brigantine's speed increased. Isabella turned her attention to land and realized they were fifteen minutes from rounding the spit of land that would give them safe passage into the sea. Within two days' sail, they would be in Tortuga Bay.

The groans of wounded men and the smell of fresh blood were all too familiar to Isabella as she made her way into the officer's stateroom. She scanned the room and saw the familiar faces of her crew. Her heart skipped as she saw a body on the mess table. Louis held the man's arm while he bit down on a cloth covering a wooden dowel. Gabrielle was on the other side as the man screamed through the rag. The rhythm of Doc's arm told her that another one of her crew would lose a leg, earning, according to their pirate Articles, another eight hundred pieces of eight. She resolved to add two hundred more Spanish dollars to his kitty, but even that seemed short of the compensation he really deserved in service to her calling.

"Louis is a hard worker and strong," Jean-Michel said.

Isabella put her hand on Jean-Michel's shoulder and rested her head. "A pirate ship is no place for a boy."

Jean-Michel heaved a big sigh. "No, it isn't, but he doesn't have a choice now."

"Perhaps we can return once the violence has settled to find his mother and return him to Port-au-Prince."

The quartermaster turned his head and gave the top of Isabella's head a kiss. "I'm afraid that won't be possible. We tried to find her when we landed to rescue you. We found her, but D'Poussant's henchmen had gotten to her first."

"That demon," Isabella cried. "She was innocent. She knew nothing about his plans. Louis was safe with you on the *Marée Rouge*."

"*L'ange de la mort* is living up to his name. I have no doubt Louis would be dead if we had left him in port that night. They were both too close to Bellecombe, and D'Poussant would not have risked his revolution based on assurances of their loyalty."

Isabella lifted her head and watched Louis work, tears filling her eyes. "He doesn't deserve this."

"No one deserves this."

"When should we tell him?"

Jean-Michel let out a short puff of air. "I'll tell him when Doc is done."

Isabella lifted her lips to Jean-Michel and kissed his cheek. *"Merci, mon ami.* I am lucky to have you, in life and battle."

Isabella opened the door to her cabin and dipped her head into the small space. A familiar body, covered by linens, occupied her cot. She slung her sword on a peg near the basin and stepped over to the bed. The early morning sunlight brightened the battered face of Juan Carlos. She lifted her palm to his cheek, taking his hand in hers, leaned over and kissed his forehead.

"I have discovered the meaning of the prophecy," she whispered in his ear. "My calling is bigger than any man or woman. I am called to show the world that freedom is the natural right of all men, given to us by a higher power. I need you to help me ensure this prophecy is fulfilled."

Juan Carlos's eyes opened, and he focused on Isabella. He squeezed her hand. She leaned over to his lips, and they kissed.

About the Author

SR Staley (www.srstaley.com) has been enamored with pirates since he was a pre-teen but didn't get to write about them until he put pen to paper to craft his first published novel, *The Pirate of Panther Bay*. Since then, he has become an award-winning author of fiction and non-fiction books that explore the uncomfortable realities, everyday heroism, and ethical dilemmas faced by contemporary children and adults in a society that values personal freedom and choice. Staley's stories take readers from the sweltering jungles of the eighteenth century Caribbean (*The Pirate of Panther Bay* and *Tortuga Bay*) to the brutal concrete playgrounds of inner-city gangs (*A Warrior's Soul* and *Renegade*) in books recognized for their realism, action, and layered characters. For additional inspiration, he draws on his extensive experience traveling to more than one hundred cities and forty-three states in the U.S. as well as countries as diverse as China, Peru, Guatemala, India, France, and England. In fact, he has traveled to China more than thirty times.

An economist by training, he is director of the DeVoe L. Moore Center at Florida State University in Tallahassee, Florida. He earned his B.A. from Colby College in Waterville, Maine, his M.S. from

Wright State University in Dayton, Ohio, and Ph.D. from The Ohio State University.

SR Staley enjoys participating in book club and classroom discussions. He can be contacted at sam@srstaley.com and discussion questions can be found at www.srstaley.com.

www.srstaley.com
www.campusninjaselfdefense.com
http://blog.srstaley.com
Twitter (@SamRStaley)
Facebook (SR Staley and Path of the Warrior)

Discussion Questions

1. Only a handful of women pursued the pirating life, even during the "glory days" of Caribbean pirating (the early 1700s). Why didn't more women become pirates? What makes Isabella's story different?

2. Can you identify three elements of *Tortuga Bay* that reflect the real world of pirates during this period of history? How does this contrast with modern pirating, either off the coast of Somalia, in the current Caribbean, or in Asia?

3. How would you characterize Isabella's leadership style as captain of the *Marée Rouge*? How does this contrast with Jean-Michel's style? Which do you think is closer to the real world of pirates in the 18th century Caribbean?

4. Isabella is haunted by a prophecy told to her by her mother. Why is the prophecy important to her? How does the prophecy motivate her?

5. Why do you think Juan Carlos is attracted to Isabella? How does this put him in conflict with Rodriguez? With Muñoz? With Jean-Michel?

6. What values does Isabella struggle with when she experiences the voodoo ritual with Madame Rêve-Cœur? What does the voodoo priestess mean when she says she feels the pull of many spirits in Isabella?

7. Why do you think Isabella is vulnerable to the persuasion of Dr. D'Poussant? Is this typical of people in leadership positions today? What are the implications for her ability to lead and for the slave revolt to be successful?

8. The values of the American Revolution (1776) are often contrasted with those of the French Revolution (1789). What are their respective core values? Do you see these values in conflict or reinforcing each other in *Tortuga Bay*?

9. How has Isabella's character changed over the course of the novel? How has Jean-Michel's? Juan Carlos's?
10. Juan Carlos and Captain Muñoz are in conflict through much of the story. What is the source of this conflict? How does this complicate their decisions and actions at the end of the story?

CPSIA information can be obtained at www.ICGtesting.com
Printed in the USA
LVOW06s0253121015

457867LV00001B/98/P